THE BYRNE BROTHERS

# VICIOUS SEDUCTION

## JILL RAMSOWER

Editor: Editing4Indies

❀ Created with Vellum

# VICIOUS SEDUCTION

## JILL RAMSOWER

# ONE

FREE DIVERS TRAIN THEIR HEARTS TO SLOW TO A MERE ELEVEN beats per minute. I learned that from some television documentary and was fascinated. If only I'd been interested enough to remember how they acquired that kind of control.

My heart thudded with such ferocity that I was certain it would crack a rib.

That was what I got for voluntarily returning to the Olympus Club—the elusive playground of the city's most wealthy and powerful. My sprinting heart rate wasn't a result of excitement, however. I knew all too well that wealthy and powerful were just polite ways of saying entitled, hedonistic assholes who didn't care who they trampled to get what they wanted.

1

I would know. I was born into that world.

General knowledge of the Olympus Club was extremely limited outside of the most elite circles. And within those groups, membership was highly coveted. People would do almost anything to get inside these solid mahogany doors—a fact I wished I didn't know so well.

I'd been lucky enough to go as a guest several times now with the man I'd been seeing for the past couple of months. Lawrence Wellington—shipping mogul and one of the city's most eligible *mature* bachelors. He had a son not much younger than me, but I'd never met him. Fortunately, Lawrence didn't exactly look his age. He still had plenty of dark hair with a touch of silver at his temples and kept himself fit with regular exercise.

Lawrence was taking our budding relationship surprisingly slow. I wasn't entirely sure if it was out of caution or an innate indifference to anything but the acquisition of power. Not that he needed more. The stuff radiated off him like the dirt cloud around that Pig-Pen character in the *Peanuts* cartoons. Everyone around him seemed to respond as though that aura of power scrambled their brains, making them prattle inanely or shower him with compliments.

Knowing he was used to such lavish attention, I wasn't sure he'd give me a second look when I approached him. I went with a more aloof approach, and it worked. That and my often coveted genetics—blond hair, blue eyes, full lips and a statuesque frame of long legs and a large chest. All of it natural. A gift and a curse. All I had to do was walk into a room for all eyes to be drawn my way. I'd prefer to be invisible, but we didn't choose our genetics. And I couldn't totally complain. My looks had benefited me almost as much as they'd hindered me.

Tonight, I was using them to my full advantage. Scarlet-red dress hugging my body, the back open nearly down to my ass. The cut had to be perfectly tailored for the dress to stay on. I'd pinned my hair up in a stylish pile of curls to expose my neck and accentuate the dip of the dress.

In my experience, men loved the sight of a woman's neck. Delicacy and vulnerability were always attractive to predators. In this instance, I was happy to be the prey.

And to ensure my success, I painted my lips and nails the perfect shade of crimson. If all eyes weren't drawn to me before, they certainly were now. I looked like I was walking the red carpet for the Oscars, and though it might have only been an average Wednesday night, this was the Olympus Club. Every night was a red carpet night at Olympus.

"What did you think of the duck? Last week, it was overcooked," Lawrence asked as he sat back and sipped his wine.

I patted my lips with the white linen napkin, not a hint of lipstick marring the cloth, then placed it beside my finished plate. "It wasn't bad tonight and paired well with the white you chose." I took a sip from my glass. "Cards tonight?"

"Taking money off someone at the card table might help me overlook a less-than-ideal day at the office." He downed his last drops of wine and stood before helping me from my chair.

The dining room was small but not crowded. Everything about Olympus was intimate yet opulent, with a dark color palette and warm accent lights. A modern version of old-world wealth, the decor of wood and stone finishes was softened with warm leathers and velour fabrics but not in the ornate style from the past. Everything was very tastefully designed, with clean lines and simple elegance. I had to give the designer credit for a job well done.

Across from the dining room was a gaming room used for socials and after-dinner entertainment. Each of the four times

Lawrence had invited me to the weekly club dinner, there'd been poker tables in play throughout the evening. Tonight, it appeared four tables were already occupied, leaving one available.

Lawrence paused our progress, his hand at my lower back creeping around my waist to signal our stop. When I peered back at him, I was shocked to see the hint of a snarl twist his lips.

As far as I'd been able to tell, Lawrence Wellington didn't show emotion.

"What is it?" I asked discreetly.

"It would seem entry standards here are growing lax."

I followed his gaze to the two men conversing at the far table. One was bearded with a scholarly bow tie and an epic comb-over. I could only see the other man's profile, but it was all that was necessary to know he was breathtakingly hand-some. Chiseled jaw, strong brow line, and a well-propor-tioned nose over full lips, the bottom larger than the top. His dark brown hair was styled back, not a strand out of place, and his black tux squared his broad shoulders to the exacting specifications of an expert tailor. Nothing about that man denoted riffraff. And judging by the gumball-sized diamond on the other man's pinky finger, he wasn't hurting either. I was curious about what Lawrence found distasteful.

"We could always call it a night," I offered, hoping he might finally ask me back to his place. I'd been seeing the man for three months, and not once had he taken me home with him.

"No. No one is running me out of this club or anywhere else." He walked us to the back table, his stride measured yet confident.

A quick peek at Lawrence told me the handsome younger man held his ire. Interesting.

4

"Wellington, good of you to join us," said the bearded man. "I'd like to introduce you to Oran here on his first night with us. He's just joined the club."

The man named Oran stood and turned to greet us, and I nearly gasped at the sight of him. His profile was impressive, but full-on, he was exquisite masculine perfection. And tall. I'd grown used to standing eye to eye with men. In conservative heels, I was an inch taller than Lawrence. But the gray-eyed Adonis before me had to be at least six-four and every inch brimming with swagger.

Gorgeous *and* loaded? He'd probably never been told no in his entire life.

I was repulsed.

"I'm familiar with the Byrne family. You are a Byrne, aren't you?" Lawrence managed to look down his nose at the man who stood several inches taller than him. It was almost impressive.

"I am." The man's steel gaze cut to me, an invisible lasso wrenching tight around my middle and squeezing the air from my lungs. "Oran Byrne." He held his hand out for mine.

I obliged, not wanting to be rude, hating the flush that crossed my cheeks when his lips grazed my knuckles.

"At your service," he murmured, eyes never leaving mine while his hand lingered longer than appropriate.

Lawrence's hand was still on my back. Couldn't he see that? Who the hell did he think he was, making such an overtly seductive move right in front of my date?

"Lina Schultze," I offered in return with a tight smile.

Wellington pulled me closer against his side as though reasserting his claim. "You aren't honestly telling me they're considering you for membership here."

"Not considering. It's done. Tonight is my first official night as a member here at Olympus."

"Surely, there are more … *appropriate* social organizations for someone with your interests."

His interests? What was Lawrence getting at? Who was this Oran Byrne?

Oran's answering grin was so devastatingly attractive I could hear the subtle whoosh of panties dropping to the floor all around me. "Let's not be too hasty, Lawrence. We're not so far apart, you and I."

My date scoffed.

Oran raised a hand. "How about this, then? We'll let the cards decide. If you win, I'll withdraw my membership, and you'll never see me here again."

Lawrence's hand fell away from me, his chin lifting. "And if you win?"

The way Oran's stare burrowed into mine, I half expected him to ask for me. It was an absurd thought. I wasn't even sure where it had come from, nor the tinge of disappointment when he didn't.

"If I win, you allow me to discuss a business proposition with you." Oran finally cast his stare back at Lawrence. I did, too. Even the bearded stranger who'd grown silent during the exchange seemed fascinated with hearing Lawrence's reply.

Smugness tugged at a smirk on his lips. "Sounds like I have nothing to lose." Lawrence pulled out a chair and seated himself at the table.

I reached for the chair beside him, my hand colliding with Oran's. His strong fingers circled mine before I could pull away. "Please, allow me." He was being overly polite, adding yet another layer of tension to the already suffocating pressure in the room.

He released my hand to pull out my chair, but only after his thumb stroked a sensual caress up, then down the center of my palm. The tiny movement was invisible to everyone else, but I felt like he'd stripped me naked, splayed me wide open on the table, and swept his tongue the length of my center. I had no idea the palm could be so erotic.

Oran knew exactly what he'd done, according to the hint of a smirk teasing at his lips.

My legs suddenly as unsteady as a newborn fawn, I sank to my seat before anyone could detect my distress. These men weren't the only ones schooled to maintain an impeccable facade. I gave a slight dismissive nod to Oran and turned to my date—the one and only man in this room who deserved my complete attention.

Someone needed to relay that message to my heart. It had resumed its frantic sprint, convinced I needed to run for my life.

Maybe I did.

Judging by the tension around me, I was in the middle of a serious pissing contest. Lawrence sat to my right, and Oran sat a little too close to my left. I was the delectable piece of meat between them.

"Gentlemen, place your antes." The dealer began to shuffle.

Oran pushed a stack of three pink chips to the center of the table. Each represented ten thousand dollars. Lawrence motioned to the gaming supervisor for a stack of chips that would be debited from his club account. He tossed his ante haphazardly onto the table as if it didn't represent the price of a midsize sedan.

The air filled with testosterone so thick that it clotted in my lungs.

This wasn't how I'd seen my night playing out, but there was no stopping it now. Oran's appearance at the club had interrupted my plans and left me with no option but to take a slow, deep breath and watch the show unfold.

Oran

# TWO

Lina's composure was impressive. Though, I should have expected as much. No one but an ice queen could possibly be frigid enough to date a man like Wellington.

Lina was flawlessly impassive. A living, breathing Barbie doll with no greater purpose than to be played with and admired. It was a shame, in a way. Like opening a meticulously wrapped Christmas present to find nothing inside, and her packaging was nothing short of perfection. She reminded me of a 1950s pinup model—Marilyn Monroe with the most vibrant blue eyes I'd ever seen. And that voice. *Jesus Christ*, that voice. The natural huskiness made every word sound like something whispered naked in the dark.

All together, it was enough to make a man forget his own name.

I knew from experience, however, how deceiving appearances could be. The woman I'd married had seemed like quite a prize—not as innately alluring as Lina, but enticing enough to lull me into a false sense of security. My soon-to-be *ex*-wife taught me a valuable lesson on how easy it was to be deceived by a pretty package. Caitlin had looked and acted like the perfect wife for a whole goddamn year before I learned she was a fucking lunatic and a traitor.

Our marriage had been arranged, so it wasn't like we'd started with a strong foundation of loyalty, but I'd still been blindsided. My family unearthed her secrets, and now she was behind bars for murder. It was a fucked-up series of events, but it reminded me how important it was to always keep my guard up. A healthy dose of skepticism kept a man breathing. It was a lesson I wouldn't soon forget.

Lina had an agenda. I'd bet my life on it.

Her motive was probably as simple as finding someone to bankroll her lavish lifestyle, but that was still an agenda. I was glad. Someone so shallow would be easy to manipulate once I proved to her that I was just as powerful as her current conquest, with the added bonus of being able to get it up without a little blue pill. I couldn't fathom how someone as young and attractive as her could come to the conclusion that Lawrence *fucking* Wellington was her best option. The man was old enough to be her father. The situation reeked of Daddy issues.

Her commitment to him, however, was surprisingly resolute. I didn't miss the way she angled her body just slightly toward him—away from me—when she sat at the game table. I might have questioned my ability to succeed in my campaign to steal her had it not been for the tiny fluttering pulse point at the base of her neck.

Lina played her part well, but a person could only do so much to combat physiology. And now that I knew how my attention affected her, I would wage a war of seduction until she was on her knees begging for my touch. Until she forgot Lawrence Wellington ever existed.

# THREE

Tense didn't begin to describe the atmosphere. For a solid hour, Lawrence and Oran stalked one another from either side of the card table. Neither stood from their chairs, but both were on the hunt.

Watching them was fascinating. Especially Oran. Though I tried not to give him my attention, his motivations left me incredibly curious. Would he really give up his membership if he lost? Was this some sort of machismo way of earning his place in the club, or did he really have business he wanted to do with Lawrence? And if so, why would he want to work with a man who clearly didn't think highly of him?

It was baffling. Even more so was Oran's impassive handling of it all. As though he were the one with nothing to lose, rather than Lawrence. And that was how Oran played his cards—boldly and without fear of consequence. He made such risky bets that Lawrence steadily acquired a majority of his chips.

Soon, Lawrence had him by the jugular. Sensing the time was right, Lawrence upped the ante with everything he had. Oran had to decide whether to fold and survive to play another hand or to follow suit and put everything he had in the pot as well.

Other members had abandoned their games to gather around our table. Whispers mimicked the current of electricity zipping through the now sweltering room. Each breath I took grew increasingly shallow, anticipation coiling my insides into a tight knot.

Yet again, I couldn't resist glancing at the mysterious man to my left as he decided his fate. I wondered if he wasn't a little insane. He didn't look remotely affected, as though oblivious to the fact that he'd slowly been milked clean of his chips and possibly his membership. Didn't he care? Was he unaware of how hard it was to gain access to the club?

The man didn't have a hair out of place or the tiniest dot of perspiration on his brow. If I hadn't known better, I would have said he was playing for quarters, not a priceless seat among the city's most influential residents. He was either incredibly impressive or terrifyingly unstable. Maybe a little of both.

"I suppose I can always find a new club to join," Oran said in a lazy drawl, then slid his remaining chips into the center pile.

Lawrence sucked in a swift breath as did many others, initiating a chorus of hushed whispers.

"Gentlemen." The dealer signaled for the two players to show their cards.

A Cheshire grin spread wide across Lawrence's face. He laid down two queens and three sevens—a full house. Again, the room around us buzzed with chatter.

"Olympus was the wrong place for you anyway. You'll be more comfortable somewhere else."

Oran grimaced and nodded. "You may have a point." He set his five cards down in a stack and slowly spread them apart, revealing a perfect straight flush. Five cards in numeric order, all in the same suit. "But I'm gonna stick around, nonetheless."

He'd won. The bastard had done it.

The room erupted in cries of shock and laughter.

Lawrence shot to his feet, his face blistering red. "I will *not* tolerate a cheat," he barked over my head to the man seated beside me.

Feeling like the flimsy wire fence separating a ravenous lion from its dinner, I slowly scooted my chair back.

Relaxed as ever, Oran pushed back from the table and casually crossed his legs. Remaining seated somehow conveyed a confident authority despite his lower ground, and he knew it. He was adept at navigating social situations, especially ones involving conflict. I wondered how often he found himself in this sort of face-off.

"Like you said in the beginning, you haven't truly lost. All I want is for you to hear me out, but if that's really so repulsive…" He slyly cut his eyes to me. "You could always let me have Lina here instead." His baritone voice thickened to a sultry cashmere that teased across my skin.

When his words registered, however, my spine went ramrod straight. He'd caught me by surprise, so much so that I was speechless at his audacity and my shamefully weak initial reaction.

*"You're out of line,"* Lawrence hissed through clenched teeth.

Oran raised a placating hand. "My apologies. Just thought I'd throw it out there as an alternative. You seem like a man who likes options."

Lawrence's already thin lips pressed tightly together, making them nonexistent. "Meet me at 106 East 71$^{st}$ Street. Tomorrow, nine o'clock. I'll give you ten minutes and not a second more." He held his hand out to help me from my chair. "Come, Lina."

I stole one last glance at Oran from the corner of my eye. The smug bastard wore a smirk, his stare colliding with mine as though he'd known I'd look back at him.

How infuriatingly arrogant. And the playful, amused glint in his gray gaze made me want to scream with frustration because it made him so damn beautiful.

What the hell was wrong with me that I could be attracted to a man who'd just tried to take me as his prize for winning a game of cards? What was wrong with him that he'd think it was okay to even ask?

Audacity wasn't a strong enough word.

He was nothing but a self-important, pretentious egomaniac with the arrogance of a career politician. That was more like it.

As I followed Lawrence to the elevator, I had to fight the urge to stomp my feet. Rigid and distant, he was equally as perturbed by what had transpired.

"The membership committee must have lost their damn minds," he grumbled as we rode down the elevator. "But I admit that I'm mildly intrigued by the man."

I wasn't surprised. Oran probably reminded him of himself twenty years earlier.

"Who is he?" I'd been dying to ask earlier but never had

the chance.

"His family is the strongest contingency of Irish … *businessmen* in the city." He held the elevator door for me to exit.

Businessmen? Did he mean organized crime? Was Oran Irish Mafia?

Jesus. This kept getting better and better.

It was no wonder the man thought the rules didn't apply to him. Although, that was true of most men at Olympus. When I thought about it, I wasn't sure he was any different at all except for the label. Plenty of purportedly upstanding citizens were shady as hell. At least the Mafia didn't pretend to be something they weren't.

I wanted to ask more questions but didn't want to upset Lawrence. What I really needed to do was defuse the situation and focus on my own agenda.

We walked to where Lawrence's driver waited in a black Town Car. When Lawrence opened the back door for me, I faced him instead of getting in. I slowly ran my fingers down his lapel as if to straighten it, then peered up at him through my lashes. "I'm sorry the night didn't go your way. I hate to leave you on a sour note."

*Come on, Larry. Invite me back to your place.*

It'd been almost three months since we started seeing each other, and the man *still* hadn't taken me home with him. In all honesty, he'd been a perfect gentleman, and it was driving me up a fucking wall.

Lawrence cupped my jaw with his hand, then swept his thumb slowly across my lips. I started to get excited that maybe we were finally getting somewhere, but then his face fell as if … disappointed? *Why?* I practically offered myself up on a silver platter. Did the little blue pill not work for him? What else could he possibly be disappointed about?

"If you want to help, you could come to my place

tomorrow sometime before nine. If I have to see the man again, at least I can remind him of what I have that he doesn't."

Finally. A glint of hope that our relationship just might be progressing. It was the first sign I'd seen of Lawrence feeling possessive over me.

"I'd be happy to." I grinned up at him. "Can I bring you some coffee? Maybe a pastry?"

"I start my day early, so that won't be necessary. Now, get in the car before you freeze. I can't have you getting sick."

I placed a quick kiss on his cheek, then did as he instructed. A few minutes later, he dropped me off in front of my apartment building. Or so *he* thought. It was the building I'd told him I lived in, but the truth was, I shared a much older, smaller apartment in an adjacent building. One that had yet to be renovated in an area quickly being gentrified into a thriving community.

I waited in the lobby until the car was out of sight, then left the glitzy new construction and hurried across the street toward the old relic I called home. It wasn't much to look at, but at least we had an elevator. A very old, sketchy elevator that smelled a little too much like urine for my liking. But when you lived on the eighth floor, you took what you could get so long as it wasn't the stairs.

"Honey, I'm home," I called in a somewhat weary tone when I opened the door and saw Jessa cuddled up watching television. God, I was jealous. I would have given my left tit to have been in her comfy house shoes tonight rather than swimming with the sharks at Olympus.

"How was your night?" she asked with a smile.

"Better, I suppose."

"I can't believe you've been seeing this guy for three months, and he still hasn't come up here."

*Get used to it because that's not happening.*

"Yeah, he's pretty private." Jessa knew me well enough from living together over the years, though we weren't overly close. It was probably my fault. I was more guarded than most, but the living arrangement worked well for us. Jess knew bits and pieces of my past—enough to paint a picture without giving too many details. And she knew my estranged family had come back into the picture, but I hadn't told her more because I preferred to pretend that part of my life didn't exist, Lawrence and Olympus included. "This one isn't long-term, trust me." I tossed my clutch on the coffee table and slid off my heels. "How was your evening?"

"You're looking at it."

My shoulders sagged as I sighed deeply. "You lucky whore."

She burst out laughing and threw a pillow at my head. "Hey now, you could have been just as lucky. You chose to go out."

My laughter faded at the thought of just how wrong she was. "I suppose I did." I unzipped my dress and turned away from my roommate, hoping she didn't see my face fall. I couldn't help it. Her words were a reminder of just how little choice I really had.

Bemoaning my circumstances only made me hate myself more than I already did.

I was to blame for my situation—for everything that had happened—so it was my responsibility to make it right. I had no business complaining.

I put on my pajamas and settled into my sewing station near the window. The main living space in our apartment was oversized by city standards, which was good because it served as my bedroom, closet, and office, along with our living, kitchen, and dining rooms. Jessa had a small bedroom and paid a premium share of the rent for that privilege. My futon sofa was all I'd needed when my focus was so absorbed in my design career.

"You working tonight?" she asked, clicking off the television.

"Yeah, I want to get a little further on this one dress before I call it a night." Plus, sewing was therapeutic for me. When I cleared my mind to focus on the delicate stitches that went into a designer garment, all my worries evaporated. When I was sewing, I was free, and I needed that right now.

"Sounds good. I'm gonna head to bed."

"Night, Jess."

"Night."

I clicked on my task light and let the world fall away. It was a feeling I knew well—my favorite part of every day. Except this time, I couldn't clear my mind. As I examined the expensive blue silk, I was reminded of the tiny hint of navy sheen to Oran's tuxedo. That thought triggered a phantom touch down the center of my palm, which morphed into a full-body shiver.

The man was sex on a stick. Unapologetically seductive. Relentlessly charming. He was an over-the-top rom-com hero come to life minus the com because nothing about his potential to devastate was funny. Tropical storm Oran was on the horizon with Cat 5 potential.

*Get a grip, Lina. You have to ignore him.*

I'd gotten my first invitation to the Wellington mansion. I couldn't waste the opportunity, whether it was Oran joining us or the Pope. Being there with Lawrence was all that mattered. Oran Byrne was irrelevant.

*Oran Byrne couldn't be irrelevant if his life depended on it.*

Hell, I was in trouble.

Oran

# FOUR

THE DECEMBER AIR ON MY OFFICE BALCONY CUT DEEP, BUT THE two-hundred-year-old malt I sipped bit back. I liked the burn of both. They kept my head focused, and I needed that right now.

Tonight had been the first big step in my plans. I had to make sure everything played out perfectly, and I couldn't afford distractions like a certain ice queen whose glacial stare I couldn't seem to forget. I should have been running through scenarios to prepare for tomorrow's meeting. Instead, my mind was plagued with curiosity about Lina and her relationship with Wellington.

After spending an hour at the gaming table beside her, I grew increasingly intrigued. She'd come off as intelligent, confident, and intuitive—it was just a first impression, but mine were rarely wrong. Why the hell would a gorgeous woman like that be with a man like Wellington?

I did a brief internet search and saw that she came from money. That didn't necessarily mean *she* had money or would inherit her family's money, but was Wellington really necessary? What other motivation could she have besides money?

Daddy issues. It had to be.

I almost felt bad for her. Almost, but not quite.

No one grows up without a few issues. She had the money to get a fucking shrink. She should have done that instead of hooking up with men twice her age. Or at least had the wherewithal to find someone halfway decent to cozy up to. Wellington hadn't even pulled out the goddamn chair for her. And when I'd suggested a night with her, just to see how he'd react, he'd considered it for a fraction of a second. I saw it in his eyes. I would have missed the telling flash had I not been intentionally watching for it.

What a fucking pig.

I couldn't wait to see his smug face once I'd crippled his shipping empire and muddied his name so badly that no one in a thousand-mile radius would look at him.

It was coming. Soon.

And while Lina might not have been his one true love, I'd take her from him too. The man had an ego to rival a self-appointed dictator, and I wanted to cut him down in every way possible.

Death would have been too easy. Wellington needed to suffer.

He'd enabled sex traffickers. He knew his son was a fucking psychopath abusing and killing women, yet instead of stopping him, Lawrence Wellington set him up with a source to ensure his fetishes weren't discovered. One of the women he'd killed had been an acquaintance of mine—a girl who'd worked at one of our clubs. When I learned how he'd been involved, I decided to take on a mission of vengeance. Wellington had to pay for his actions just as dearly as the people he'd hurt. I was going to savor every minute of his downfall, and only when he was at his lowest, once he knew his entire life had been an utter failure, would I consider killing the fucker. Slowly and painfully.

♦

The Wellington mansion was an austere memorial to days past. A stone exterior with carved elements that had to have cost a fortune even back when it was first built, it was one of a handful of well-preserved single-family mansions in the exclusive Lennox Hill neighborhood.

Many properties had been updated or fallen into disrepair. Wellington's statuesque home looked almost as pristine as it had one hundred years ago. Not even the steadily falling rain could soften the foreboding look of the place.

I could see why Wellington had selected it. I hated it, but I could see why *he* would have chosen it. No one would dare question the clout of a man who owned such an obelisk of history and wealth.

*Fucking narcissist.*

When I rang the bell, a short, older woman answered with a smile. "Can I help you?"

"Yes, I have an appointment with Mr. Wellington."

"Your name?"

"Oran Byrne."

She dipped her chin and stepped back to allow me inside. "Mr. Wellington is expecting you. If you'll wait there in the lounge, he'll be with you shortly."

She took my coat from me, the heavy wool dotted with rain, and hung it on an ornate entry piece off to the side. The inside of the home lived up to every expectation the exterior had created. The entry floor was a checkerboard of black and white marble with a polished sheen. A large spiral staircase wrapped around the edge of the circular room, the decorative iron spindles supporting the rail only outdone by the plaster carvings beneath. Every wall was detailed with gold wainscoting, and the chandelier overhead could have belonged to Rockefeller himself.

No expense had been spared. No detail bypassed.

And the lounge to the right was the same. Even the high ceilings were artfully decorated with a coordinating plaster embossing, and large palatial windows were dressed with tassel-lined satin drapes. The place could have been a museum. It was unquestionably impressive and just about the worst place to live I could imagine.

I was conducting a loop around the room when a section of wall hinged open beside me, and Lina rushed out. She collided flush with my chest, gasping as she bounced off me. I grabbed her arms to keep her from stumbling backward into what appeared to be a small powder room.

That was when it hit me that she was soaked.

Her ivory silk blouse clung to her like a second skin, exposing every intricate detail of the black lace bra she wore beneath. Lips parted and hair still clumped in damp, wavy strands, she peered up at me with wide blue eyes. It was the sexiest goddamn thing I'd ever seen.

*Fucking Christ.*

# FIVE

"You can let go now." Why the hell did I sound like I'd just had the best orgasm of my life? Breathless and disbelieving. In awe, if you will. Not at *all* how I wanted to sound when stumbling into Oran Byrne's arms.

My body had a mind of its own where he was concerned.

I was usually a pro at appearing unruffled, but I'd been thrown off my game by a damn coffee delivery truck. The blazer I'd been wearing wasn't ideal in the rain, but I managed fine until the matchbox-sized mini truck raced through a puddle by the curb and shot up a rooster tail of water that completely drenched me. I'd been scrambling to mentally catch up ever since.

"Trust me," Oran said in a dark murmur. "I know exactly what I can and can't do."

His hands stayed put for several eternal seconds before lowering. It was as if to ensure I knew he was releasing me because he was ready, not because I'd asked. I hadn't realized how warm his hands were until they were gone, the loss making me shiver.

Or was that my body responding to his overbearing proximity?

Oran had let go, but he hadn't backed away. If anything, he felt even closer—something about the heat radiating off him, just out of reach. My already hard nipples felt like they were straining for him.

That's when I remembered that my damn blouse was so wet, I was practically naked.

"*Touch*." I announced, hands going to my hips as I owned all sixty-nine inches of my full height.

"Excuse me?" His molten silver eyes lifted from my chest to my cutting gaze.

"That's what you can't do. You might be able to look, but you can't ... *touch*." I didn't back away. I refused to let this man or any other think he could intimidate me.

"And Lawrence? Does he get to touch?"

"What I do with Lawrence is none of your business."

A guttural rumble of amusement resonated from deep in his chest.

"And if I make it my business?"

I got the sense he'd meant to tease me, but his words had a predatorial edge to them, the deep timbre reminding me of a hungry jungle cat. Why did his voice have to be so damn seductive?

My heart did a stutter step that made my head spin. I wanted to believe it was the menace in his tone that affected

24

me, but that would have been a lie. Every shallow breath was owed to the graphic image that burst into my mind of Oran fucking me against a wall while my legs were wrapped around his middle. It was so hyper-realistic that it could have come from a memory, but I'd never once been with a man like Oran. I would have remembered.

"Then you'd be an unwelcome intrusion." I tried to keep pace with him, but my thoughts were all over the place.

He raised his hand so slowly, I had an eternity to wonder what exactly he planned to do before his knuckles finally made contact with my neck. He swept his hand upward, coming away with a drop of water transferred to his skin. I watched raptly as he lapped up the tiny droplet with a slow swipe of his tongue.

"*Liar.*" His exhaled word feathered across my skin.

"Who are you?" I breathed, my voice abandoning me.

"I'm whoever you want me to be, so long as you want me."

I didn't have time to process his offer before footsteps sounded in the foyer. Reality came crashing back to me like an icy bucket of water all over my already freezing body. I lurched backward and hurriedly retrieved the hand towel I'd dropped at my feet.

"Lina? What on earth happened to you?" Lawrence stood across the room, gaping at me.

"Poor city drainage and a reckless delivery driver, that's what happened. I was just toweling off when Oran arrived." I abandoned the man beside me and crossed the large sitting room to Lawrence.

His brow furrowed disapprovingly. "I thought you'd be joining us, but not like that. It's too cold to run around soaking wet. You should probably get home and change."

I smiled reassuringly. "I came all this way to see you. I'll be fine now that I'm drying off." I tried so hard to ward off the chatter in my teeth, but I couldn't hold back a shiver that started in my shoulders and shook me down to my toes.

Lawrence shook his head, pursing his lips. "Why do women always have to be so damn stubborn? Find Hannah. Maybe she'll have something you can change into." He looked over my shoulder to Oran. "My office is back here."

"One second." Oran walked past me into the foyer. When he returned, he had his coat in his hands. "Before you freeze to death," he mumbled gruffly as he draped the heavy wool over my shoulders.

"Thank you."

He grunted, then returned to Lawrence. I sensed he was irritated, but I wasn't sure why. Wasn't he the one offering himself to me minutes earlier? And he didn't have to give me his coat. I would have been fine without it.

As if lashing out in argument, my body shook with another shiver.

"Yeah, yeah. I get it. I needed the damn coat."

Good grief, the man was so confounding he had me talking to myself out loud. Leaning into my already ridiculous behavior, I breathed deeply when the sandalwood scent lingering on his coat enveloped me.

God, it smelled good. *He* smelled good.

My conscience rained down a shower of acidic guilt, searing my insides. Why the hell was I wasting time acting like a hormonal teen? I needed to stop screwing around. This was the first time Lawrence had invited me to his home, and I'd been left to my own devices for who knew how long. I had to make the most of it—look around and see what I could learn, but quickly.

I needed Lawrence to trust me. To let me in past that outer barrier he kept up. Anything I could find to help speed along his opening up would be a huge win. I was running out of time. Each day, the desperation I'd been consumed with for months withered a little more into a desolate sense of hopelessness.

Focus returned, I hung Oran's coat back on its hook with a touch more aggression than necessary, then quietly hurried up the grand staircase to the second story. I wouldn't have long. Considering how irritated Lawrence was to see Oran last night, I doubted he'd give the younger man much chance.

Peeking into the first room I came to, I suspected it belonged to Lawrence's son who'd recently moved away. I hadn't had a chance to meet him, which was probably best. I was closer in age to Stetson than his father. That could have been awkward.

I gathered that the two didn't have a good relationship. Stetson hadn't returned to visit since he'd left two months ago. Or maybe that was just my jaded nature coloring my perspective. It was easy for me to understand wanting to escape your parents.

The room was still decorated with field hockey memorabilia but no pictures or anything particularly personal. He'd likely taken that stuff with him. I didn't have time to dig in any drawers, but I did make a mental note to ask Lawrence more about Stetson. Parents generally liked talking about their kids either out of pride or irritation. It would be a good conversation starter.

I moved on to the closed door across the hall. I only needed a quick peek to know this room was rarely occupied. While Stetson's room had traditional-style furniture built in the modern day, this bedroom seemed to be a tribute to the past. Each ornate piece looked like it could have been original to the house, intricately carved with gold leaf embossed on some design elements. If I stayed there, I'd wake each morning feeling like I'd fallen into an episode of *Downton Abbey*.

At the end of the hall was a cozy yet luxurious family room with a huge television and a giant sectional to match. Everything looked professionally designed, and it was the most modernized room I'd seen so far. The downstairs had been painstakingly kept in its original design.

Feeling each second ticking by like water through my fingers, I rushed to the other end of the hall only to find three more meaningless guest rooms and a small stairwell to a third level I didn't have time to explore.

My first big break, and I hadn't learned a goddamn thing.

I was so frustrated I could have screamed. But I'd come too far to ruin things now with a lapse of control. Instead, I steeled myself and slipped back downstairs to search for Hannah, the housekeeper. I'd had to rush to the bathroom to dry off when I first arrived, so I hadn't had a chance to talk to her. If anyone could tell me about Lawrence, it would be her.

I found my target in the kitchen, slicing vegetables by the sink. "Hello? It's Hannah, right?"

"Oh! Yes, come on in. I'm just getting some soup ready to simmer for tonight. I figured it would be perfect with this rain."

I grimaced. "Yeah, sounds like it's still pouring out there. I can't believe I ended up soaked."

Hannah shook her head sternly. "Those fool drivers never think of anyone but themselves. I was almost hit crossing the street a few weeks ago. Just ridiculous."

I leaned against the island and smiled ruefully. "Life's so busy these days, it's a miracle any of us know which way is up."

"True," she said, sadness entering her voice.

"I suppose it's been quiet here since Stetson moved out." I

snatched the opening she'd presented and tried to fish for information on Lawrence's son.

Hannah's gaze drifted to me somewhat warily. I sensed that her warm personality didn't translate to loose lips. It was still worth a shot.

"He had his own place in the city, so things haven't changed all that much. Did you get to meet him before he moved?"

"No, unfortunately. But I hope I'll get the chance soon."

"That would be nice. I'm looking forward to a visit from him as well."

"Maybe with both of us asking, Lawrence will make it happen."

"Oh no." She cast a scandalized look my way. "I wouldn't bother them with something so silly, same as I didn't fuss about not getting to say bye before Stetson left. It's not my place to make demands of them."

The kid had moved without coming by to see her? That was sort of strange. I adored our housekeeper growing up. She was more of a mother to me than my own.

Had I been off in thinking that Hannah had been with them for a long time?

"I take it you've been working for Lawrence for a while?" I joined her, scooping her carrot scraps into the waste bin she'd set beside her.

"Oh! You don't have to do that."

"It's no problem. I like helping."

"Well, thank you." She seemed flustered, giving me the impression she wasn't used to the family joining her. "You seem awfully comfortable in the kitchen."

"I've always been stubbornly independent. I started cooking for myself at an early age." If you could call microwaving ramen cooking. It took me a while to acquire the tools and skills, but eleven years after leaving home, I was more than a little competent in the kitchen.

Hannah hadn't answered my question, but it seemed out of place to push, so I let it go.

"We had a housekeeper who taught me a few things. Once I moved out on my own, I put those lessons to the test."

"It never hurts for a young person to learn self-sufficiency." Her tone grew matronly, and I got the sense it was an argument she'd raised more than once in her employment.

"Agreed. You never know what the world will throw at you." I knew that hard truth all too well.

An echo of male voices carried down the hall.

"Sounds like they're done talking. I better get back out there."

"Thanks for the visit. It's nice having a little female company around here," she said conspiratorially.

"Absolutely. Hopefully, I'll see you again soon." I smiled warmly, then returned to the foyer where Lawrence was closing the door behind Oran.

"How did it go?" I asked with a smile.

"Hard to say," he murmured distractedly, then looked me up and down. "You're still in those wet clothes. Come on, I'll run you home. I need to go into the office now anyway."

My shoulders sagged a fraction. I'd hoped to get a glimpse of his home office—what I imagined would be his inner sanctum.

"I'd appreciate that." I forced a smile.

Even if I didn't have anything tangible to work with, the morning had still been a success. I'd gotten a look around the Wellington mansion and talked to his housekeeper. It was a big step in the right direction.

As for Oran, he'd proven just how dangerous a distraction he could be. I could only hope I never saw the man again.

Oran

# SIX

"My son has been missing for months, and the woman he was dating is now *married* to a Byrne. Do you really expect me to believe those two facts are unrelated?" Wellington stared icily at me from across his desk.

I was struck by how dispassionate he was on the subject. He believed my family was responsible for his son's disappearance, yet he didn't show an ounce of outrage or resentment or even the tiniest bit of pain. If my child had gone missing, I would have been an inconsolable ball of fury shredding the very fabric of the city until my child was back home.

Wellington acted like it was a car that had been stolen, not his son.

"I expect you to be a man of business capable of using logic. My cousin was married to his wife well before your son went missing. If I was going to look for a culprit, I might be more interested in a certain Russian you've been doing business with. Did he tell you how he miraculously ended up with our stolen guns, then came after us when we confronted him?"

Wellington studied me intently. I knew very well that he didn't know anything about our business with the Russian and that he certainly wouldn't know I'd muddied the truth. All I needed was to nurture the uncertainty he was already facing about his son's disappearance. The truth was, my family *had* killed his son, but Wellington had a shit ton of enemies. Figuring out which one of us was to blame would be a monumental task. How likely was it that the man sitting across from him putting forth a business proposition had been responsible?

Oh, the irony.

"What is it you're here to say?" he demanded gruffly. He hated for me to be right, but he couldn't deny I had a point.

I took the win graciously and reserved my gloating for a later date. "As I mentioned, we've had an issue with stolen shipments recently. We need to make new arrangements."

"And what could possibly entice me into helping you?"

This was it. The lynchpin.

I'd thought long and hard about this question because having the right answer was crucial.

"Aside from the fact that we own half the police force in the city, which makes life a hell of a lot easier, my cousin is now married into the Moretti family. Conner Byrne recently married Renzo Donati's niece." I let the information sink in.

As the owner of one of the largest shipping companies in the world, Wellington would be familiar with the Italian family who controlled the docks throughout New York via the dock workers union. Wellington and all other shipping companies were in never-ending negotiations with the dock workers. Having an inside connection would be priceless for him.

"I'd say family dinners with the Donatis would be enticing for a man in your profession. I wouldn't have come here if I didn't believe we have enough common ground to form a mutually beneficial arrangement."

Wellington steepled his hands together in contemplation. "What exactly did you have in mind?"

"Once a month, I'll need a quarter of a container. That's it. And as for Donati, how does dinner on Sunday sound?"

"I suppose we could see how dinner goes..." He trailed off, his gaze unfocused as he contemplated the possibilities.

"You could bring Lina with you. She's absolutely stunning." I decided to test the waters, wanting to see his reaction. "I don't suppose you're the sort to share?"

I hadn't expected him to lash out. He wasn't the type. But the degree to which he was unbothered was somewhat unexpected. Not even the slightest twitch in his eye or flare of a nostril.

"In this world, nothing is off-limits for the right price."

*Wrong answer, asshole.*

"Good to know. Our first sit-down might not be the place for her, but it's something we could explore."

His answering smirk was so goddamn slimy, I was going to need to shower off the filth when I got home.

I couldn't understand why the hell she put up with a man like him. I wanted Lina as part of my plans to humiliate Wellington, but I'd be doing her a favor. I had to win her over so she'd leave the bastard. Lawrence Wellington only cared about power. That was frighteningly evident to me now more than ever. His son. Lina. He didn't care about either of them.

A glance around the room didn't reveal a single family picture. Not one. Instead, framed news articles of Wellington's business acquisitions and personal accolades adorned the walls. Meaningless decorative bobbles and crystal placards engraved with awards he'd received throughout the years lined his bookshelves. I wondered if he wasn't legitimately certifiable—some sort of sociopath incapable of love and empathy. He was a narcissist at the very least.

The one good thing about his limitless ego was the fact that he was so absorbed with himself that he failed to detect his own downfall sitting before him. I wondered if he could hear the clock counting down to his own Armageddon.

I could hear it, and the steady beat was music to my ears.

# SEVEN

"You never cease to amaze me." My business partner and dear friend, Cosmo, stepped back to admire a bust I'd outfitted with the red dress I'd sewn last week. He took in the piece as a whole, then moved close to examine the seams and stitching.

"I hope that's a good thing." I grinned, knowing exactly what he meant.

"Girl, this dress is even better than I imagined. I don't know how you do it." He paced around to the back and adjusted the straps. "You think it'll stay on? There's not much to the back."

"I know it will because I wore it out last night."

Cosmo spun around, spearing me with a salacious stare.

"You don't seriously think you can say that without telling all, do you?" He rested his hand on a cocked hip. "Where, why, and *who*? I want all the deets."

I chuckled and sat in one of the workshop chairs. We rented a thousand-square-foot studio as our base of operations. It was a converted factory building, so the rent was good, and the light was even better. It housed bolts of fabric, a sewing station, a standing-height cutting table, another smaller table for business discussions, and racks and racks of clothing. It was a good workspace, but I preferred to work at my home office. I liked to shut out the world when I worked. As much as I adored Cosmo, he could be more distracting than a small tornado.

"Just a guy I've been seeing. We went to dinner—nothing special." I hadn't told Cosmo anything about Lawrence because he would have gone into cardiac arrest if he had known the details. Cosmo could be a smidge overly dramatic.

One perfectly sculpted brow arched high on his forehead. "This dress and nothing special could never exist in the same world, let alone the same sentence."

I shrugged. "It is what it is."

"Well, maybe I should get his number because if he didn't instantly try to put a ring on it in this dress, he must be gay."

A laugh burst past my lips at the absurdity that a simple dress could motivate a man to marry. As I laughed, however, I remembered the way Oran had touched me and how his stare had burrowed into mine—and I started to reconsider. He'd acted like he was seconds away from claiming me for himself. Then there was the way he'd looked at me in my wet silk blouse. Like I was Little Red, and he was the ravenous Wolf.

I had to clear my suddenly parched throat. "Life is a little more complicated than that, but I appreciate your endorsement."

Cosmo huffed. "I suppose if he doesn't make the effort and appreciate all this"—he motioned up and down my body with fluttering fingers—"then he doesn't deserve it."

"Absolutely," I agreed.

"Good. Now that that's decided. I'll take this beauty and the two black ones to Faith at Chiara. They'll make a perfect addition to the pitch for next fall's collection."

"Sounds good to me! I'm going to head home. I have a few more hours, and the navy silk blend will be done."

"The one with the halter neckline?"

"Yes. That fabric you sourced was *perfect*, almost black with a touch of navy sheen. It's gorgeous."

"This time, if you get a chance to wear it out, I better see a pic," he chided me playfully.

That wasn't happening because I had no reason to wear such a statement dress, but I saluted anyway. "Understood." I gave Cosmo a quick hug. "I'll be in touch."

"Counting on it."

I'd been incredibly lucky when I met Cosmo in design school. We were an excellent complement to one another, making for a remarkably functional business model. We designed together in late-night binge-eating sessions that left me exhausted yet immensely fulfilled. I did most of the actual sewing while he schmoozed and sold our designs to labels. After five years of busting our asses, we'd finally made a name for ourselves and even contemplated hiring an assistant.

The pride bubbling with warmth in my chest fizzled out as I thought about who I'd wanted to hire for the job. It would have been the perfect setup for my sister, but I never got the opportunity to tell her. She'd been gone for three months now. I'd spent every single minute of that time fighting to get her back, but the more time that drew on, the more I worried I'd lost her forever.

I descended the stairs to the subway, shivering as the suffocating helplessness that had been my constant companion for months wrapped me in its arctic embrace. Remorse and despair had loomed over me daily, making their presence known the most when I went home for the night because I should have moved out of the apartment with Jessa months ago. I tried not to show it, but seeing my roommate was a stark reminder of how horribly things had gone wrong. And once Jessa went to bed, the solitude of my quiet apartment, while providing the perfect sewing atmosphere, also denied me an escape from myself and the incessant thoughts that assaulted me day and night.

Was I doing enough?

Why hadn't I made any progress?

What else could I possibly do?

I felt so fucking helpless, and I hated it.

I slumped in my seat on the subway train home. My vision blurred with watery regrets as I stared at the dirt-speckled floor. I'd tried so hard to make good choices and be a decent human being, yet I'd fallen damn short of the mark. Maybe it was defective genetics. An insidious selfishness that manifested itself no matter how hard a person fought to overcome.

I had to wipe my eyes when the tears broke free.

What I wouldn't have given to go back to the beginning of summer and do it all again. Life wasn't like the movies, however. There were no do-overs. I could only move forward and try not to make another mistake—especially not an enigmatic, disarming mistake with eyes so piercing they thwarted all my defenses.

Oran was the worst sort of mistake and a distraction I couldn't afford. One missed opportunity could be the difference between life and death. I had to stay focused on my mission or risk hating myself forever.

I almost dropped my phone when it vibrated in my hand, startling me from my thoughts.

**Unknown: It sure is a waste, Lina**

*What?*

I didn't give my number out often, so a text from an unknown number was unusual. And it had come from someone who knew my nickname. The only new person I'd met recently … it couldn't be. How would he have my number? If not him, then who? Not one person came to mind.

Getting the text when I'd already been thinking about him was too fitting. He felt omnipresent like that—saturating my thoughts and senses. I was just telling myself how important it was to steer clear of him, and there he was, luring me back in. The curiosity. The intrigue.

I wasn't sure what the text meant, but it sounded like something he'd say. Something to keep me off-balance and guessing.

Telling myself it was just a text, I typed out a response.

**Me: Who is this?**

**Unknown: Wrong question.**

The authoritative response sent a thrill of awareness down my spine and out to my fingertips.

I was right. Oran was texting me.

I wanted to ask how he'd gotten my number, but I knew his answer already. *Still the wrong question.* I could have blocked him. I should have. It was the logical thing to do, but responding to him wasn't so much a decision as a compulsion. I *needed* to know what he'd reached out to say. Needed to feel the heady rush I got from his attention. I'd been in such a dark place for so long that I craved his spotlight.

**Me: What's a waste?**

**Unknown: Every minute you spend with him.**

There it was. Warmth spread from my chest down to my belly and onward. He was wrong about my time being wasted, but I liked knowing it bothered him.

**Me: Jealous much?**

A tiny smile perched at the corners of my lips.

**Unknown: It's hard to be jealous of something that's already mine.**

That got an audible laugh.

**Me: I was wrong.**

**Me: You're not jealous. You're arrogant.**

I practically salivated for his response like a junkie anticipating her next hit. This man was so damn dangerous for me, but I couldn't stop myself. Truth be told, I didn't want to.

I waited a solid minute, staring at my phone screen for his reply.

**Unknown: I'm right.**

I started to text a response, then deleted it, a hollow void expanding in my chest. What the hell was I doing? Engaging him was pointless. If anything was a waste of my time, it was texting Oran Byrne. I needed to get my head out of the clouds and stop letting myself get distracted.

**Me: As if you'd be any different.**

I wasn't sure I believed it, but the despondency I felt was seeping through.

**Unknown: Let me show you.**

Exactly. It was pointless. I shook my head slowly and started to shut down the conversation when he sent another quick message.

**Unknown: Look in your purse.**

My heart teased its way up my chest and into my throat.

I glanced around, suddenly aware of the people on the train with me, feeling like they all surely heard my thundering pulse. After assuring myself no one was paying attention, I slid my hand into the moderately sized leather tote-style purse I'd been carrying lately. I wasn't the sort to carry a ton of unnecessary items around, but being on the go in the city meant needing a good number of things on hand at any given time.

I jostled a few items before I saw a photo-sized piece of white cardstock paper that I didn't recognize. When I pulled it out, I discovered that it was an invitation.

*A cordial invitation to*
*The Bastion Club's*
*5ᵗʰ Annual December Masquerade*

Beneath the listed address was a date. Tomorrow.

**Unknown: Give me a chance, Lina. Come by tomorrow —I'll be there all night.**

I didn't reply. My mind was too busy racing.

Olympus wasn't the only club Oran belonged to. What sort of club was Bastion? The invitation looked formal, with elegant embossing on expensive cardstock. Maybe it was silly of me, but I was surprised I hadn't heard of it.

*Maybe it was just as secretive as Olympus.*

Using printed invitations? That didn't track. So ... not secretive, but maybe still elite? Maybe that was why he'd joined Olympus, though—because it provided something other clubs didn't.

Unease coalesced into a thick sludge in my stomach.

Was I being ridiculous? I couldn't tell anymore. My body responded to him unlike it had to any other man. I didn't understand. He was the same as the rest, wasn't he? He was angling to do business with Lawrence—that meant his morals were definitely questionable. He wanted me to give him a chance, but I could never trust him. Use him? Maybe. But never trust.

My phone buzzed again.

I took a slow, deep breath to prepare for what he might have said next, only the message wasn't from Oran. It was a thousand times worse. The message was from my mother.

That sludge in my belly turned rancid.

**Eliza: We need to talk. Can you come by the house?**

The gall. I wouldn't step foot in that house if it started raining acid, and that place was the only shelter.

**Me: No. If you need to say something, say it.**

**Eliza: I'm not texting about this, Carolina.**

I should have told her to fuck off. That was what she deserved. Hell, I would have had her number blocked if I didn't suspect she knew more than she was telling me. I didn't trust my mother or her asshole husband, but on the off chance she had real information, I couldn't ignore her.

**Me: Meet me tomorrow, 1pm at the Applebee's on 50<sup>th</sup>.**

**Eliza: You can't be serious.**

If I had to see the woman who birthed me, then I would make the most of it. Seeing her mortification at the possibility of being spotted entering her equivalent of a food brothel would fill my heart with joy.

**Me: You'll survive.**

I grinned.

She didn't deign to reply.

Lina

# EIGHT

I ARRIVED AT APPLEBEE'S EARLY SO I'D ALREADY HAVE A BOOTH, forcing Eliza to make the walk of shame through the restaurant. I even asked to be seated in the back. A vision came to mind of Cersei Lannister walking naked through the streets of King's Landing in *A Game of Thrones*, the people throwing food at her and calling out "shame."

I grinned. This wasn't the same, but close enough. I'd take what I could get.

Eliza arrived wearing large dark sunglasses and a scarf tied around her hair, neither of which she removed upon entering the restaurant or sitting down. She perched on the edge of her bench so stiffly, I would have thought it was lined with broken glass. Such a bitch.

"What do you want?" I asked dryly.

"Don't you think this has gone on long enough?"

"I'm not stopping until I get answers."

"If there was something to find, you'd have found it by now."

"Not necessarily. I think we both know how well you and your cronies keep secrets." Secrets like how they'd do anything to acquire status as New York elite, and they weren't above using their children in the process.

"You've dangled this over our heads long enough. You need to start looking somewhere else." Her words struck a nerve, and all my frustrations surfaced. So much time had slipped by, and I was no better off than when I started this hunt. I couldn't fathom how she could be right, yet... Maybe I could use her impatience to weasel information out of her. I'd gone to her in the beginning, but of course, she swore she didn't know anything. Would her answer change now? I'd had to blackmail her to get my foot in the door at that fucking nightmare of a club. I wondered what she'd offer up at this point to get me to disappear.

"Do you have reason to think I should focus my efforts elsewhere?" I raised a brow as I bit into a french fry.

She sneered, her body listing backward in the booth. But as she considered my words, she seemed to sober, her blue eyes going glacial. "Maybe you should ask that handsome new stranger about how he acquired his membership at Olympus."

Her insinuation shocked me, but I'd come prepared with my best poker face, so I didn't show any reaction. But then, neither did she. I couldn't tell if there was any truth hiding in her comment. Could Oran be the man I was looking for? He and Lawrence had known one another, at least tangentially, which would explain Lawrence's role. I knew Lawrence was involved, but could Oran be the one truly responsible?

Everything inside me rebelled at the notion. I didn't want it to be true, but I had to admit the theory had merit.

"It's time you left Lawrence alone," she added for good measure, sensing she had my attention. The fact that he'd started dating me had to have eaten her alive. He was like the Grand Poobah of their little band of miscreants. Warning him away from me would have reflected poorly on her, and that wasn't an option. Image was everything to my mother.

"I'll do exactly as I damn well please, *Eliza*," I said coolly.

Her eyes narrowed behind the dark lenses. "It doesn't matter what name you use. It will never change the fact that I'm your mother, Carolina." My given name on her lips was nails down a chalkboard to my ears.

"Maybe to you, but as far as I'm concerned, you surrendered that title eleven years ago, and you will *never* get it back. We're done here. You can leave." I took out my phone and began to type out an inconsequential message to Jessa purely to be dismissive. I refused to storm away from my mother. A rebuff was much more satisfying, and doing it without the slightest tremor in my fingers was orgasmic.

Fuck.

Her.

Eliza huffed, scooted herself from the bench, and marched out of the restaurant. The sight of her tucking tail and running brought a smile to my face.

"I'm so sorry I didn't get over here quicker. Did she want to order anything?" The young server looked worriedly over her shoulder toward the exit.

"Not at all. She just popped in for a word."

"Okay. Is there anything else I can get you?"

"Actually, I think dessert is in order. Let's do an Oreo shake."

"Whipped cream on top?"

"Oh yeah. I'm fancy like that."

The girl grinned wide at my cheesy reference to the Walker Hayes song lyrics. "Coming right up."

While I waited, I sat back and considered what I planned to do about Oran. I didn't want to screw things up with Lawrence on the off chance that he did have information, and I just hadn't unearthed it yet. I knew his mansion had been involved at the very least. That was plenty of justification to keep him as my number one suspect. He had to know something. But if he wasn't the only one with information, wouldn't it make sense to broaden my search?

Sliding my hand into my purse, I pulled out the invitation still floating inside. The Bastion Club.

I entered the name into Google and scrolled through the resulting pictures and references. It was a social club, not totally unlike Olympus, but clearly not as secretive. It had a web page and an address listed. There were even pictures from inside—formal events and gaming tables.

The club appeared legitimate enough to be safe for a night. There would be plenty of people present. What did I have to lose? I had to start making progress soon, or I'd never learn the truth. Oran wanted me to give him a chance? I would, but not in the way he hoped.

◊

The difference between Bastion and Olympus was like the difference between Prince William and Prince Harry. Both swam in money and power, but one was imprisoned by it, and the other saw it as a means for freedom.

Where Olympus was posh and stuffy, Bastion was warm and inviting. The gaming tables boasted the same extravagant antes. The decor was equally lavish, but the atmosphere in Bastion was ten times livelier. It made me uneasy to think about why anyone would seek out Olympus when they already had access to Bastion. His motives didn't bode well, knowing what I did about Olympus.

The smiling faces and laughter helped ease my nerves, that and the fact that I hadn't overdressed, which I'd been worried about. Despite what I'd told Cosmo, I did wear the halter dress—one of the perks of being the seamstress was using my own measurements for samples. I'd also stopped by a locally owned hat shop that sold handmade Derby hats and masquerade masks. I found an absolutely stunning mask with one side black and the other side an ornate butterfly's wing in shades of iridescent blue. It represented how I felt— striking and bold yet still so fragile.

I had no idea what to expect when I arrived, but I wouldn't let my insecurities show. I kept my shoulders back and chin high when I showed my invitation to the woman at the reception desk. From there, she directed me upstairs to the main club. The large room was already bustling with people, which was nice. No one noticed my arrival. The mask also helped, but I still went immediately to the bar. New social situations always seemed more manageable with a drink in hand. I didn't think alcohol was wise tonight, considering I was alone in an unknown environment, but the contents of the drink were irrelevant. The glass itself was the important part. It served as an icebreaker and a shield—a sort of social talisman to aid in mingling.

"Soda water with a lime, please. And a straw." The straw was important—that made it look like an alcoholic drink.

The bartender smiled and quickly threw together my

drink. As he slid it across the bar, two hands braced on either side of me, a warm body closing in at my back.

"You came." *Oran.*

Had he seen me come in? I knew he would recognize me, but I hadn't expected him to zero in on me quite so quickly.

"How did you know I was here?" I didn't turn around. Instead, I sipped from my drink and pretended I didn't feel a magnetic pull urging me to lean back and mold my body into his.

"I've done nothing but watch for you since we opened the doors." He was smooth. I'd give him that.

I finally peered over my shoulder and turned, prompting him to give me a few inches of space. Not enough space, yet somehow too much.

"We?" A hint of breathlessness feathered the word.

Oran was handsome on a bad day—wearing a mask accentuated his angular jaw and the liquid mercury of his heated stare. He looked utterly mesmerizing.

"My family owns the club." He motioned to the busy room. "Shall I show you around?"

"Yes, thank you." They owned the place. That was unexpected, though it shouldn't have been if they were mafia. I wasn't sure of the implications, so I stored the information away for future consideration.

His eyes lifted to the bartender behind me. "Mark, you need anything before I go?"

"Nah, boss. We're covered here."

Oran nodded and grabbed several napkins, which he then wrapped around the side of my glass to keep my fingers from getting cold. He did it matter-of-factly as if we'd been together for years. As if it was so customary, it didn't even register that he'd done anything. But I watched every careful movement of his hands as though he'd performed a fascinating magic trick. In my experience, men like him didn't do things like that. I didn't know what to think or how to react.

Oblivious to my discomposure, he gestured for us to start our tour. Leaning a bit closer, he spoke softly. "Forgive me for not saying so earlier, but you look absolutely stunning tonight."

"Thank you." Was that warmth in my cheeks? Dear God, was I blushing?

I couldn't fathom what had gotten into me.

Needing to ground myself, I redirected our conversation. "How did your meeting with Lawrence go?" This seemed like a perfect opportunity to explore their connection and focus on my goal.

Oran didn't answer immediately. I snuck a glance at him, surprised to see his jaw tightly clenched and a storm darkening his eyes.

"It went well enough."

"I wouldn't have guessed that by looking at you right now. You look ready to strangle someone."

He peered at me out of the corner of his eye. "Come with me where we can talk more privately." He didn't wait for a reply. Taking my hand in his, he led me to a small hallway with two closed doors opposite one another. When he took out a set of keys to unlock one of the rooms, unease sent a spike of adrenaline through my veins.

"No, Oran. I'm not—"

The door pushed open, revealing a private gaming room. The tension in my shoulders eased a fraction.

"We can leave the door open, if you prefer." He studied me, his perceptiveness unnerving me even further. "I thought you might prefer if we weren't overheard."

I nodded, ready to do anything to be free of his scrutiny.

True to his word, he left the door open after following me inside.

"I'm not telling you anything you don't already know when I say that Lawrence Wellington is no good for you."

I was struck by the hypocrisy. How could Oran think he was any better than Lawrence when both were drunk on their need for power? Fancy clubs. Beautiful women. Enormous mansions and fast cars—anything and everything to be seen and envied. That type of person took what they wanted without a second thought. They didn't care about anything but themselves.

"And why is that?" I asked, acid dripping from every acrid word. "Because he's a criminal, the same as you? It seems like someone in organized crime shouldn't be casting stones at others."

"Our income sources have nothing to do with it."

"Then why is he so bad? Because he's not you?"

Oran took a menacing step closer. "He doesn't appreciate you."

"Tell me something I don't know."

"If you know, then why the fuck are you still seeing him?" He ripped off his mask and tossed it to the floor, unleashing the full brunt of his scathing stare. His anger spurred my own.

"Because life is fucking complicated," I shot back at him while jabbing my finger into his broad chest. "Because I was born to a woman who would rather sell her goddamn soul than risk being *ordinary*."

He snatched my hand and brought it to my back, pulling me close against him in the same motion. "What the fuck is that supposed to mean?"

"If you want to know, go ask her yourself. She's a long-time member of your precious Olympus Club." My temper flared out of control, and I spewed things I had no business saying. Realizing what I'd done, I clamped my jaw shut. I could feel my nostrils flaring with the need for oxygen, but I refused to open my mouth and risk saying more.

Oran's head shook slowly. "Oh no. The time for silence is over."

"I can say or not say whatever I damn well please. You don't own me. *No one does.*"

His free hand lifted, trailing his fingers down the delicate column of my throat. "Then prove it," he challenged in a hoarse murmur. "*Kiss me.*"

Oran

# NINE

Lina's eyes dilated until only a halo of her perfect sky-blue iris was visible. Her pulse point fluttered like the wings of a butterfly. And for one breathless second, I thought she might actually do it. She wanted to. I had no doubt of that. She studied my lips as though she could already taste them. I could have closed that gap for her and ended the torment, but something told me she had to be the one to do it. She had to make the choice to give in.

In the end, she wasn't ready. Something held her back.

When she finally pulled away, rage singed my insides. She was choosing him over me. Choosing to remain in her fucked-up situation rather than take a chance at making a change.

Why? It didn't make any fucking sense. And why the hell did I even care?

My mind raced to come up with possible reasons. I wanted to understand because no matter how hard I tried, I couldn't eviscerate that pathetic optimist in me who wanted to see good in people. That side of me was weak and dangerous. He insisted Lina was trapped and in desperate need of help, but it was more likely that I was yet again being manipulated by a woman and her schemes.

"I should go." Her voice was ragged like she'd just fought a ferocious battle and barely won.

I wanted to refuse to let her leave until she explained herself, but my pride wouldn't let me. The fact that I entertained the possibility she was in trouble spoke volumes about where my head was. Her dysfunctional relationship with her mother wasn't my problem. My job was to lure her away from Lawrence Wellington. That was it.

With that in mind, I choked back my frustration and took her hand. "I'll walk you out."

She didn't pull away, and I chose to ignore the satisfaction that brought me. Once we'd retrieved her coat and were outside, she stopped and crossed her arms over her chest to ward off the chilly night air.

"Tell me one thing, Oran. Why did you join Olympus? If you have all this—" She motioned toward the building. "Why Olympus?"

Her question seemed to come from left field. Why did it matter why I'd joined? Of all the things she could ask, why that? I considered conditioning my answer on one of her own but decided against it. I was trying to gain her trust. That was going to require more finesse than I'd anticipated.

"Networking." Vague but not entirely a lie. I needed to meet Lawrence and weasel my way into his world.

"Your club here doesn't provide that already?"

"A part of my job for my family is to be in the know. To have friends in high places. Olympus is perfect for that."

She studied me as though my answer was crucial in her estimation of me. Yet again, I was in the dark as to why.

"I'm sorry to see you go. I would offer to take you home, but I doubt you'd accept."

"You're right. I wouldn't." The sadness in her smile clawed at my doubts and insecurities.

As I watched her walk away into the night, I wondered if I was making a mistake by not listening to my gut. I'd second-guessed myself ever since I learned about Caitlin's betrayal, but before that, my instincts had always been adept.

A healthy dose of cynicism was necessary in the life I led. So were well-honed instincts. If I didn't learn to trust myself again, I'd be stuck in perpetual uncertainty.

My gut told me Lina was in trouble.

If that were the case, the next question was, what did I plan to do about it?

♦

"Don't you think it's time to downsize? A four-footer on a stand or a table would be just as pretty and a whole lot less work." I stared at the half-fluffed fake Christmas tree I'd been wrestling with for a half hour and grimaced.

Nana whacked me with her cane. "I'll downsize you, Oran Byrne, if you even think about it."

Paddy cackled with laughter from his recliner.

I glowered at him. "Thanks for chiming in your support."

"Boyo, you know she loves Christmas. Don't be daft."

Nana plopped into her own recliner and waved her cane

in the air. "The girls got out all the other stuff. All I need from you is the tree. That's not so much to ask."

"You're very right, Nana." I bowed my head with exaggerated contrition. "I'm not sure what came over me."

She huffed as I returned to my task of fluffing the branches. At least she'd agreed to upgrade to a pre-lit tree two years ago. Stringing the lights up and down every branch the way she insisted it was done was a fucking pain in the ass. And I was a week late getting the tree down from the attic, so I was already walking a fine line. Nana really did love everything about Christmas.

"I know exactly what's gotten into you," Nana offered sagely. "You've not been the same since Caitlin."

*Great. Here we go.*

"It'd be pretty worthless for me not to learn from my mistakes, Nana."

"Ach, there's a difference between being cautious and locking away your heart. You, Oran Byrne, have shut out everyone these past months. Caitlin was as crazy as a loon, agreeing to an arranged marriage hoping to tear down our family. It's rare to come across someone that secretly damaged. T'was a shame, but it won't happen again. And if you live your life like it might, you let her win. You really want that? Think of how delighted she'd be to know how changed you are."

Nana wasn't totally wrong. It really fucking annoyed me, though it shouldn't because the eighty-five-year-old was somehow always right. And intuitive. Every year, I expected to start seeing signs that the old woman was slipping, and every year, I was relieved to see her as sharp as ever.

"I'm just trying to be smart like you, Nana," I said with obvious flattery, hoping to tease my way out of the conversation. "I don't want to be blindsided again."

"Psh. Tell yourself what you like, but deep down, you knew she was off."

"Really?" I asked wryly. "And how is it you know what I knew?"

She leaned in, pointing a gnarled finger at me. "Remember last Christmas when your brother mentioned possibly leaving his two little ones with you and Caitlin for a weekend, and you told him you didn't think that was a good idea? I've seen you with those boys, Oran Byrne. You adore them, and you've watched them in the past."

"How did you even know about that conversation?" I would have been more bemused if she hadn't regularly proved that she had eyes and ears everywhere.

Nana chose to ignore my question. "And then there's the fact that during your year-long marriage, your mother arranged three girls' nights, and Caitlin never made it to a single one because you either made other plans for her or didn't pass along the invitation. Now, you can try to tell me they were coincidences, but you know what I think of those."

"Codswallop, I know."

"Exactly. Now, you say you don't want to get blindsided again, but you had the intuition then, and you have it now. You just need to listen to it. What you're doing at the moment is forcing everyone out so you don't have to rely on instinct at all. It's understandable. Acknowledging doubts about the person you married would be devastating for anyone. Rather than face that again, you've shut yourself off. But there's no need for that extreme. You just have to listen to that little voice when it pipes up."

"Easier said than done when a slip in judgment could cost someone their life." I'd lost my father because of Caitlin. She'd given his location to an enemy who gunned him down. Ever since I'd learned she was responsible, I'd carried the burden of knowing he'd still be here if I'd seen through her deception earlier.

"Now you're just feeling sorry for yourself," she said flatly.

"No good deed goes unpunished, does it?" I muttered, suddenly wishing I hadn't stopped by to help her decorate.

"Well, it's true. Your father chose to live a risky life. We all agreed to the terms of being a Byrne on one level or another. Brody Byrne knew the score as well as anyone. I should know; he was my son." Her accent thickened as she continued, her voice graveled with age. "You're telling me if your ma died in a car crash tonight, you'd not drive a car again? Ach, of course you wouldn't'a. Tis the same to think you can't trust anyone ever again."

Hell, she was right.

It was no wonder the woman had been the de facto matriarch of our family for as long as I'd been around. She had a way of seeing things that others couldn't. She'd taken my perspective of what had unfolded months ago and turned it on its head.

I'd thought my instincts had failed me by not seeing what Caitlin was up to, but Nana was right. I *did* have suspicions, and I didn't heed them. I hadn't wanted to admit it because that meant I shared in the blame. It was time to step up and face the truth. I'd been suspicious about Caitlin for months, a cloying discomfort weighing on me whenever I was around her. It wasn't the same sort of unease I felt around Lina, but fear whispered that it might be just as dangerous. I didn't want to repeat the same damn mistake as before.

I shook my head. "You never cease to amaze me, Nana."

"Well, now, Oran. Maybe you are a little slow if you've still not caught on that I'm the brains behind this operation."

A chuckle rumbled from deep in my chest. "I'll try to

catch up from now on." Surprised that Paddy hadn't chimed in, I looked back to find him asleep with his mouth wide open.

"Well, then. If that's settled," Nana continued, "tell me more about these plans of yours. I understand you've got payback on your mind." Her eyes glinted with mischief.

"Why, so you can scold me on the pointless nature of revenge?" I teased.

"Agh, don't be absurd." She waved her hand at me. "A little vigilante justice is good for the soul and society. Helps cleanse the riffraff from the gene pool."

I started to smile, but it fell short when I thought of Lawrence Wellington as part of the gene pool and Lina pregnant with his baby. I wanted to think he was too damn old to knock up anyone, but plenty of old bastards had proven it was possible. Christ, I had to get her away from him for so many reasons.

"This is personal, is it?" Nana's tone grew somber.

"It wasn't supposed to be—not really." I sat on a step stool with my elbows resting wearily on my knees. "My plan was to learn everything I could about Lawrence Wellington. Insert myself into his life, then pull the rug out from under him. Bankrupt his shipping empire. Ruin his reputation. Aid in criminal charges being filed against him. And the cherry on top was supposed to be stealing his girlfriend, leaving him a shell of his former self."

"Ahhh, now I see."

"What do you see? I haven't told you anything yet."

"You've told me all I need to know," she shot back defiantly. "You meant to use this girl, but something's changed. You want to help her, but your ex did a number on you and convinced you that helping a woman will only lead to pain. It's all there plain as day."

My lips parted, then snapped shut. Words escaped me.

"You ever been accused of witchcraft?" I asked once my gears started turning again.

"That would be the least of the accusations I've faced in my day."

"Well, you may not be totally wrong, but it doesn't change the fact that the girl isn't my problem."

Nana smacked my arm with a strength she shouldn't be capable of. "Oran Marcus Byrne. I didn't let you shadow my every step as a wee one so you'd grow up as dense as a stone."

"The girl is part of Wellington's circle and swimming in secrets. I have no reason to give her the benefit of the doubt."

"If that were true, you wouldn't be worried about her. She's given you plenty of reason to believe in her; you just need to get your head out of your arse."

How was I supposed to argue with that?

A wry smile teased the corners of my lips as I shook my head. "You know, someday you just might be wrong. It could happen."

"Doubtful, but even so. Today is not that day. Now, tell me about this lass."

I took a deep breath, my gaze dropping to my hands. "Her name is Lina Schultze, and the cursory search I did showed that she uses her father's last name even though her mother remarried when she was young."

"Not a stretch to understand a child wanting to keep ties to her father," Nana noted.

"Agreed, and the family seems normal on paper, but appearances are meaningless." I paused as Lina's anger toward her mother played in my head. "She has a younger sister who lives with family in Paris. I wouldn't want my kid living a continent away, but it's not unusual for that bougie sort—boarding schools and all that crap."

"Aye. Some tend to be less hands-on than I think is proper. You think she's in some sort of trouble, do you?"

"I know she is," I admitted reluctantly. "I just don't know what."

Nana patted my hand with a knowing grin. "Sounds like she crossed your path for a reason."

"To punish me." I scowled. "I must have really fucked up in a past life."

"Don't make me hurt you, boyo," she said in a playful tone edged in warning. "It's time for my coffee. Get your nana a cuppa, and don't forget the uisce beatha." *Water of life.*

As usual, Nana took me from a grimace to laughter in under a minute. "Aren't you too old for whiskey in your coffee?"

"Don't be an eejit."

I tipped my head back and laughed from deep in my belly.

♦

After spending the afternoon with Nana and Paddy, my evening was much less lighthearted. As promised, I arranged for dinner with Wellington and Renzo Donati. It was the longest hour and a half of my life. I imagined launching myself across the table and spearing Wellington with my steak knife at least half a dozen times.

We didn't delve into the docks or any particular arrangements with any detail. Instead, we framed the meeting as a get-to-know-you opportunity to set the groundwork for a lasting relationship. I got a small amount of satisfaction knowing it was all a ploy, and we were playing Wellington for a chump. He was clueless. By the time he departed for his black Town Car, he was in high spirits, patting my back and laughing like we were long-lost family.

Boy, was he in for a surprise.

Once he was gone, Renzo and I lingered out front for a private word.

"I want to thank you again for doing this," I said quietly. "I'll definitely owe you."

Renzo rubbed his palms together as if in anticipation. "We appreciate you bringing this to our attention. The Moretti family has zero tolerance for trafficking, especially on our own goddamn docks."

When I first went to them about Wellington, I hadn't been sure how they'd respond. Plenty of organizations on our side of the law dabbled in the skin trade. They could have been partners with him for all I knew. Thank God that wasn't the case. The Donatis quickly stepped up and offered to help with my plans in any way they could. No matter what Renzo said, I definitely owed him.

"Just give me a little time to get matters in order. I want Wellington to crash and burn, and to do that, I need him to think he's untouchable."

"Understood. So long as you plan to gut the fucker, we'll follow your lead."

With that, the final pieces of my plan fell into place ... aside from Lina. What had seemed like a given in the beginning would end up being the greatest challenge. Difficulty hadn't stopped me before, and it wouldn't this time around. After my talk with Nana, I finally felt confident about what needed to happen. I had to get Lina away from Wellington, one way or another.

Lina

# TEN

THE ONE GOOD THING I COULD SAY ABOUT MY MOM WAS THAT she chose not to raise me herself. Granted, it was probably a selfish move to avoid dealing with me rather than an inciteful acknowledgment of her lack of maternal instinct, but whatever. The result was the same.

In her endeavor to ensure she could be as hands-off as possible, she'd chosen one of the kindest, most nurturing replacements imaginable. Gloria Ruiz came into my life a month before my father died of an aggressive brain tumor. At the tender age of six, I was told that my father, my world, was sick, and a month later, he was gone. Mom started dating Charles two months later and married him within a year.

Gloria became my rock. I was certain she was the only reason I wasn't a complete sociopath.

When I left home years later, I never once returned, but every few months, I made a concerted effort to stop by Gloria's small apartment in Queens to check on her. She still worked for my mother and seeing her there would have saved me time, but I'd sooner have swum naked in a bathtub full of jellyfish than go back to the Brooks house. I wouldn't even visit my little sister, Amelie, at the house. I went to her dance studio or dropped by her school to eat lunch with her. As far as I was concerned, my family home didn't exist.

Gloria knew I didn't care for my mother. She assumed that was because Eliza had been emotionally unavailable. I never told Gloria the extent of my mother's depravity. That would have devastated her. She would have quit her job on principle, and I'd needed her to be there for Amelie.

My little sister was only six when I left home. The age gap kept us from being close at the time, but I wasn't going to leave her in that house alone. I did everything I could for her, but it still wasn't enough.

*I miss her so damn much.*

"There's my little Lina, mija, how are you?" Gloria wrapped me in a crushing hug that a seventy-two-year-old waif of a woman shouldn't have been capable of. The welcoming smile on her face was ecstatic, and her joy infectious.

"Hey, Mama G. It's so good to see you." I'd never met anyone else who made my soul smile the way Gloria could. "I'm sorry it's been a bit longer than normal. I've been crazy busy."

Truth be told, I'd avoided seeing her out of shame. She'd never intentionally make me feel guilty—I brought that on myself. If I wanted to make anyone proud, it was Gloria. She didn't even have to be aware of my failures for me to feel worse about them in her presence. It was enough that I knew, and I hated feeling like I let her down.

"You don't need to worry about me." She swatted away the idea as if ridiculous. "You and your sister are busy girls with full lives. I may be old, but I still remember those days. Now come sit at the table with me. I'll get you some caldo to warm you up. This winter seems extra cold already. I'm dreading January."

"You know I can't refuse your caldo."

"Good, because I made more than I should have. I wish I could send Mellie some soup, but the shipping takes too long. I looked up the weather in France, and it doesn't seem like it gets quite so cold. Hopefully, she's staying warm." She took out a Tupperware from the fridge and poured the contents into an old pot over a gas burner. "That'll be warm in no time, and while we wait, you can tell me all about what you've been up to. How is the design business?"

Hearing my sister's nickname carved a ragged gash into the surface of my heart. My hand pressed flat against my chest over the lancing pain.

"It's really good. Cosmo is … *Cosmo*," I said with a dramatic wave of my hand. "We're wrapping up summer contracts and getting started on designs for next fall."

"So soon?"

I shrugged with a small smile. "Now that we have a solid pool of buyers, we've been able to line up collections further in advance."

"Oh, *mija*, that's wonderful!" She squeezed my hand. "And what about that love life of yours? Meet any handsome young men lately?" She wiggled her eyebrows at me, making me laugh.

"You are incorrigible."

"You mispronounced *hopeful*. I just don't want you to be alone, little Lina. You know that."

"I know, Mama G. That's very sweet of you, but no white knights on the horizon." The words hadn't left my mouth before the image of silver eyes peering out from behind a black mask surfaced in my mind.

Knight or villain? I couldn't decide.

Days earlier, when I'd waltzed into the Bastion Club, I would have said I was confident he was a villain. It made sense. All the evidence pointed in that direction.

But then his challenge shook my foundations.

*Kiss me.*

It wasn't the words themselves. It was the overwhelming urge to comply that had me at a loss. I trusted myself. I didn't fall for smarmy men. I didn't even own a pair of rose-colored glasses. So why had every fiber of my being gravitated toward him?

I was scared to answer that question.

"Maybe that's the problem," Gloria said in a sage tone. "You don't need a knight; you just need someone who loves you with their whole heart."

God, she was the best.

Gloria had a way of seeing the very best about the world, and I adored her for it.

"Thanks, Mama G. I'll try to remember that." My voice was thin as it squeezed past the lump in my throat.

She patted my hand just as the first drops of bubbling caldo boiled over, sizzling on the hot burner. "*Aye, Dios mío.*" She jumped up to move the pot from the heat. "Time to eat!"

As always, the food was delicious, and the company filled me just as heartily as the soup.

I left Gloria's feeling re-energized and ready to make progress in my hunt for information. It was Wednesday, and

Lawrence had asked me to join him for the weekly club dinner. I had to make the night worthwhile. I needed to manifest some answers, and that called for confidence. As any woman knew, the perfect set of matching lingerie was essential to achieving a queen's mindset. I went straight from Gloria's to my favorite lingerie shop.

The pieces they carried were made with exquisite quality, which was reflected in the prices. As a seamstress myself, a quality garment was always important. I struggled to justify buying something I could have made better myself. Not that I had the time, but it was the principle. Conscience of my budget, however, I didn't usually splurge on such luxuries. Today was an exception.

When I saw a red silk set with a black lace overlay, I instantly fell in love. The lace flowers extended beyond the silk cup with a red mesh backing so fine it was almost transparent. The effect was stunningly beautiful. I wasn't sure what I'd wear over it, but that was almost irrelevant when I knew what waited beneath.

I thanked the store clerk and walked back to my apartment with long, energized strides. I even managed to keep from stumbling when I spotted Oran standing outside the building adjacent to my own—the one I'd listed at the club as my residence. His eyes were locked on my approach.

My insides begged to liquefy with nerves and melt into the dirty concrete seams, but I forced my chin up and continued forward.

"If I didn't know better, I might start to worry you were stalking me."

"The difference between stalking and dating is a simple matter of attraction. In this case, the attraction is mutual, so stalking isn't an issue."

I raised a brow at him.

He answered with a lupine grin. "Careful throwing around challenges like that. I might be forced to prove you wrong."

God, I wanted to ask how, but that was exactly what he wanted. It would have been an invitation. And while the words were on the tip of my tongue, I forced myself to swallow them back.

"What are you doing here, Oran?"

He took a step closer, his eyes darkening. "Say it again."

I considered being obstinate and asking my question, this time without his name, but I knew what he wanted. I knew it, and I liked seeing how badly he wanted to hear it. I was just as hungry for his ravenous stare as he was for my voice.

Dear God, I wanted Oran Byrne.

The realization clamped down on my lungs, making it hard to breathe.

I licked my suddenly parched lips and gave him what he asked for, not because I had to but because I wanted to.

"Oran," I said in an unintentionally husky voice. "You still haven't answered my question."

He prowled a few inches closer. "I'm here because I started to look into you—into your family—like you suggested at Bastion."

"I was just venting. There's no reason to overreact." I never should have opened my damn mouth that night.

"Regardless, I decided I wanted to hear it from you instead. I don't want to ask your mother why you hate her. I want *you* to tell me."

*I want to tell you, too. I'm tired of carrying this burden alone.*

God, I did want to tell him. I was shocked at how strong the compulsion was to lay all my problems at his feet, but I couldn't give in. He was doing business with Lawrence, and the two had some sort of past. I couldn't afford to forget that he was one of them, no matter how tempting the lure.

"I never should have said those things—I was lashing out. If you were hoping for an explanation, I'm afraid you're in for a disappointment."

The heat in his eyes smoldered. He seemed to contemplate his next move when his gaze snagged on the bag in my hand. He might not have known the store, but it wasn't hard to guess what sort of shopping I'd done. I held a small white gift sack-type bag with black tissue paper. The name of the store was scribed in elegant black script on the side. It practically screamed intimates.

Oran held out his hand in a silent demand.

I smugly handed over the bag. Let him squirm, knowing what I wore beneath my clothes. It served him right, considering how thoroughly he'd distracted me lately.

I watched him intently as his large, strong fingers lifted the delicate red silk from the bag. The molten desire I expected in his stare never appeared. Instead, he turned eyes sharp as silver daggers on me, every muscle in his body stiffening.

"You are not fucking wearing this for *him*."

Oran

# ELEVEN

I was too pissed to play Prince Charming. Fuck that. I'd sooner throw her over my shoulder and lock her away than let that geriatric bastard see her in what should have been meant for me.

Jesus, I didn't know where these thoughts were coming from.

I was out of control and couldn't find it in me to care.

She started to answer, and I could tell by the fire in her eyes that I wouldn't like what she was going to say. I cut her off before she got the chance to say a word. Clutching her wrist, I hauled her around to the alley on the side of the building. It wasn't particularly private, but it was better than having it out with her on the goddamn sidewalk.

"Is Wellington taking you to the club for dinner tonight?" Just saying the words made my jaw ache with strain.

"Yes." Defiance. So much bloody defiance.

"You don't want to be with him, I know it. You came to Bastion for a reason. I didn't make you—you came on your own. So why the fuck are you still going to see him?"

"I told you, it's complicated."

"Nothing's that fucking complicated."

"Maybe for you," she shot back angrily.

My mind raced as I stared her down. I needed to handle this carefully, but my frustration tinged my vision with red, making it hard to see anything but my need to gain her submission.

The lighter was in my hand before I knew it, and I flicked it open.

"Can you swear on your life he'll never see it?"

"You *wouldn't*." She gaped at me.

"Baby, you have no idea the lengths I'd go to."

She crossed her arms over her chest and narrowed angry blue eyes at me. "Fine, I swear no other man will see the lingerie."

My smile was slow and lupine as it crept across my face.

"Wrong answer."

She could try to sass me, but it wouldn't get her far. The small flame barely kissed the thin black tissue before the hungry flame devoured the paper.

Lina's jaw plummeted, her eyes going wide with horror. And was that … a touch of … *sorrow* mixed in?

Shit, I didn't want to hurt her. I'd been trying to prevent that. Being near Wellington, clothed or not, was dangerous for her in so many ways.

I tossed the smoking bag away from us and caged her in

70

against the stone wall, forcing her watery gaze to mine. "Look at me, Lina."

Questions and uncertainty spun in her eyes like little blue whirlpools of chaos. "Why, Oran? Why are you doing this?"

Only an inch separated us, and my body screamed with the need to close the gap, so much so that my breath grew choppy and shallow.

"Because you need me to. You need my help, whether you want it or not."

It should have been a lie—a line I fed to her to win her over—but instead, it rang with sincerity even to my own ears. Where she was concerned, my actions were no longer purely motivated by revenge. I didn't know what that meant for me and didn't want to think about it.

I lowered my face to hers, drawn by an invisible force impossible to ignore. My lips ghosted over her skin—her temple, her cheeks, her lips. I never touched her, though. I made sure of that. My body vibrated inside with restraint, but I kept control of myself.

Lina trembled beneath me.

Her lips parted a fraction, and I felt her warmth as her chest lifted and strained closer to mine. We lingered in a time-less moment of suspense, all the while the whisper of my words from the club echoing in the air around us.

*Kiss me.*

*Kiss me.*

*Kiss me.*

Like a needle to a balloon, chaos exploded when Lina launched herself at me, her lips colliding with mine and arms tugging me close.

*Thank Christ.*

I responded with equal abandon. Pulling her luscious body against mine and devouring her kiss. The sweep of her tongue along mine turned my cock to solid stone. It pressed so hard against my zipper I worried it would leave a permanent mark. My physical reaction to her was undeniable. What amazed me even more was my emotional response. The second her body melted into mine, I went feral with the need to own her. To possess her so thoroughly she forgot any other man had ever existed.

Her submission to the desire pulsing between us was a sign that I was making progress.

It made me ravenous for more.

The small glimpse of what it would be like to have her for myself had my world tilting on its axis. The breathless moan that snuck past her lips. The tug of her fingers in my hair. The nip of her teeth on my bottom lip.

How could kissing anyone else ever compare to this?

It was impossible.

She'd decimated my prior standards and permanently altered my perceptions. She'd marked me in a way that couldn't be seen, but I knew it was there, and I'd be damned if I didn't find a way to return the favor.

I hated how much I wanted her.

She wasn't even hiding the fact she was keeping secrets, and I'd sworn I would demand nothing short of absolute transparency in any future relationship. Lina was the epitome of everything I didn't want. I couldn't understand what was wrong with me, and the loss of control over my own desires was maddening.

We reluctantly came apart in our need for air. Her eyes remained closed as if savoring the moment. Or regretting it. Both were equally likely where she was concerned.

I released a deep, resigned breath, my forehead coming to rest against hers.

"This doesn't change anything, does it?"

Slowly, so agonizingly slowly, her head shook side to side, a gentle caress against my skin like a whispered apology.

"Good thing I don't give up easily," I murmured, the hint of a smile fish-hooked the corner of my lips at the small chuckle I drew from her.

"You're impossible." She pulled back, her eyes cutting over to the now flaming bag of paper and silk. "And you owe me a new bra and panties set."

I waited to respond until her eyes returned to mine. "Baby, you tell me I'm the only one to see you in them, and I'll buy you the whole goddamn store."

"I don't want a store."

"And I don't want you to go near him."

Her teeth tugged against her bottom lip. "I have to go now."

I allowed her to slip away, a frosty chill lancing through my chest.

Lina's previously confident strides were now measured and cumbersome as if burdened by the weight of the world. Something or someone had a hold on her with a death grip. Figuring out exactly what had her in its clutches would take time, which was in low supply between my plans progressing more quickly than expected and my patience rapidly dwindling.

Now that I'd tasted the desperation in her kiss, I made the easy decision that it was time to force the issue. It would be best for everyone involved. She'd be free of Wellington, and I'd no longer have to worry about falling for the wrong woman because Lina would hate me once I executed my plans. Any longing in her eyes would turn to pure resentment.

It was the smartest move I could make, and I fucking hated it.

Lina

# TWELVE

If Oran Byrne was sent as a test to challenge me, I was failing. He was creeping under my skin a little more with every interaction, wearing down my resolve and confusing my priorities.

I was supposed to go home with Lawrence that night. The lingerie *had* been for him, and I'd left the shop committed to seducing my way into his bed. Our relationship had been purely ornamental—I'd been the very definition of arm candy. I had no idea why Lawrence hadn't sought more from me. Most older men in his position would jump at the chance to use me to boost their ego. All Lawrence seemed to want was to be seen with me on his arm. That wasn't enough. I had to find a way to take the relationship to the next level to gain his trust. Without trust, I'd never get information on the Society.

The Society was Olympus's dirty little secret. A club within the club. A group so secretive, there weren't even whispers of its existence. I only knew about it because my mother and stepfather were members. So was Lawrence Wellington, and he was also the key to getting my sister back.

It was my fault they'd gotten their hands on her, and I wouldn't rest until she was home with me where she belonged. She hadn't even turned eighteen, for Christ's sake. She should have been my only focus, but Oran had muddied the waters so badly that I kept losing my way.

His jealousy over me being with Lawrence shouldn't have factored into my decisions, yet when the club dinner ended, I made my excuses, claiming a headache, and left alone.

The following two days were a barrage of guilt and frustration. How could I have possibly let Oran sway me into missing an opportunity to gather information? What if a night with Lawrence unveiled a clue that helped me get my sister back? No matter how grotesque the situation, it would have been worth it. I would have done anything for Amelie.

I'd already sacrificed so much, and it would all be for nothing if I failed. I refused to allow myself to stray from my goals.

Oran was just another rich bastard who wanted what he couldn't have. They were all the same. I wouldn't let him get in my way again.

Thankfully, another opportunity presented itself days later when Lawrence invited me to a charity dinner event. I was so relieved to have another chance that my nerves barely acted up. Normally, I had to fight back my visceral reaction to the man and everything he represented. Tonight was different.

I hovered close to Lawrence as we mingled with the city's

most influential residents. I leaned into his touch and looked at him admiringly when he spoke. I played my part perfectly, and as the evening drew to a close, I was more determined than ever to ride the wave of momentum and push the relationship to the next level.

*It's just sex. You've lived through worse, Lina. Think of Amelie. You owe it to her.*

*Think of Amelie.*

*Think of Amelie.*

I chanted that phrase in my mind on the way to Lawrence's car. Once we were closed off in the back together, I angled myself toward him and ran my hand up his thigh.

"You haven't even tried to touch me, Lawrence. Don't you find me attractive?"

He sighed. "There are two types of women, Lina—those you keep on your arm for the world to see, and those you fuck. That truth is especially important for a man like me who has … *particular* tastes."

*Of course.* Why hadn't I thought of it before?

"You like kink," I said quietly.

"What I like is something a woman of your standing would never tolerate."

"You don't know that."

"I do."

I held his hard stare with resolute conviction. "You do know who my mother is, right? I have *particular* tastes as well. How will we know whether our tastes are compatible if you don't give me a chance? I could make you *very* happy." I said the last words in a seductive, slightly unhinged voice while cupping his erection.

His eyes flared. He cupped my jaw, his thumb swiping my bottom lip like he'd done before.

"You like it when the lipstick smears," I surmised. That was why he'd been disappointed.

"That and waterproof mascara are the worst things to happen in modern beauty." He spoke in a daze as though lost in the recollection of days past.

Lawrence got off on degrading women—it was so obvious now. Of course! It all made so much more sense now. That was the reason he hadn't tried anything. It was the same reason he was a part of the Society and why he had to be linked to my sister's disappearance. All of it was related.

And now, I had a chance to get some answers.

But at what risk? How extreme was his kink? What would I have to endure for that chance?

*Would you really want to live knowing you didn't try?*

*Think of Amelie.*

*Think of Amelie.*

I lowered myself to my knees on the floorboard of the back seat and bowed my head. "Please, Sir. Show me."

My heart was a drum thundering in my ears. I didn't look at Lawrence, but I could hear his swift intake of breath.

"Adam, drive until I tell you to stop," he said into the intercom, his voice ragged.

The city blurred past the heavily tinted windows above me while the air in the car grew stagnant and stifling.

"You're nothing but a worthless *slut*, aren't you?" His callous words pierced me deeper than I expected. He'd meant to degrade me, and he'd hit his mark because that was all I was at that moment. A woman willing to give her body in exchange for a price.

And it wasn't the first time.

*Think of Amelie.*

"Is that what you want?" he continued, unbuckling his belt. "To be used because that's all you're good for?"

He seemed to want an answer, but I'd lost my voice. I'd thought I was prepared for anything he could throw at me. I was wrong. All I could do was nod.

His hand gripped my chin harshly and angled my face up to his. "You treat me with the respect I'm owed and answer me with words. Is that understood?"

"Yes, Sir," I answered quickly, surprised at the fire in his eyes. It was the first time since I'd started seeing him that there'd been true emotion in those soulless depths. He was such a sick bastard. I refused to give his words any merit. They were meaningless because he didn't know me at all. He didn't know the degree of sacrifice I was willing to endure for the people I loved.

That wasn't weakness. It was bravery.

If anything, I was using him. Not the other way around.

I allowed him to think of me as subservient, my gaze falling back to my knees.

He took his cock into his hand and began to stroke himself. "Take down your hair, then lay your head on my lap."

I did as I was told in an Oscar-worthy performance. He wanted to break women? I'd give him sad and broken. Then I'd break him.

"Is this what you expected, little whore? Or did you think I was joking?"

"You're giving me exactly what I wanted, Sir. Thank you."

"And when I shoot my cum in your hair, you'll still thank me? Or will you run home crying like a spoiled little brat who got her feelings hurt?"

I sensed his control had grown as ragged and thin as his voice. His hand thumped my head with each savage stroke, his breaths shallow and gasping. He was getting close.

"I want everything you have to give me because I deserve all of it. I'm so dirty and worthless."

"*Ahh, fuck, yes.*"

I could feel the spots of warm ejaculate seep through my hair to my scalp. And if that wasn't bad enough, he then used his hand to rub it in, petting me like a dog.

Fuck, I would have to scrub to get that shit out.

I didn't think he could see my eyes, but I held back the epic eye roll I wanted to make, just in case.

*Talk about worthless—a man with such a pathetic self-image that he has to belittle women to get off.*

"Well, Lina. This has been a pleasant surprise."

I sat up and did my best impression of a doe-eyed anime girl as I peered up at him. "Thank you, Sir. I'm so honored to have pleased you."

"Hmm … yes, I think this might work. Find yourself better makeup—something I can smear."

"Yes, Sir."

His chest expanded on a ragged breath. "All this time, you were right under my nose, and I had no idea." He caressed my jaw. "If I didn't have to be in Chicago in the morning, I'd take you home with me. But maybe it's best to ease into things." He pressed the intercom button. "You can take us to Lina's place, Adam."

I started to rise back into my seat only to have his hand clasp my shoulder. "Oh no, you don't. Dirty sluts with cum in their hair don't get to sit in seats. You stay right where you are."

I smiled and nodded appreciatively while my thoughts flayed open his gut and scattered his innards across the leather seats.

*How's that for dirty, you worthless son of a bitch?*

Not for the first time in my life, I wondered what it might feel like to kill a man. If I was ever going to find out, Lawrence would be well deserving. It was something to keep in mind.

Oran

# THIRTEEN

FROM THE MINUTE I STARTED LOOKING INTO LAWRENCE Wellington, I set up cameras outside his Upper East Side mansion to monitor who came and went from his home. I had a cyber team tracking his online activities and placed a GPS tracker on his car. That man didn't take a shit without me knowing about it.

I knew right away that he'd taken Lina to a charity dinner. The event sponsors had posted photos to social media throughout the evening, so even if I hadn't tracked her cell phone as well, it wouldn't have taken me long to figure out she was his plus-one.

I hated that she'd gone anywhere with him. I even considered crashing the damn event.

But the real test of my patience came when the evening ended, and I watched his car on my location map cruise the length of 54th Street, then back down 53rd, only to circle back to 54th and repeat. They spent a full ten minutes driving aimlessly before finally stopping at Lina's building. It was the longest goddamn ten minutes of my existence.

I couldn't stop thinking about what might be happening in that car. It was enough to drive me insane.

I slammed my laptop shut and grabbed my keys. Enough was enough. I couldn't undo the last half hour, but I could make sure it never happened again.

On my way out, I texted to arrange a meet-up with an old friend, though we might not be friends after he heard what I wanted. He owed me big, and I was calling in that favor in an even bigger way.

Casper was mostly legit. He'd been on the force for twenty years and was one of the few who wasn't on the take from one organization or another. He was married to my nana's niece's cousin, so we were related in the way that all good Irish Catholics were related. That was why he'd come to me when he needed help—we were family but far enough removed that ties were thin. Two years ago, Casper's daughter was assaulted by a boy she'd been dating. Casper made sure the girl filed charges, but like any halfway decent father, he felt like the kid needed a bit more punishment than the law allowed. I was happy to help.

Now, it was his turn.

"I knew I'd get that text one day," Casper said as I approached him outside an all-night diner. "I just hoped it wouldn't be midnight in the dead of winter. I suppose it's too much to hope for that we're going in for a hot cup of coffee."

"You'd be right. Come on, let's take a walk."

"*Fuck me,*" he muttered under his breath, making me smile.

"You're getting old if the weather's starting to bother you that bad."

Casper was closing in on fifty. His real name was Bryan Fahey, but his extreme pallor and less-than-athletic physique had earned him the nickname Casper when he was a kid. The name had stuck.

"I was getting old ten years ago," he grumbled. "I've arrived. And being out in the cold makes me grumpy as fuck, so why don't you tell me what I'm doin' out here."

"Fair enough." I outlined my plan, including his role. As I explained, his gait slowed until he finally came to a stop.

"You're asking too much, Oran." All humor was lost—his voice now as harsh as the December night air. "It's too risky."

"It's not. This doesn't have to go beyond you and me."

"This is my fucking life we're talking about here." He got in my face like he meant to intimidate me.

I had his coat clenched in my fists and his back to a wall in two seconds flat. "You forget who you're talking to, Fahey."

"I didn't forget *shit,*" he shot back at me. "What you're planning wouldn't just ruin my reputation—I could end up in prison, and my family would lose my pension. You're asking me to risk their entire livelihood."

"It's already at risk. If word got around about what happened to that kid…"

His lip arced in a sneer. "The fuck is wrong with you, Byrne? You're not the man you used to be."

Jesus, he was right. I'd lost my goddamn mind.

I released Casper and paced for a second, letting the cold air clear my head.

"Look, I wouldn't have asked if it wasn't important. I

swear on my life none of this will ever come back to haunt you. In fact, you do this, and I'll owe you."

He straightened his coat and scowled at me. "Fuckin' pain in the ass. It's too fuckin' cold for this," he muttered, then barked, "When?"

"About two weeks."

"You'll owe me. Big." He pointed at me, brows raised for emphasis.

"Yeah, Cas. I'll definitely owe you." Finally, I could breathe.

"I'm outta here. I'm sure you'll be in touch." He shoved his hands in his pockets and marched down the sidewalk away from me, muttering under his breath about "fucking family" and "shoulda known better."

I didn't care so long as he held up his end of the bargain.

Tomorrow, I'd strategize the rest of my attack. I'd devised this plan as a backup, hoping it wouldn't be necessary, so I hadn't worked out all the details yet. It would be a busy two weeks between my new plans for Lina and my ongoing efforts to destroy Wellington. Hopefully too busy to second-guess myself because what I was about to do had the potential to backfire in my face.

Certain gambles were worth the risk, and Lina was one of them.

♦

I didn't see Lina for five more days—an entire week since our kiss. During that time, I'd embraced a cool resolve to see my plans through. I'd done nothing but work on my plans because anything less left me with time to think about what she might be doing with Wellington.

I couldn't bear to dwell on those thoughts. I refused to even pull up her GPS. It would drive me insane.

I'd even debated showing up to Wednesday dinner at the club. In the end, I couldn't stay away. I needed to see her, but something dark and scaly slithered beneath my skin when I did. It wasn't seeing her that bothered me; it was seeing the way Wellington hovered near her at all times. Touching her. Claiming her.

Something had changed.

I didn't know what had gone on between them, but something was different, and I fucking *hated* it.

When dinner ended and people gathered in the gaming room, I went straight to the bar and got a whiskey neat. I wanted to down it in one go, but the drink wasn't for me.

Smiling, I joined Lina and her psychotic date. "You up for a game tonight?" I asked Wellington.

"Not tonight. I've been out of town for several days and want to spend some quality time with Lina. We're just staying for a drink before we go."

"That's too bad. I was hoping to talk to you about a visit I'd had with Donati this weekend." It was bullshit. I hadn't talked to Renzo, but Wellington didn't need to know that.

"In that case, let me get a drink, and we can talk." He nodded and made for the bar.

I immediately leveled Lina with an arctic stare. "When he comes back over, you will excuse yourself to go home and change, and you will stay there the rest of the night. Should Wellington offer to take you home, you will urge him to stay and talk with me. Is that clear?"

"What?" she asked with wide eyes. "Why would I do that?"

I lifted my glass until it was flush with her breast, then

mechanically poured its entire contents down the front of her dress. Her jaw dropped, arms going out to the sides in shock.

"Go home, Lina," I instructed harshly one last time.

"What's happened here?" Wellington returned with exceptional timing.

"Oh, Lina. I'm so incredibly sorry. What a clutz." I snagged a cocktail napkin off a nearby table and tried to pat at the golden stain down her creamy sheath dress.

Finally collecting herself, Lina snatched the napkin and shooed my hands away. "I've got it. It's no problem. I'll just run home and soak the dress before it sets. Is that okay, Lawrence? I don't want to keep you two from visiting."

"Yes, you need to clean yourself up. We'll talk tomorrow."

"Okay. I'm so sorry." She gave him an apologetic smile, then shot daggers in my direction before stepping away toward the elevator.

*Just wait, Lina. You'll really hate me when it's all said and done.*

But she'd be safe, and that was all that mattered, right?

Right.

# FOURTEEN

IF I BELIEVED IN A GOD, I'D HAVE SAID HE WAS PISSED AT ME. And I'd have had definitive proof that God was a man because women had too much shit going on to find time to be so vindictive.

I mean, *really*.

What other explanation was there besides the universe colluding against me?

Something had prevented me from seeing Lawrence for two weeks straight. Each time I made plans with him, something had come up on his end or mine.

After Oran spilled his drink on me, I spent the next two days confined to my apartment, unsure whether I had the stomach bug from hell or had eaten something rotten. The entire weekend was a wash. Lawrence ended up with unexpected business out of town the first half of the week, then Cosmo got word that a huge Parisian design firm wanted to see our work while they were in town and insisted both designers be present. I had to spend three days wining and dining them.

Granted, the pitch had resulted in an incredible contract—more money than we'd ever pulled in before—but the timing sucked. Any excitement I felt for our success was leached of joy by my frustration and growing despair whenever I thought of the days slipping through my fingers.

Lawrence and I both had other obligations during the week of Christmas. We weren't close enough to spend that time together. Cosmo and I did a Christmas Eve celebration with friends every year, and I had spent Christmas Day for the past eleven years with Mama G. That wasn't something I was willing to give up.

The next opportunity to see him was the Wednesday club dinner on the twenty-ninth. I was all keyed up to manipulate information from him using his need to humiliate, but at the last minute, I got a notice from the city about an emergency gas test being performed in my building due to a suspected leak. They were asking for one member of each household to be home, and Jessa wasn't available.

I started to question whether I was cursed.

It would have explained a lot through the years. But if I didn't believe in a god, then I wouldn't believe in curses either. Sometimes shit happened.

Tonight, however, would be different. I was going to the club with Lawrence for its annual New Year's Eve party, and *nothing* would stop me.

My makeup was water soluble. My hair was up but only loosely. My dress was a pale blue silk that complemented my eyes and would leave the perfect stains when I cried fake black tears. I was certain I would make the most of the night.

When a knock sounded on my door, I'd never hoped with such fervor to find a Jehovah's Witness on the other side. Lawrence thought I lived in another building, so it wasn't him. Jessa had already left for the night. None of the remaining options looked promising.

Hands starting to sweat, I peeked through the peephole. Three armed police officers stood in formation facing my door—not remotely what I'd expected to see. I wasn't sure what I'd expected, but *that* wasn't it.

"Carolina Schultze? This is the NYPD. Open up."

*Oh shit! They're here for me?*

My first instinct was to assume they'd knocked on the wrong door. But that wasn't the case.

Heart in my throat, I slowly opened the door and kept my hands in view. "Hello, can I help you?"

"Carolina Schultze?"

"Yes."

"We're here to execute a warrant to search your premises."

I couldn't have been more confused if he'd told me a three-armed monkey had broken out of a science lab and was hiding in my apartment.

"A warrant? To search for what?"

Their only answer was to angle their way inside. One man stood next to me as if ensuring I didn't dive for a weapon while the others began rummaging through our stuff.

"What on earth is going on?" How did they get a warrant and *why*? "I have a right to know what's going on."

"Ma'am, it's best if you remain quiet. In the event that anything—"

"Found it," called the cop by the window who'd gone

straight for my sewing supplies. He held up a metal box I used for keeping zippers, of all things.

"That your box, ma'am?" the officer beside me asked.

"Yes, why?"

The man holding the box opened it, revealing a baggie full of white powder the size of my fist. My jaw hit the floor. If the men said anything else, I didn't hear them due to the ringing in my ears.

I forgot how to breathe.

The world spun around me until strong hands gripped my arms on either side to keep me upright.

"That's not … I've never seen it … I don't understand…"

How could this be happening? What the hell was I going to do?

"Let's get down to the station, and you can talk it over with the captain."

Could I even afford a lawyer? How much would this sort of thing cost? And would it even do any good? They'd obviously gotten some sort of tip-off and confirmed the report with their discovery. *Someone* was going to prison for it.

Could the stash have been Jessa's? I didn't think she was into drugs, certainly not selling, but nothing else made sense. How could that much coke end up in my apartment? I would have said the cops planted the drugs, but I'd been observing as the guy started looking through my workstation because everything over there was precious to me. I'd been watching intently, and that baggie had been exactly where he found it. In my box. How long had it been there? How did it get there? I had no answers.

I walked in a daze with the three officers surrounding me. They had the decency not to cuff me. Of course, it was pretty obvious I wasn't concealing anything in my dress. I'd been too shocked to even grab a coat on my way out. No coat. No purse. I hadn't even locked the damn door behind me. All I had was the blue silk gown I wore and enough crippling terror to last a lifetime.

The police station was eerily empty, though the place would likely be buzzing with activity in a few hours. For the moment, every available set of hands was out on the streets getting ready for one of the most chaotic nights in the city all year. If I'd had my faculties about me, I'd have questioned why officers were messing with executing a warrant on a night like this, but fear had scrambled my ability for logic. When it came to fight or flight, my brain had most definitely fled.

I was taken to a small interrogation room. It didn't look quite like they did on TV—no two-way mirror and metal table bolted to the ground. The small closet-like room had two chairs and an empty desk against the wall. A rounded CCTV camera lens poked out of the ceiling in one corner.

It would be easy to assume the camera was there to record suspects, but as I sat alone battling back tears, I realized it had another purpose. Something about knowing someone was watching you at your lowest made everything ten times worse. The shame and fear. The pressure and uncertainty. All of it was compounded with the insufferable weight of eyes watching me.

When the door finally opened, my breath hitched with the start of a sob. I was on the verge of coming unglued until I saw who had joined me. It was so unexpected that I wondered if this whole thing wasn't some wild hallucination.

Oran Byrne towered over me in the doorway. In his black dress coat over an immaculate gray suit, he was the spitting image of a romantic hero swooping in to save the day. His hair was perfectly styled, and he had a vengeful glint in his eye that would make anyone think twice about crossing him.

I rocketed to my feet with a burst of elation and relief. "Thank *God*, you're here! I've been completely freaking out and haven't even had a chance to call anyone, though I'm not sure who I would have called. I don't know if they're keeping me or what on earth is going on. They just dropped me off in here and then disappeared. No one has even come to talk to me yet." My babbling withered to silence when Oran's face remained eerily impassive as he closed the door.

"Have a seat, Lina." He motioned to the chair I'd been in while taking his own seat at the desk.

Hope drained from my heart faster than the blood from my cheeks. I allowed my now wobbly legs to drop me back into my seat. "How did you know I was here, Oran?"

Had he been watching my apartment building? Did he even know where I lived? It seemed far-fetched to think he'd put a general watch out for me with the police department, but I wasn't sure how else to explain his presence. All I knew was that something was off. But then, nothing made sense in this whole crazy situation—the drugs, the police, and now Oran.

My spine fused straight.

The fine hairs on my arms and neck pulled taut.

"Did you have something to do with this?" My question was no more than a whisper. My voice abandoned me as though I'd been punched in the gut.

"I told you to stay away from him," he said with a hint of irritation as he stood and shrugged off his coat. When he tried to drape it around my shoulders, I jerked away from him like a caged animal, shooting back to my feet.

"Get away from me, you—"

"Lina, *listen*." His hands clamped around my upper arms, neutralizing my efforts. "You're fucking freezing. You can still be pissed at me wearing the coat."

"How *could* you?" I hissed in his face.

He waited until my body stilled before lowering his hands. "What you should be asking is why."

I contemplated kicking him in the shins but decided to hold off for now. "You and your damn semantics. Who cares if I asked how or why? Are you going to explain yourself or not?"

"I did it because I can, and because I can just as easily *un*do it."

I considered his words, but no matter how I looked at them, I didn't understand. "Why would you go through the trouble of setting all this up if you planned to turn around and make it all go away?"

"Because I can ... *if* ... you agree to my terms."

Blackmail. That was what this was about. Oran was blackmailing me.

I should have known. They were all the same. How stupid did I have to be to think he might be different?

"What do you want from me?" My tone sounded as hollow as my heart felt.

"I want you to be mine."

Had I heard him wrong? I must have. "What?" I squinted my eyes as if it might help me understand.

"I want you to agree to a fake engagement. It'll be temporary, but it has to be convincing. Those are my terms."

My night was one big fun house, each room more confusing and unexpected than the last. Oran had set up my arrest—*framed* me for drug charges—in order to then *blackmail* me into being his fake fiancée.

Had I been given a million chances to predict how my New Year's Eve would go, I never would have gotten it right.

"But ... *why*?" The word was saturated with disbelief.

His hands lifted to cup my face, a thumb trailing softly over one cheek. "Does it matter?"

He was right. It didn't change anything, but I still wanted to know why all my efforts were about to be flushed down the toilet. He wasn't going to tell me, though. His resolve was clear in the set of his jaw and the impenetrable wall behind his eyes.

I was only a pawn in his grand scheme.

What did that mean? Was he trying to show up Lawrence? Or was the show meant for someone else, and I was simply the unlucky fool he chose to play the part?

"The clock is ticking, Lina. You need to decide. Are you walking out of here with me or not at all?" His hands fell to his sides, but he didn't back away.

We stood toe-to-toe as I weighed my options.

I could have refused him. I could have hired an attorney with money I didn't have and battled the charges for God knew how long. Chances were, I'd still end up convicted. Even I thought I looked guilty as hell. I couldn't see even a remote possibility where that scenario worked out in my favor.

*Think, Lina. Think.*

And if I agreed? What would that mean for me and everything I'd worked toward?

Oran was a member of Olympus, which might still be helpful, but I was almost certain he hadn't yet joined the Society. They were too secretive to take on a new member so quickly unless he already had a connection on the inside. Someone who knew him well enough to unveil the group's existence. Even then, I suspected he would have to be a member at Olympus for some time while they vetted him.

*Even if you were seemingly engaged to Oran, would that deter Lawrence from wanting more time with you?*

He was so morally corrupt that an engagement would probably enhance my appeal. If I still had access to Lawrence and could add Oran as a possible information outlet, maybe this wouldn't have to be a total disaster.

I hated that my choices were being stripped away from me yet again by an entitled asshole who thought he could have whatever he wanted. And to think I'd almost been taken in by his charm. I was embarrassed by my naivete and whimsical fantasy that a selfless, kindhearted man might swoop in to save the day. That type of mythical creature didn't exist.

"Only in public," I demanded. "I'm not fucking you." If we were doing this, I wanted to be clear on the terms.

"Assuming you don't want to." A fire lit his eyes. "Never say never, Lina."

"Honestly, how do you even fit through the door with that ego of yours?"

He tipped the tiniest bit forward. "Very. Carefully." Then he breathed deeply in through his nose, his brows knitting together as if savoring the flavors of a fine wine. "Now, get out your phone. You need to text Wellington and tell him you're not attending the party."

"Why not? Don't you want to show off your new *fiancée*?"

"Not tonight. We have a wedding to attend tomorrow."

He wouldn't. He *couldn't*, could he?

*Look at everything else he's done. What makes you think he wouldn't?*

The world spun.

Oran

# FIFTEEN

Shit, she was going to pass out.

"*Breathe*, Lina." I pulled her against me to keep her upright. "You can relax. The wedding's not ours," I quipped sharply. "My cousin's getting married, and you're my date."

The woman knew how to humble a man.

I'd meant to toy with her, but she acted like I'd threatened exile in Siberia.

Surprising me again, she shoved my chest, a fire lighting in her eyes. "That wasn't funny, asshole."

I let a wicked grin darken my face. "Depends on who you ask."

"This is my *life*, Oran. Not some fucking game."

"Considering the clown you've been dating, I'm not sure you know the difference."

The slap came without warning. It resounded in my ears and stiffened my cock. I wasn't sure why, but seeing her feisty side made me want to bend her over the desk until the entire precinct heard her come.

"Glad to see you still have some sense left." Hunger clawed at my voice, leaving it raw and guttural.

"No thanks to you."

"Remember you said that."

"Oh, I will. I'll remember every infuriating second of this night so long as I live, and I won't let you forget it either."

I leaned in, bringing my lips close to her ear. *"Promises, promises."*

Turning, I led us from the room and back through the police station. I didn't look back, but I could hear her heels clacking behind me, and it helped me breathe easily for the first time in weeks.

I was helping Lina, whether she wanted to believe it or not. Admittedly, my methods were extreme, but she only had herself to blame for that. I'd tried to play nice and charm her away from Wellington. The damn woman wouldn't cooperate even though her entire body practically purred with desire when she was near me.

That look on her face when I walked in the door? Christ, I'd never forget it. Like I was the storybook knight she'd been waiting for her whole life. The sight nearly undid me, but it only lasted a heartbeat. Her skepticism and stubborn wariness set in as soon as her questions surfaced, coloring everything I'd done in shades of hostility and corruption.

I needed to be grateful. Her response would help me stay focused on my goals. I'd gathered most of the intel I'd needed over the past month. While I'd had to push things along a bit faster than I'd have preferred so that I could get Lina away from Wellington, my timeline was still functional. At least now I didn't have to worry about her safety on top of everything else.

In a month or so, she'd be free of me and able to seek out another toxic relationship, if she was so damn insistent upon it.

I accidentally slammed the car door after helping her in, pissed at the thought of her with another undeserving asshole. I didn't understand why it irritated me so badly. I knew she'd hate me, so her response came as no surprise. But it still grated on every one of my nerves.

"I don't have my phone," Lina mumbled when I joined her in the car. "I left it with my jacket and everything else at my house."

I almost forgot I'd told her to text Lawrence. She was a constant distraction like that.

"Stand him up for all I care."

She sighed heavily as I merged the car into traffic.

"I'd give you my address, but clearly, you already know."

"If it's any consolation, it wasn't easy to find."

She harrumphed and cast her face toward the side window, remaining quiet for the rest of the short journey. When we arrived, I turned off the engine and started to exit the car.

"You don't have to walk me up."

"Do you always get your hackles up when people are polite?"

"I do when they have ulterior motives."

"And what, pray tell, is my ulterior motive in walking you to your apartment?"

"It's impossible to know what's going on in that twisted head of yours."

A bellow of genuine laughter seized me—something that rarely happened when I was with anyone but family. As it subsided, I glanced at Lina and was surprised to see a flush cross her cheeks. For the millionth time, I wished I knew what she was thinking. Watching her in the elevator, I speculated that it would likely still baffle me even if I had access to her complicated mind.

I held the doors open, then followed her to her apartment, which she opened without a key.

"You always leave your place unlocked?" Irritation seeped into my words.

"I was a little distracted by the prospect of life in prison."

"Not life, just ten to twenty," I said distractedly as I looked around. I'd known this place would be much more dated and humble than I'd initially expected of her when I discovered her real address, but the reality was even more surprising than I imagined. The fake city inspector I'd used during our staged emergency gas test had been the one to plant the drugs, so I'd yet to see the place.

What shocked me the most was that she had a room-mate in a one-bedroom apartment. Lina Schultze had hundreds of thousands of dollars sitting in a bank account. Why the hell would she choose to live here … with a *roommate*?

I wanted to peek into the bedroom, but the door was closed.

"I'm safely home, now. You can leave." She crossed her arms over her chest.

I picked up her phone from the coffee table and handed it to her.

She rolled her eyes, typed out a short message in hyper speed, then held the screen in my face. "Happy now?"

I prowled closer, ignoring the device. She relented and

lowered her arm to her side, lifting her delicate chin defiantly. God, I wanted to bite it.

"This won't work if you can't pretend to like me." I stalked closer.

She retreated, one step for each of mine until her back was against the wall.

I lifted my hands and savored the way her body reacted to the uncertainty of my touch. As much as she wanted to hate me, her body wasn't so sure. I trailed my fingertips along the neckline of her gown until they met in the middle between her breasts, then back up before slipping my coat from her shoulders.

"Evening attire for the wedding. Nothing too fancy. I'll be by to get you at five. Don't be late." I walked away with a smug grin as her shaky exhale filled my ears.

It hit me that if I'd found my first wife this intriguing, maybe I wouldn't have ended up wanting to kill her.

*What's to say this won't end the same?*

Not a goddamn thing.

# SIXTEEN

Who the hell got married on New Year's Day? The world was hung over and exhausted. No one wanted to get dressed up and sit through a boring-ass ceremony of two people who would probably just end up divorced.

*And when did you become a grumpy old shrew?*

Ouch.

Okay, I deserved that. But this wedding business was seriously stressing me out. I'd gone through my wardrobe no less than a dozen times and still couldn't decide what to wear. My mood had morphed from righteous indignation to something befitting a poisonous cactus—prickly and possibly deadly.

I couldn't believe Oran was making me meet his entire

family one day after framing and *blackmailing* me into a fake engagement. Who did that?

Oran Byrne, the most pigheaded, insufferable man I knew, that was who.

He would be here any minute to pick me up, and I was still in my underwear. I'd already done my hair and makeup, but it was the wardrobe that got me. Nothing seemed to say *strong, independent woman being held against her will by her not-so-real fiancé.*

Go figure.

The wardrobe challenge was enough cause to have me running late, but holding up Oran's schedule was also the best protest I had available to me. If he didn't like it, he could hijack some other girl's life.

I lowered the dress I'd been holding up, my stare unseeing as I envisioned how easily Oran could charm the pants off any girl he wanted. The image soured my mood even further—not because of how easy it would be for him but because of the odd irritation it stirred in me. The feeling stunk of jealousy, which was the very last thing I should feel where Oran Byrne was concerned.

By the time his knock sounded at the door, I was certifiably petulant.

"You have to wait. I'm not ready," I hollered through the door.

"Open the door, Lina. I'm not waiting in the hall."

"I will when I'm dressed."

"I'll give you to the count of three," he called dryly.

I couldn't believe he was serious. What the hell did he plan to do? Break down the damn door?

"Three."

I crossed my arms and mentally dared him to do his worst.

"Two."

And he would most *certainly* be paying for the damages.

"One."

I braced for him to burst through the door, my lips pursed tightly together, but the key turned in the lock, and the door opened with ease. I was so shocked that I forgot I was wearing nothing but a bra and panties.

"How the hell do you have a key to my apartment?"

Oran's gaze licked down my body with ravenous hunger.

"Maintenance," he murmured distractedly.

Realizing I was practically naked, I almost ran for the bathroom, but then my outrage took the reins and plotted a totally new course. Hands on my hips, I let a venomous smile twist my lips.

"Like what you see?"

His gaze tore from my body up to my icy stare, but he didn't respond.

"Good, because it's never. Going. To. Happen." I yanked a dress off the futon and strutted past him to the bathroom. I didn't even look to see what I'd haphazardly chosen until I was alone behind the closed door.

Black. *Excellent.*

I slid on the expensive wool sheathe and took in my reflection.

Elegant. Sophisticated. All business.

It was perfect.

I needed to select a pair of shoes but wasn't ready to exit, so I sat on the toilet and started scrolling on my phone while rehearsing the scathing remarks I'd have for maintenance. Had he paid them off or just stolen the damn thing? There was no telling with him. Either way, I was pissed.

The knock I'd been waiting for took longer than I'd expected.

"I may not have the key to this one," Oran said evenly, "but it would be easy enough to break down. Do I need to count to three?"

What a pain in my ass. "I'm on the toilet." Technically true.

"Three."

"Two."

I jumped up and hurried to the door, swinging it wide open and glaring at my tormentor. "*You…*" I was too irritated to come up with a good insult.

Oran smirked. "Me? I'm not the one being difficult."

"I can't help it if you're rushing me. These things take time, you know."

"Not for you, Lina," he said in a velvet caress. "You'd be beautiful without even trying."

A few softly uttered words, and he'd sucked every bit of air out of the room. My lips parted then shut as if I were practicing my fish impersonation.

*Smooth, Lina. Real smooth.*

Unsure how I felt, I chose not to say anything and slid on the red heels closest to me.

"Good girl. Now, let's go. We're already late." Then the Neanderthal erased any kind thought I might have had with a resounding slap on my ass.

I glared at him. "Try that again, and I'll cut off one of your fingers."

"So long as it's not this one." He held up his hand and curled his middle finger as though signaling me closer. "I've been told it's rather … *skilled* in certain situations."

I may have blushed, but at least I managed a comeback. "Women say all sorts of outrageous things to protect men's fragile egos."

"There's one way to know for sure." He smirked, eyes hooded.

"Let's hope your prowess is better than your memory. I said it's never happening, and I meant it." I leaned back against the elevator wall opposite Oran and truly took him in for the first time that evening. His suit was impeccable. Black on black with no tie. His gray eyes ringed with thick black lashes were even more prominent, like shimmering diamonds set on a black velvet display.

"Keep looking at me like that, and it *will* happen right there against that elevator wall." The hint of warning in his gravelly words told me he wasn't joking.

A bowl of cotton sprouted in my mouth and sucked out every bit of moisture. I kept my lips sealed the rest of the way to the church.

♦

Oran wasn't lying when he said we were late. We missed the entire ceremony and walked into the reception just as the groom launched the garter at the crowd. Only, the garter missed the group and landed smack against Oran's chest like a heat-seeking missile. He reflexively caught the scrap of satin, waving it good-naturedly above his head as if he'd planned the whole thing.

The room burst into cheers. All eyes were on us, each curious stare pricking at my skin like a swarm of hungry mosquitos. Fortunately, the crowd quickly dispersed back into smaller groups, alleviating the tension until I realized the bride and groom themselves were walking our way along with another couple.

This was it. Time for the show.

"Congratulations, you two." Oran hugged the groom and

gave the bride a small kiss. The newlyweds made a lovely pair. She had a wholesome beauty to her, and the smitten look in his eyes was enviable. He was head over heels in love and didn't care who knew. I respected that in a man.

"I'm so sorry I was late, but it couldn't be helped. You see, we have some news of our own to celebrate." His words rang in my ears, horror enveloping me.

He wouldn't. Not at someone else's wedding. Surely, he knew better.

"Everyone, I'd like to introduce Lina Schultze, my fiancée."

*Mother. Fucker.*

Apparently, he didn't know better. Or he just didn't care. Either way, I was mortified.

The two couples gaped at us with such shock that my palms tingled with unease. His announcement was unexpected—that was a given—but his family stared at us as if he'd told them he planned to move to Antarctica and spend the remainder of his life studying penguins.

"Oran, what a wonderful surprise." The bride regained her composure first, giving Oran a hug before turning to me. "Lina, I'm Stormy. It's lovely to meet you."

"Thank you, Stormy. I'm so sorry to hijack your day. I told Oran he needed to wait." It was a white lie. We hadn't discussed the matter, but hell if I was going to get on their bad side before I'd even met them. I had no qualms about throwing him under the bus.

"This calls for a toast," announced the man with a striking redhead on his arm. Or she would have been striking if all the color hadn't drained from her face.

Between her reaction and the twitch I'd noticed in the groom's eye, I felt more conscientious than ever. I was unwelcome here.

How dare Oran put me in this situation? Especially with no warning.

I was so freaking pissed, I could have strangled the man. Instead, I chose a more passive-aggressive route. I had to comply with our agreement, after all.

When the server presented a tray of champagne flutes, I *accidentally* knocked a glass down the front of Oran's beautiful suit. It was a shame, really, but the man deserved it.

Hell, he'd done the same to me two weeks earlier.

"Oh, baby! How *clumsy* of me." Each word was more saccharine than the last.

"It's no problem, *sweetheart*." He began to dab at his shirt with a napkin, leaning toward me. "You can lick it off me later," he added in a voice that was not nearly quiet enough for my taste.

*In your dreams.*

I smiled at the bride as she placed a hand on my arm. "I'm so glad you two could make it, and congratulations again." She quickly turned to the redhead, and the two scurried off to the restroom.

Oh well. It wasn't the first time I'd been the subject of rumors, and it wouldn't be the last.

I took a slow, deep breath in preparation for a night full of maddeningly awkward conversations. I was going to have to find a way to pay back Oran.

Maybe a kiss…

With my fist…

To his face.

And with that thought, I returned to mingling with my first genuine smile of the night.

# SEVENTEEN

BRINGING LINA TO THE WEDDING CAME ABOUT SO QUICKLY THAT I didn't have a chance to warn Nana that Lina was coming. Now, the two were about to meet, and I wasn't entirely sure what my feisty grandmother might say. The possibilities were unnerving.

I considered tactically avoiding her side of the room but decided her wrath, if I did, would be even worse, and that was a guarantee. There was at least a slim chance Nana would play it cool.

"Nana, I have someone I'd like you to meet."

"Well, lassie. I thought Oran here had exaggerated when he told me how bonny you were, but I can see for myself it were the God's honest truth. You must be Lina."

*So much for playing it cool.*

"Lina Schultze," I said, "I'd like you to meet my grandmother, Nana Byrne." When I looked back at Lina, she studied me with an intensity that made my skin itch.

"Nana, it's lovely to meet you." She extended her hand with effortless grace. Every awkward situation I'd thrown at her, whether intentional or not, she'd waded through with practiced ease. I was impressed. Though I liked it better when I saw the true Lina—the fury and snark that lived beneath the aristocratic facade.

"I'm so glad you could join us," Nana beamed. "Can you believe such a marvelous celebration was thrown together in only a week?"

"You're kidding!"

"Not at all. They were ready and saw no need to wait, but that's the way of these Byrne men. Not a lick of patience among them." She held up her hand the second I opened my mouth. "Don't you argue with me, boyo. You're a Byrne through and through." She continued talking to Lina as though I weren't there. "The whole family came together, the ladies especially, of course. It was a group effort, and I'd say it's a splendid show of how well we work together." The old woman was damn proud. I had to smile.

"I'm shocked they could get a florist to do an event like this on such short notice."

Nana shrugged nonchalantly. "Sometimes you just have to know how to talk to people."

"Alright, Nana. That's probably enough out of you." I didn't know what information she might have or what she planned to say, but I wasn't risking it. "We still need to make a few introductions."

She gave me a deadpan stare, then turned to Lina. "See! What did I say? Not a lick of patience." She reached out two wrinkled hands and clasped Lina's affectionately. "It was a pleasure to meet you, Lina dear. Take care of my Oran. He's not so tough as he lets on."

*Jesus H. Christ.*

Lina looked like she was ready to split at the seams with laughter. "I'll do my best. And trust me, the pleasure was all mine."

"Ignore her. She's completely senile," I grumbled as I herded Lina far, far away from Nana.

"Interesting. She seemed lucid to me."

"That just goes to show how questionable your judgment is."

"Careful, that's your fiancée you're talking about." She shot me a look filled with sass.

I gave her a quick tug, bringing her back flush with my front, and wrapped my arms around her. "You have any idea what that mouth of yours does to me?" I rasped quietly, my cheek close to hers.

Lina shook her head. I lowered one hand to her belly and pulled her against my thickening cock. I felt rather than heard her sharp intake of air.

"A little something to remember next time you feel like being smart."

"That's who I am," she said, her voice gone husky. "I suggest you get used to being *painfully* embarrassed."

I took her hand and spun her as if we'd been dancing, then pulled her front flush with mine, my cock now pleasantly pressed into her lower belly. "Sweetheart, I don't give a fuck who knows I'm hard for you." I brought my face closer, my stare melding with hers. "Now, unless there's something more … sophisticated on the menu, it's time for cake. I'm famished."

"Cake," she breathed, nodding sharply. "Yes, cake would be good."

I released her with a wolfish grin, thrilled at how thoroughly I'd managed to disorient her. We took our cake slices to a vacant table and sat with a view of the room. I grabbed a glass of champagne for each of us, smirking when she downed half in one go.

"Oran," she said quietly after she'd finished her cake. "Why are you doing this?"

"Why do you think?" I asked back with a good amount of genuine curiosity.

Lina shrugged a shoulder. "Hurting Lawrence would make the most sense, though being here is hardly necessary for that, and stealing me away from him is bound to hurt your business relationship."

"Maybe I enjoy torturing you."

Her gaze raked over me. "Possibly."

"Or I could just be succumbing to family pressures to marry."

She smirked. "You're such a good catch you had to blackmail a girl into it, huh?"

I shrugged. "Fewer emotions involved that way. A lot less complicated."

"True, but you had me agree to a temporary engagement, not a marriage. That's hardly going to satisfy a Catholic grandma." She sipped on her drink, eyes roving around the room. I, on the other hand, couldn't tear my eyes away from her.

"There's always the possibility I'm doing it for you," I said evenly.

She looked back at me and chuckled. "This is all for my benefit, is it?"

"I suppose that's one way to interpret it." If only she knew.

Her head cocked to the side. "Do you get off on being cryptic? I'd love to have just one straight answer from you. Just once."

"I tell you what, we get one question each, but only one. Agreed?" It was dangerous but too tempting to pass up.

Her eyes flared. She nodded.

"I'll start. Why do you live with a roommate?" The roommate question was informative while not overly invasive. I didn't go for one of the more burning questions I had because I wanted her to tell me herself. I wanted her to volunteer the information.

*You want her to trust you.*

The realization sat heavily on my chest. It seemed I was doomed to repeat the same damn mistakes I'd made in the past. Only this time, it was worse because I was doing it with my eyes wide open.

Lina stared at me as if she'd misheard. "You can ask me anything, and you want to know about my roommate?"

"Not about her. *Why* her. You come from money, Lina. You don't need to live in an old building with a roommate."

"You're right. I *came* from money. That's not my money; it's my mother's money, and I want nothing to do with it."

"But if you don't use their money, how do you afford to wear designer clothes?"

Her chin lifted, but her gaze dropped to her hands. "They aren't designer—not exactly. They're mine. I made them. That's what I do."

I thought back to the sewing station in her apartment. I knew she was in the design business, but it hadn't occurred to me that she made the clothes she wore.

Jesus, she was talented.

"The blue gown last night?"

A nod.

I looked down at her perfectly tailored dress.

"Yes, this one, too," she confirmed. "I put myself through design school, then started a company with a classmate. It took a while to make a name for ourselves, but the business has recently taken off. I'd planned to move into my own place at the beginning of the year, but..." She paused, her teeth raking over her bottom lip. "Things came up, and I was too busy to mess with a move."

"What things?"

Her eyes locked with mine again. I thought I might actually get an answer, but she slowly shook her head instead. "You got your answer, plus one. It's my turn."

I motioned for her to ask away.

She thought for all of five seconds, then asked, "Why did you join the Olympus Club?"

I had given her cart blanche to ask anything she wanted of me, and that was what she chose? Why the hell did she care about my reasons for joining? She could have asked why I'd forced the fake engagement or how I'd figured out her real address or whether I planned to hold up my end of our arrangement. She could have asked *anything*. Why the club?

I was already planning on being honest, but it felt even more imperative, considering the importance she must have put on the answer. "To get close to Lawrence Wellington."

She stared unmoving except for a single blink as though my reply left her speechless. I didn't think it was all that outrageous, but she'd apparently been expecting something else.

"Why do you want to get close to Lawrence?"

I smiled wryly. "The Q&A is over."

Lina frowned, and it was disturbingly adorable. I wanted

to bite that pouting bottom lip, then soothe the burn with my tongue. "I gave you one extra."

"Lucky me," I mused.

"Hey, Oran," a voice called over, interrupting our moment. One of the younger cousins in training approached with a broad grin. "Got your captain for you. Name's Willis."

Fucking Christ. He was bringing up my plans for Wellington's shipping empire demise right here in front of Lina. He was so goddamn eager to impress me that he hadn't paid one bit of attention to his surroundings. It wasn't the end of the world in this situation, but it was a mistake he couldn't afford to repeat.

I shot to my feet and had my hand around his throat so fast he didn't have a chance to flinch. The kid might have been loose-lipped, but at least he knew better than to fight me. Both his hands clasped my wrist while his eyes bulged with a need for air.

"Don't you ever talk about family business again without being absolutely sure of your surroundings. Do you *fucking* understand me?"

I didn't give a fuck that the entire room watched. This dumbass had to learn a lesson.

His eyes cut to Lina, then bulged even more. He nodded as best he could, gasping and patting my arm like we were playing a game and he was tapping out. Wrong. In our world, following the rules was a matter of life and death. There was no mercy rule.

I kept my grip tight until he went limp from passing out, then eased his body to the floor.

When I turned my attention back to Lina, she stared at me as if seeing me for the first time.

Good.

I hoped it gave her something to think about when she was tempted to go back to Wellington.

"Time for us to go." I held out my hand and thanked Christ when she placed hers in mine without hesitation. Fear could have motivated her, but I didn't care. I was just relieved to have her comply without question for once. More than relieved. Her submission was a shot of adrenaline straight into my bloodstream—a high I could easily begin to crave.

Feisty Lina was enticing. Captivating.

The more pliant, yielding side of her could bring a man to his knees.

I hoped I never saw it again.

*Lina*

# EIGHTEEN

WAS ORAN TELLING THE TRUTH? HAD HE REALLY JOINED Olympus just to get close to Lawrence?

As we drove back to my place, I watched the buildings pass by, but nothing I saw registered. I was too confounded by the fact that all my instincts told me Oran had been honest. I hadn't necessarily expected him to tell me outright that he was looking to join the Society, but I thought he might hint at something more nefarious.

Maybe the answer he'd given was only part of the truth. Getting close to Lawrence could be his method for gaining membership to the Society. Maybe he saw them as one and the same.

But if that were the case, stealing me away from Lawrence would hardly help his cause.

I wasn't sure what to think. A part of me wanted to believe there was a chance he was different from the others, but just because he wasn't involved in the Society didn't make him safe. He was still an associate of Lawrence's. A criminal. Just look at what he'd done when his own cousin had upset him. If I'd had any question about his family being in organized crime, that had swiftly been put to rest. Not a single person had batted an eye at the outburst.

My mother had insinuated Oran knew more than he let on. Could he have been involved in Amelie's disappearance? Without an answer, I would have to stay on guard, which normally came naturally to me after years of necessity. Yet somehow, whenever I was near him, I seemed to forget every hard-fought lesson I'd ever learned.

Watching him with his family made things even more confusing. Everyone seemed so … *genuine*. It felt foreign. Like I'd stepped into an alternate dimension where people cared about one another and valued their time together. In my experience, that wasn't how family worked. Family were the people you were shackled to by blood.

As we stepped onto the sidewalk in front of my building, I gave voice to my thoughts. "You're a lucky man. You have an incredible family." Even if they did kill people.

"You're not close to yours." It was an observation rather than a question, but I answered as if it were.

"No."

"None of them?"

An ache radiated from the sinkhole that had slowly devoured my heart over the past few months.

"Not as close as I should have been." The words felt so heavy, I was surprised they carried at all.

Sensing he'd struck on a sensitive subject, Oran didn't push for more. I wondered why. He'd made no promise to be kind or even tolerable during our time together. If he wanted answers, he could force them from me. I wasn't some Navy SEAL badass trained to withstand interrogations. Given the right circumstances, I'd fold like a cheap lawn chair.

Maybe acting like a gentleman and showing me his family was all a manipulation. Maybe he was trying to get me to drop my defenses. But to what end?

I had no clue, but regardless, his tactics were working. I didn't want to admit it, but I felt at ease with him in a way I hadn't expected. Like I didn't have to put on a show or behave a certain way.

*And when he has you where he wants you, what then?*

I sighed heavily as I stepped onto the elevator.

Oran pressed the button for my floor. "I need you to stay away from Lawrence. No contact whatsoever. Understood?"

"What are you going to do if I don't?" My thoughts triggered my defenses, and his command only worsened things.

"Lock you in my apartment."

"You wouldn't," I scoffed. "You couldn't. People would look for me."

He used the side of his fist to press the red emergency button, forcing the elevator to come to a jarring halt. Oran prowled across the small space and placed his hands against the metal wall on either side of my body.

"Tell me I can't do something one more time, and you'll see just how capable I am of many, *many* things." He wasn't joking. Not even a little. In fact, I got the sense he was almost begging me to give him a reason to follow through. If I gave him the slightest provocation, he'd have me chained to his bed, proving just how adept those fingers of his were.

God, why was I so tempted?

He brought his lips to my ear. My lungs quit working.

"Do it, Lina. I can see how badly you want to test me. Just give me one ... little ... reason." His whispered words flooded my core with such intense desire that I had to press my thighs together to alleviate the ache.

What about this man was so damn irresistible? I should have been repulsed. I should have told him off, then kneed him in the junk for good measure. Instead, my treacherous tongue trailed over my bottom lip as I grappled for control.

"Okay," I forced past my throat. "Message received."

He waited several more seconds for emphasis before slowly pulling away and putting the elevator back into motion. I could feel his eyes devouring me but couldn't convince myself to meet his stare. If he saw how close I was to throwing caution to the wind, we wouldn't have left that elevator.

I practically ran through the elevator doors when they opened and burst into my apartment. Jessa was home. I wasn't sure what to do, but when Oran didn't turn to leave, I hesitantly allowed him inside.

"Hey, Jessa. This is Oran."

"Hey! It's great to finally meet you." She stood from the comfy chair and shook his hand.

I wasn't sure what was worse—for Oran to think I'd been talking about him or for him to realize Jess had him confused for Lawrence.

I grabbed him by the hand and led him over to my sewing area. "So how will this work?" I asked quietly, hoping he got the drift that I'd prefer my roommate didn't know I'd been coerced into dating him.

"I'll pick you up for Wednesday dinner at the club. In the meantime, I'll explain to Wellington how circum-stances have changed. You don't need to say or do a thing." Meaning I wasn't allowed to communicate with the man.

"It's still going to be awkward as hell. You know that, right?"

"If anyone can get herself through an awkward situation, it's you."

Was that … a compliment? I wasn't used to those and felt horribly out of my depth.

"Yeah, well. We'll see," I muttered.

He started to turn toward the door but pulled up short, tugging me close against him, my thighs intertwined with his. His lips feathered over my ear. "Night, baby. And be good. I'll be watching." With that, he left, taking my equilibrium with him.

Jesus, what had I gotten myself into?

# NINETEEN

I WASN'T JOKING WHEN I TOLD LINA I WOULD BE WATCHING HER. Cameras, GPS, spyware on her computer—I was locked in where Lina Schultze was concerned. She wouldn't be able to sneeze without me knowing.

So why did I feel like I was minutes from losing my shit after only a few days away from her?

I was going insane. Why else would I have already developed such an intense need to be near her? I had a sneaking suspicion I wouldn't breathe easy unless she was within reach or until Wellington was dead. Neither of those options aligned with my plans, which meant I'd had to make some adjustments.

Originally, I'd wanted to save my big reveal that Lina was

mine as part of the grand finale—my way of kicking Wellington when he was down. Instead, the news was served as an appetizer with a full five-course meal of devastation to follow.

We needed to touch base one more time about the arrangements for our first shipment transaction. He didn't want to meet in public, so I stopped by his office and used the opportunity to share the big news of my engagement.

Considering how blasé the man had been about sharing Lina, he grew surprisingly agitated when I told him. He fidgeted in his seat—a very uncharacteristic action—and a pulsing vein bulged from his forehead.

"I hope you understand," I offered disingenuously. "Sometimes two people are just meant for one another. It's just one of those crazy things. I might have worried, but after our initial talk, I knew you were a businessman through and through. Besides, I'm sure you keep your options open anyway."

Crimson blotches crept up his neck like steam overtaking a bathroom mirror.

"So that would explain her absence and excuses over the past two weeks." He lifted his chin, clearly battling over whether it was better to look unaffected or to defend his claim. In the end, the weasel in him won out. "No matter. I've always been of the opinion that the dependence on any one person is a detriment. Where women are concerned, the supply is unending."

Pathetic.

It was that same callous mentality that allowed him to continue working with traffickers.

*Get ready, asshole. Judgment day is coming.*

Soon.

"Glad to hear it." I stood and extended my hand. "You

know where to reach me if anything comes up before the shipment date."

"And Donati? He's still on board? I haven't heard from him or any of the Morettis."

This time, my smile came easily. "I spoke with him yesterday. He's just as committed to this joint venture as I am. I promise you that." *Committed to fucking you over.*

Wellington had navigated the first of his misfortunes, but two days later, I planned to put his pride to the test by taking Lina to Wednesday night dinner at the club. And not long after that, his entire world would begin to crumble.

♦

"Take it off. Find something else to wear."

Lina gaped at me. Hell, I was internally gaping at myself.

"Why? You were the one who told me to wear the damn dress." She was right. I had.

The red dress she'd worn at the club the first night after I'd joined had been incredible. I thought having her wear it would be the perfect jab at Wellington. The problem was, now that I'd seen her in the crimson fabric that clung to her like a second skin and exposed her entire back in the most seductive way possible, I couldn't stand the idea of sharing her—even the sight of her—with anyone. Not when I knew every dirty bastard in that club would jack off to the memory of her.

I would know. I'd done the same more than I cared to admit.

"It's cold out. You'll freeze," I told her.

"I'll wear a coat."

"Jesus, can't you just follow a simple instruction for once?"

"No, I can't. If that's what you wanted out of your *fake fiancée*, you chose the wrong girl." She glared at me with rabid intensity. I met her stare with equal fervor, speaking clearly without saying a single word that she was exactly who I'd meant to choose.

"Fine," I finally grumbled. "Get your coat. Let's go."

She snatched a heavy black dress coat off the back of a chair. After sliding an arm in one sleeve, I helped her with the other. She gave me an odd look but allowed me to assist.

"You know, it's a little strange that we're supposed to be engaged, but I don't have a ring. Not to say you have to buy one," she hurried to add. "I would have worn something I already owned if I had anything appropriate. Just thought it might sell the story better." Her gaze darted everywhere but at me.

I'd wanted to fuck the feisty side of her two minutes earlier, but this rare glimpse of vulnerability didn't make me want to fuck her.

It made me want to *own* her.

I pulled out a small velvet box from my coat pocket and opened the lid. I'd known the ring was hers from the moment I saw it at the jeweler. The asscher cut of the main diamond along with the three baguettes on either side gave the ring an Art Deco look—sophisticated and unique. Exquisite, like her.

When I took the ring in my fingers and held out my hand for hers, Lina stared in shock.

"Your hand," I prompted, fighting back my amusement.

Her left had floated upward without her eyes leaving the ring. "Oran, it's breathtaking. You didn't have to ... I mean, I hope you didn't spend too much."

I slid the ring on her finger, and fuck if it wasn't the most satisfying thing I'd ever done.

"You did spend too much," she whispered as she took a closer look. "And I'm not giving it back."

I slid my hand around the back of her neck, bringing her wide gaze to mine. "Wouldn't have given it to you if I wanted it back."

Fuck if I didn't want to kiss her senseless, but I was already swimming in a dangerous cocktail of emotions. The last thing I needed was to confuse the situation any further and end up drowning.

I allowed my thumb one slow caress of her cheek before I let my hand fall away. "Time to go."

♦

Our arrival at the club went as expected. While we got drinks at the bar, we were the subject of stares and whispers as word got around about our sudden engagement.

I was extra attentive to Lina, but it wasn't just part of the show. I found myself wanting to be near her to shield her. A tendril of guilt had slithered into my conscience over the position I'd put her in. When I'd switched tactics and coerced her into the relationship, I hadn't exactly thought through how she might feel about being a spectacle—the girl who'd jumped from one man's bed to another in a small social circle. It wasn't a flattering light.

In my original plan, she was a witless bit of arm candy who wouldn't care what others thought as long as she'd secured the biggest fish in the pond. That wasn't Lina. I didn't know who she was exactly, but it wasn't a gold digger.

I was even hesitant for her to leave my side when she excused herself to the bathroom before dinner. If I was going to put her in a vulnerable position, the least I could do was protect her as best I could. Had escorting her to the toilet been an option, I would have done it. Though I was glad I hadn't when her stepfather approached me the moment she disappeared. I was eager to finally meet him.

Charles Brooks was the stereotypical result of new money. In the seventies, he'd made his initial fortune from a sizable investment in high-risk, high-yield stocks. From what I'd gathered about the man, he was quick to leave his immigrant parents and modest upbringing in the past. Charles had money, and he liked people to know it.

I hadn't had the opportunity to talk with either of Lina's parents yet and had been hoping to get the chance. They'd lost her favor in a big way. Now that I knew her better, I suspected I wouldn't like them either, but I wanted to see for myself.

"Charles Brooks." The waif-like man extended his hand. "We haven't had the chance to meet."

"Oran Byrne." Shaking his hand was like holding a cold, wet chicken cutlet. I had to fight back the urge to wipe my hand on my pant leg afterward. "You're Lina's stepfather, correct?"

"Yes, and I hear congratulations are in order. Quite the surprise." He lifted his drink in the air, and I mirrored him, though neither of us drank.

"Sometimes these things fall into place unexpectedly."

"Good for you. I mean, if you're the sort who doesn't have a problem sharing his wife..." His comment wasn't just in poor taste. It was malicious and condescending.

My temper spiked from zero to volcanic in an instant.

Thank God I had better control over that sort of thing than many of the men in my family. Charles Brooks might have already been bleeding out by now.

Considering how disrespectful he'd been to me and my future wife, that might still be his fate.

"What exactly do you mean by that?" I allowed my tone to vibrate with menace.

He raised a hand, and his brows lifted to his thinning hairline as though suddenly realizing his unintentional slight. "Oh, nothing to get upset about. I just mean that she's not ... *pure*, if you know what I mean. I didn't want you to end up feeling misled down the road."

That was the most fucked-up thing he could have said, and the worst part was, it was a load of bullshit. He'd backed off whatever he meant to imply and had gone with something he thought was docile in comparison.

"I wouldn't expect her to be a virgin at twenty-eight." Each word was stiff with restraint. "As a man who married a widow with a daughter, I'm surprised you found that sort of thing worth mentioning."

"A widow is different from someone who..." His eyes cut to mine assessingly. "I'll just say that if your intent is to advance in the club, her presence will only hinder you."

What in the ever-loving fuck was he talking about? Advance in the club? And what was he implying about Lina?

My entire body quaked with the need to force some answers out of Charles Brooks. I'd happily break a bone for every minute he made me wait.

*Remember your goal, dickhead. You're not here for Lina. This is about Wellington and justice.*

But if I was out to kill a wasp and happened to uncover an entire nest, why wouldn't I torch the whole bloody thing?

Something was off about the Olympus Club and its members. I started to wonder if Lina's involvement with Wellington was actually about the club rather than a relationship. If Brook's statement stood alone, I'd have said he was just a whack-job trying to scare me away from his stepdaughter the best way he knew how. But when I factored in

Lina's odd reluctance to leave Wellington behind and her animosity toward her mother, I couldn't ignore the likelihood that something was up.

"I appreciate the advice," I said coolly, reining in my temper. "Any other suggestions?"

"Not at all. I can see now that you're the sort of man who can handle himself. I'm sure you and Carolina will be well matched." His eyes drifted over my shoulder just as an arm hooked around mine possessively.

I didn't have to look to know it was Lina. She fit at my side as though we'd been made as part of a matching set, only just reunited.

At almost the same time, Eliza Brooks appeared at her husband's side like troops rallying behind their commanders. The four of us squared off across from one another.

I placed a firm hand over Lina's where she held my arm. A message to her *and* her parents. Lina was mine, and I wasn't about to tolerate any disrespect. Judging by the way Eliza's blue eyes sparked, she either didn't get the memo or simply didn't care.

# TWENTY

I EXITED THE BATHROOM TO SEE MY STEPFATHER STANDING WITH Oran. I hated it. I felt a visceral need to run full-tilt at Charles Brooks and shoulder-check him into next week. I didn't want him anywhere near Oran.

Embarrassment as thick and greasy as motor oil coated my insides, knowing that Oran was getting a dose of my family's ugly nature. I wanted to drag him away so he didn't see the filth I came from. My urge was so vehement, I had to question the reason. Why did I care what Oran Byrne thought of me or my family? Wouldn't it be best if he thought the worst and left me alone?

My stomach bottomed out, making the emptiness in my chest feel even more prominent. I'd had to face my greatest struggles in life alone. It hadn't been easy, but I managed. I hadn't realized until now how much I craved the support of a partner. My relationship with Oran wasn't even real, yet I was scared of losing what amounted to the mere illusion of companionship.

*And? Come on, Lina. Be honest with yourself.*

I liked having Oran at my side. There, I admitted it. I was scared of losing him.

I was picky as hell about who I allowed close to me. That was why I didn't have many friends. Looking at Oran standing there with my stepfather, I realized I cared what Oran thought because I wanted him to like me. I didn't want him to think I was trash.

God, I was in trouble.

The last thing I needed was to develop some misguided crush on the man.

I shook myself from my stupor and crossed toward them. No matter how unwise it was for me to encourage this insane fake engagement situation, I would rather swallow a fist full of nails than let my mother and stepfather detect the truth. In the same vein, I wanted to make sure Oran knew that I was *not* my mother or her worthless husband. I was nothing like them at all.

Adrenaline burned like gasoline through my veins as I wrapped my arm around Oran's and stood defiantly at his side. I could have kissed him when his hand came to rest over mine. I hadn't been sure how he'd respond to my sudden show of unity, but he matched my stride and went headlong into battle at my side. That was how it felt when my mother approached—us against them.

The solidarity was fortifying.

I'd had innumerable showdowns with my mother and

stepfather, but this was the first time I hadn't had to face them alone.

"Mr. Byrne, Carolina." Eliza Brooks flashed a broad smile, reminding me of the wicked stepmother in *Cinderella* with comically high eyebrows and malice in her heart.

"Eliza, Charles," I responded in kind to keep us on equal footing.

"I suppose the rumors are true, considering the way you're glowing. When can we expect the new addition?" That was her not-so-kind way of implying I looked like I got knocked up and had to marry Oran, as if we'd suddenly teleported back to the nineteenth century.

I was about to respond when Oran beat me to it.

"I should be so lucky. Maybe one of these days, but for now, we plan to enjoy our time together." He handled Eliza's crass comment with tact and decorum. I couldn't have handled it better myself.

Gratitude flooded my cheeks with warmth.

Eliza waved a hand flippantly. "Well, I could have sworn you'd already put on a little baby fluff." Her tone was rife with mock confusion. "Regardless, I'm a little surprised you came to dinner tonight. Not exactly your finest showing of sensitivity after snubbing poor Lawrence."

My turn for a little condescension. "As if you'd know sensitivity if it slapped you in the face, Eliza."

"The apple doesn't fall far from the tree, then," she shot back, finally giving way to outright animosity before slipping her mask back into place with a grin. "I suppose it's good you came. We have a visitor with us that you haven't had the chance to formally meet. Oh, Ron!" She turned and waved over a middle-aged man from across the room. He was smartly dressed in a three-piece suit, swirling a tumbler of amber liquid in a hand outfitted with a large diamond pinky ring. His salacious smile made me queasy, but it was the sound of his voice that brought bile up to burn the back of my throat.

"Carolina, you can't imagine how happy I am to see you again."

I hadn't realized I'd begun to squeeze Oran's arm like a hungry python until he took a brief glance at my face. I couldn't let go. Nor could I tear my eyes away from the monster across from me.

My mother chuckled. "I was hoping you'd remember." She reached a hand across to touch Oran's hand like a heart-felt friend. "These two knew each other a long time ago, but it's nothing to be jealous over."

She'd mounted a counterattack and struck me at my most vulnerable.

A steel trap clamped its vicious teeth through the tender flesh of my heart. It wasn't blood but agony that poured out of me. Agony and shame and horror.

Eliza Brooks would have liked nothing more than to see me run from the club and never return. No matter how severe the pain, I couldn't give her what she wanted—I refused to let her have the satisfaction—but I also couldn't fight back. I couldn't manage a word, but I didn't run. I didn't cower. I didn't have to because for the first time, I wasn't alone.

"So you say," Oran said with deadly calm. "But as her future husband, I'm a little overprotective. And with my past as a Byrne family enforcer, I tend to be a little trigger-happy, so it's probably best if we excuse ourselves. Enjoy the rest of your evening." He slipped his arm from mine and pressed a scalding hand to my lower back, steering me to safety.

Oran

# TWENTY-ONE

"Keep going, baby. One foot in front of the other," I murmured gently, legitimately concerned she might topple over at any moment.

The club had small studies that could be used for private gatherings. With dinner about to start, they were both available, so I steered her into the closest room and shut the door behind us. Lina walked numbly to the tufted leather sofa and sat gingerly on the edge as if ready to bolt should the need arise.

I took a long, deep breath and started to pace.

I'd been prepared for any number of situations that might have evolved after our arrival, but what just went down wasn't one of them. I felt fucking blindsided.

What the twisted fuck was up with Lina's parents? And who the hell was Mr. Three Piece Suit? She'd been understandably aloof in front of her parents, but when that man joined us, she'd gone as stiff as a board. Every ounce of color drained from her face, and she clung to me like I was the last parachute on a plane careening toward earth.

Her mother had said Lina and that man had a past, but she couldn't mean romantic, could she? The guy was old enough to be her father. But then, she'd been seeing Wellington, and he was even older. The whole thing was totally fucked, especially the way Lina's mother seemed to delight in her reaction. What kind of a person does that to their child?

Everything about the situation made my skin crawl. Fury sank its scalding talons deep inside me, pushing my control to its absolute limits. I'd desperately wanted to take my knife to someone's throat and either demand an explanation or exact revenge. I didn't know what had been done to Lina, but I had no doubt she'd suffered some injustice at her parents' hands.

I had to keep pacing to dissipate some of the murderous energy pricking my muscles into action.

"I need to know what happened," I said in the most controlled tone I could manage. I didn't need to upset her more than she was already, but being gentle wasn't easy when I was so riled.

"Just my mother and her stupid games, that's all." Her voice was weary and resigned.

"Not tonight. I want to know what happened between you and your parents and what that man has to do with it," I demanded.

Lina squared her shoulders. "Nothing relevant. It's in the past." Her voice held an eerie detachment, and I fucking hated it.

"Wrong. You're going to tell me."

"No, I'm *not*. It's none of your goddamn business." Her spark of anger was a relief, so much more reassuring than the eerie detachment from minutes earlier.

I yanked her up off the couch and spun us around until her back was to the wall. "I *will* find out, I can promise you that. But I'd rather it come from you."

"They won't tell you, and neither will I, so you better get used to disappointment."

I growled like a fucking dog. Like I had no more control over myself than a stray mutt. "You make me crazier than anyone I've ever met."

She brought her face closer to mine, straining against my hold, and bared her teeth. "*Ditto.*"

My lips came down on hers with punishing intensity. She stirred up so many damn emotions, I didn't know how I felt, only that I felt everything to extremes. As with any cacophony of sounds, drawing out a single one to identify was impossible, yet they were so damn loud all together.

And even more astounding was the way the entire chaotic orchestra faded to a distant hum the second she began to kiss me back. The whole damn world could have collapsed around us, and I would have felt nothing but contentment at the press of her hungry lips on mine.

While the world wasn't collapsing, we stood on a battle-field with enemies surrounding us. This wasn't the time or place for anything but extreme caution.

I forced myself to pull my lips away from hers. "It's time to leave."

"But we haven't had dinner." Her response was surprisingly sharp.

My eyes narrowed. "Fuck if I'm staying after that. We can grab food on the way home."

"No, Oran. I have to stay." Her voice raised with a hint of mania. "I'm not letting them chase me away."

*Goddamn, this beautiful warrior of a woman.*

I leaned in close again, resting my forehead against hers. "I've learned that the only way to win with people like that is to walk away." I brought my lips to her jaw and kissed a path down her delicate neck. "Walk away, Lina, because if you don't care, they don't matter. And if they don't matter, they have no power over you. And you—" My hand caressed up her thigh beneath her dress.

She brought her hands to my shoulder on a shaky breath, sliding her legs a few inches apart. That was all the encouragement I needed.

"You are a fucking *queen*." My hand cupped her sex over silk panties before I slipped one finger beneath the elastic edge and into her warm folds. "You bow to no one but your king."

A ragged moan sighed from deep in her throat past parted red lips as I slid a finger deep inside her.

She was the most glorious, seductive sight I'd ever seen. And when her hooded blue eyes met mine, I vowed to myself that I would never let anyone hurt her again.

Lina clung to my jacket lapel. She used it as leverage to rock herself against my hand, and when she spoke, her raw voice was heavy with desire. "And what about my king? Who does he bow to?"

I lifted my fingers to my nose, savoring her musky scent, then lowered myself to my knees and trailed my nose along her slit. "A king is never afraid to get on his knees for his queen." I slid her black panties aside and began to devour her.

# TWENTY-TWO

I DIDN'T KNOW WHAT HAD COME OVER ME. ONE MINUTE, I WAS
facing my worst nightmare, and the next, I'd propped my leg
over Oran's shoulder and surrendered to the pleasure of his
tongue lapping at my clit.

"Right there! God, *yesss.*" My fingers curled into his thick
hair, and my eyes rolled back.

The man knew his way around a woman's pussy. He
didn't just attack the clit. He teased and coaxed pleasure from
every angle. He let the orgasm build, then recede as he
moved to another area, but unlike most men I'd been with,
Oran drew out the pleasure on purpose. I even felt the
rumbling vibration of his laughter after I groaned with frustration.

"Impatient, are you?"

"You started this, finish it."

He nipped my inner thigh. "Say please."

I'd been relieved of my pride long ago and wasn't afraid to beg for what I wanted. Right then, I needed that orgasm more than I needed to breathe. I would have done just about anything for the promise of the cataclysmic release he kept dangling just out of my reach.

"*Please*, let me come."

"Mmm … one of these days you're going to beg me to fuck you."

"Not … happening." My voice trailed off on a moan as his tongue upped its pace.

"*Yet*," he whispered before unleashing a perfectly orchestrated symphony of pleasure.

An unholy orgasm tore through my body like liquid napalm. I wouldn't have been shocked if I literally started glowing. I felt like I already was. My skin tingled and hummed while every muscle in my body liquefied as little trembling aftershocks kept me in a state of bliss.

Oran rose to his feet once my quakes had subsided, a firm hand on either side of me to ensure I stayed upright. "Now that you're feeling more … *relaxed*, let's get out of here."

The man was good. His strategy was 100 percent effective because I no longer had the energy or the interest to argue.

What little brainpower I had left was spent trying to figure out what was happening between us. I couldn't understand why Oran was helping me. Why he was acting like he cared. Was I some kind of pet project to him? Doubtful. His type wasn't into charity. He had to have had his own motives; I just couldn't decipher them.

To complicate matters, my feelings about him were just as muddied. The man had framed me for possession of drugs, then blackmailed me, and I'd just let him go down on me. I should have wanted to stop him, but I didn't. I'd needed the release as an escape. I'd wanted *him* to be the one to give it to me.

I couldn't understand what was going on in my head. Hating Oran would have made life so much easier. So much more clear-cut. I didn't know what I felt for him, but it wasn't hate.

I was entirely out of my depth where he was concerned. I'd dealt with my mother my entire life, so I knew how her mind worked and how to protect myself against her. That was impossible with Oran, which meant I had no control over the situation. Control was power, and I didn't like feeling powerless.

Using him instead of Lawrence had become so much more than a change of tactics. I was now fighting a war on two fronts, and if I didn't get the upper hand soon, I would lose everything.

Oran helped me back into my coat once we were in the lobby, then opened the door for me. The winter sky had faded to black hours ago, and the air held a bitter chill with a threat of rain. Oran hadn't parked far, thank goodness, but we'd only taken a few steps down the sidewalk when my stepfather's voice called after me.

"Carolina, I need to speak with you for a moment. Preferably in private."

My steps faltered.

"Ignore him," Oran growled beside me, urging me forward with his hand at my back.

But I couldn't. Hope was the Twinkie of emotions—it simply wouldn't die. There was a minuscule chance Charles Brooks had information I wanted, and I couldn't ignore that possibility, no matter how small. Maybe he was willing to finally concede some scrap of truth to get me to disappear from their lives forever.

"It's fine. I want to know what he has to say."

"Nothing worthwhile, you *know* that."

"Yeah," I agreed sadly. "But I still have to go."

"Not alone, you don't." He grabbed my hand and marched us back toward the club entrance.

Oran

# TWENTY-THREE

LINA MIGHT HAVE BEEN BLISSED OUT ENOUGH TO DROP HER guard, but I sure as fuck wasn't. That shit show of a family introduction was still fresh in my mind. The Brooks were going head-to-head for Worst Parent of the Year. I couldn't imagine what this asshole could possibly have to say that would be worth Lina's time, but if she insisted on talking to the prick, then I was going to be there for every word of the conversation.

"What is it?" Lina asked in an impressively disinterested tone.

Charles cut a quick look up at me. "This is a family matter."

The curl of my lips wasn't at all nice. "As her future

husband, I *am* family. You have something to say, you can say it to us both."

His upper lip twitched with a sneer before he looked back at Lina. "I have just been informed that your childish antics at the club of pitting members against one another by whoring yourself around could cost us our membership if you continue to make appearances. This needs to end, Carolina. Your presence here benefits nobody."

"*Nobody*?" She inched forward aggressively. "Is that how you think of your own *daughter*?" A humorless laugh puffed past her lips. "Why am I surprised? You two wanted me gone so badly you brought *him* back here. You disgust me."

"That was your mother's idea, and you should move on because there is nothing to find here. How many times do we have to tell you that?"

I considered stepping in, but my little fire-breathing dragon handled the situation admirably. She pressed a painted nail into his chest, her narrowed stare slicing through him. "I will *never* quit searching, and anyone with a soul would understand why." She whipped around to leave.

I flashed a smug smirk, then followed her, only to pull up short when I saw Lina standing stock-still. A man in a ski mask held a knife to her chest. In a heartbeat's time, he spun her back to his front and had his arm around her neck, positioning her between us.

"Don't fucking move, man. Just give me your cash and shut the fuck up." His dark eyes darted over my shoulder, then back to me. Behind us, the door to the club slammed shut, the deadbolt clicking over.

*Fucking coward.*

Charles Brooks had bailed. Not that I needed his help.

I held up my hands to calm the masked man. "No problem. Let me just get my wallet out."

"Don't try anything stupid. I'll stick this blade between her fucking ribs so fast..." He was young—had a man's body, but his voice still had a ring of youth to it. Immaturity and desperation were a nasty combo. Made people impulsive. I wasn't going to underestimate him.

I met Lina's wide, terrified eyes with a reassuring look. The poor woman couldn't catch a fucking break. It pissed me off, but I kept that shit buried deep. I couldn't afford to show anything but perfect calm.

"I have a couple of hundred here. Take it." I slid my wallet from my back pocket and unfolded the expensive leather.

I could understand why he'd chosen us. We wore nice clothes on a dark, unoccupied street. Using a woman as leverage. We made an excellent mark, but the problem was, my looks were deceiving. I wasn't the same as the other men who came and went from this building. I wasn't about to run and hide.

"Just give me the whole thing," the guy demanded.

I stopped pulling out the bills, then closed the wallet and held it up. "We're going to trade. I'll hand you the wallet; you give me the girl."

He nodded, eyes locked on the prize. Definitely young. Anyone who'd spent time on the streets knew you never swapped. Always have the wallet tossed to the ground nearby.

Good news for me. Not so much for him.

I held the wallet between two fingers, my other hand held up in surrender until I was close enough to slowly reach toward Lina. Just as the thug's hand reached for the wallet, I let it drop, timing it perfectly to look like I'd misjudged where his hand had been. When he moved to pick it up, I grabbed Lina away from him, shoving her behind me, then stepped on the guy's hand.

He screamed out in pain. *"You fucking—"* His words were cut off when he tried to slash at me with the knife in his other hand. Expecting the move, I dodged the blade, then pounded my fist down into his cheek.

I never even worked up a sweat, and the thing was over.

The kid collapsed unconscious into a heap on the frozen sidewalk. I thought about giving him a boot to the gut for good measure, but he was just a dumbass punk. I picked up my wallet and his switchblade, closing it and putting both items in my pocket. When I peered over my shoulder at Lina, she rushed over and wrapped her trembling body around mine.

"Shh, baby. It's okay. I'm here." I held her for several seconds, enjoying the feel of my fingers woven in her silky hair. I didn't even want to examine how incredible it felt to have her run to me for comfort. I felt ten fucking feet tall. "Let's get you home," I said gruffly, annoyed that I had to separate from her, but it was cold as balls out. I needed to get her someplace warm.

My mood soured as I thought of taking her back to her place.

*Then don't. She's in no condition to be left alone.*

I peered down at the asshole who'd scared her half to death after she'd already had a shit night. I gave him that kick to the gut I'd been considering. A whoosh of hair wheezed passed his lips, and his body reflexively curled in on itself, though he never fully woke.

Satisfied, I pulled Lina to my side and led her to the car. I was ready to get the fuck out of there. I never got the chance to see Wellington—the whole point of dinner at the club—but I couldn't seem to care.

What the hell was happening to me? Didn't I care about punishing him for letting traffickers have easy access to our city? He'd killed Darina and given that poor Russian woman to his sick son to torture. He had to pay for what he'd done.

My knuckles ached from my bruising grip on the steering wheel.

When I thought about it all, I got so damn pissed, but all it took was one brief glance at the beautiful pale face sitting next to me to know I was doing the right thing. Someone had to protect her, and helping her didn't mean I had to give up my campaign for justice. I just had to divide my time between the two.

*When Wellington goes down, and the engagement's over, what then?*

Shut the fuck up, that was what.

I zipped around a car in frustration and tried not to think the rest of the way home. Lina must have been lost in her own thoughts because she didn't notice we hadn't gone to her place until we pulled into the parking garage at my building.

"Where are we?" she asked dazedly, looking around.

"Home."

Her eyes followed me as I turned off the car and unclicked my seat belt. The argument I half expected never came. The fight in her seemingly all spent, she let me help her from the car. Our silence continued in the elevator, though the buzz of unsaid words grew louder in the air around us. The confined space seemed to amplify the chatter. Maybe it was just me.

My gaze lifted to hers, and I found she was already watching me.

"Why am I here, Oran?" she asked quietly. After everything that had happened tonight, she still looked stunning in the red dress peeking out from beneath her black coat. Her hair was a bit mussed but in a sexy way. And the elevator lighting highlighted the multifaceted shades of blue in her eyes.

"Because this is where you need to be tonight."

*This is where I need you to be.*

That was the truth of the matter, but I could hardly say it. I'd had the woman arrested for drug possession, then blackmailed her into ditching the guy she was dating. She was probably scared of me already. She'd think I was unhinged if she knew how obsessed I'd become.

I sighed heavily, then held open the elevator doors for her.

Mine was the only apartment on the floor. Lina looked around the landing before realizing there was only one door. Her lips thinned.

Was that resignation? Frustration? Why did it matter to her if I had a floor all to myself? Most women welcomed signs of wealth, but I got the sense it made her uncomfortable. Just another mystery to add to the pile.

I let us inside, flipping on the lights as I went. I watched her as she took it in and tried to intuit what she might be thinking. It was pointless, though. Everything about her was a mystery to me.

I gave her a minute to look around while I grabbed one of my undershirts and a pair of lounge pants that would probably fall off her, but they were the best I had on hand.

"Here's something to change into. There are several guest rooms down the hall to your left. You can take your pick. Bathrooms should have everything you need for the night." I took off my jacket and draped it over the back of the sofa. "I don't want you going back to the club again. I don't know what happened with your family, but those people are toxic. There's no reason to ever speak to them again." Yes, it was high-handed, but I didn't care. If she couldn't cut ties with them, then I'd do it for her. Someone needed to do it before they hurt her beyond repair.

"But you're a member, and we're engaged."

"*Fake* engaged, remember?"

"Still, won't it look odd if you don't bring me?" Her voice rose with a hint of panic. "You can't just go alone."

"I can, and I will."

I thought she might argue even though it was absurd for her to want to go back there. Why the hell would she want to continue putting herself through that?

Lina's eyes darted around the room, her fists curled into tight little balls. "You can't do this."

"Do what? It's just a damn club, Lina. Unless you want to enlighten me and tell me what's with all the secrecy."

She lifted a shaky hand and wiped angrily at her eyes. "There's nothing to tell."

I shook my head with a bitter chuckle. "Right. And you're crying for nothing, then."

"No!" she yelled. "I'm crying because I don't like self-righteous *assholes* thinking they can order me around. Take me home. This wasn't part of our deal, and I want to go home."

"*No*, you're staying *here*." Each furious word was growled through clenched teeth.

We stood across from one another, a mere ten feet and a lifetime of secrets between us.

"What, am I your prisoner now? What about my things? I have a life, you know."

"I'll go get whatever you need. You were fucking held at knifepoint today, Lina. Give me a goddamn break, and let me have this." My voice bellowed off the high ceilings by the end of my rant.

The arctic glare she shot me could have frozen shut the gates of hell.

She spun around and charged down the hall, slamming the bedroom door behind her.

*Lina*

# TWENTY-FOUR

AFTER SHUTTING MYSELF IN THE SPARE BEDROOM, I DIDN'T TURN on the lights. The dark felt more appropriate when every day felt more bleak and pointless than the one before.

I stood with my back to the door. Tears cooling on my face. Heart tattered and bleeding at my feet.

How would I ever get Amelie back if I didn't have access to the people who'd taken her?

I missed my sister so fucking bad. I hadn't protected her, and now I didn't know if she'd ever come home. I was trying so damn hard to fix what I'd done, but I hit a new wall every time I turned around. Every day that passed tore us further apart. Every minute of the shame I carried shredded another piece of my soul. Was this my punishment? An eternal struggle to repent only to have the universe reject my efforts?

I slowly slid down the door until I sat with my knees at my chest. I didn't hug them to me. I didn't deserve the comfort it provided. I deserved to be alone in the dark exactly as I was.

*You're not alone, remember?*

That voice deep inside me tried to fight back the darkness like the warm glow of city lights filtering in through the window.

I wondered if I wouldn't be better off without it—the voice of hope.

Learning to manage in the pitch-black would have served me better than constantly seeking more light when none was to be had.

The possibility of Oran's help was alluring, but he was one of *them*. A member of the club—a *criminal*—and a business associate of Lawrence Wellington. How could I possibly trust him? Telling him anything was so incredibly risky.

*But what other option do I have?*

None.

I'd hit dead ends at every turn. Without access to the club or Wellington, I had no more leads. I could take a leap of faith and bet everything on Oran Byrne or continue fumbling in the dark.

Neither sounded appealing.

My fingers toyed with the hem of Oran's shirt. I lifted the soft cotton fabric and brought it to my face like a pillow, cool and comforting against my cheek. It smelled like him—clean with a hint of spice.

Another tear trickled down my cheek.

God, I wanted to believe I could trust him. I wanted to

believe some good was still left in the world. But I wasn't certain. I'd seen so much ugly.

Unwilling to entertain those memories, I scraped myself off the floor and changed into the white undershirt. I didn't feel like hunting for makeup remover or dealing with cleaning up, so I made a quick potty stop, then crawled into the tall bed.

Silence crept in around me as I tried to escape into sleep. It filled my ears with dark whispers, growing louder and louder until the silence was deafening.

I wasn't sure how long I lay there at war with myself. Hours? Days? It felt like an eternity. Long enough that my battle-weary psyche dropped her sword and fell to her knees. She prayed to a god she didn't believe in and begged for reinforcements.

As I envisioned her blood-spattered and broken, a story I once heard about a flood came to mind. A man escaped rising water by climbing onto his roof. When a boat came by and offered to help him, he refused, adamant that his god would save him. When a helicopter hovered overhead and offered escape, he declined, insistent that his god would save him. When the flood waters finally overtook his roof, drowning him beneath the debris, he asked his god why he had not come to save the man. His god asked him why he had refused to accept the help that was sent.

I might not have believed in the hereafter, but I had to ask myself if I was being blind to a possible solution because it hadn't arrived in an acceptable form.

Everything about Oran seemed dangerous. He had the potential to destroy me in so many ways, but he'd done the opposite at every turn. Even his coerced fake engagement kept me away from a monster of a man. If I was desperate for help, and he *wanted* to help me, maybe it was time to toss those dice and see where they led me.

I didn't have to tell him everything, but I could take that first step onto the ice and test its strength.

I rolled onto my side and sat on the edge of the bed, taking a deep, even breath. A sense of calm drifted over me like a gently falling leaf. That was the effect Oran had on me. I didn't understand it and opted not to question it.

Before I could lose my resolve, I left my room and went in search of Oran's bedroom.

Oran

# TWENTY-FIVE

SELF-DOUBT WAS THE EQUIVALENT OF MENTAL QUICKSAND. THE more you engaged, the deeper you sank. I was up to my fucking eyeballs and hated it. Had I been too hard on Lina? Should I have followed her to the spare bedroom and demanded an explanation? I wouldn't allow myself to wonder if I should have taken her back to her place because it wasn't an option. I needed her here, end of story.

*If you gave her what she asked for, maybe she'd trust you more.*

And there it went—the vicious cycle of uncertainty and self-doubt. I was a rat in a cage, running to exhaustion and never getting anywhere. Certainly not sleep. If I managed to set aside thoughts of our argument, my mind jumped imme-diately into memories of her grinding against my face.

I could still fucking taste her. It made me hard for more.

Or maybe it was the anger that made me hard. I wanted to sink myself inside her for so many damn reasons that they blurred together, making everything that much more murky.

I'd been lying in bed for what felt like hours and was just about to get up when I saw Lina's silhouette fill my doorway. I couldn't see her clearly, but I could tell she'd changed into the shirt I'd given her, her long legs bare beneath. She looked so damn innocent as she lingered there, battling her own uncertainty.

"Come here, Lina." I lifted onto my elbow and patted the side of the bed.

Likely relieved I was still awake, she swept forward, then sat cross-legged on the bed. She sat close enough that I could get to her but not without reaching. I had to resist the urge to yank her closer. She'd come to me for a reason, and I wanted her to feel comfortable enough to say what she needed to say.

"When I was seventeen, Ron Gaetz took my virginity."

She spoke in a slow, even tone as if she weren't talking about statutory rape, if not worse. My entire body petrified into solid stone. I couldn't have moved if I'd wanted to. I didn't even breathe as she continued.

"I didn't know who he was until tonight. I never saw his face, but I would recognize that voice anywhere."

Slowly, I coerced my body to sit upright, never taking my eyes from her. "That … *man* raped you, and your parents *knew* about it?" Fuck, her mom had been practically giddy for Lina to see him. Why? To torture her? Was it some sort of taunt? It was the most fucked-up thing I'd ever witnessed.

"It's complicated, but yes, they knew. That's why they brought him tonight. They want me to stay away from the club."

"Jesus, then why not stay away? That fucking club isn't

worth it." I tried so hard not to get frustrated, but what in the actual hell? Why would she do that to herself?

"My mother has always used and manipulated me." A tremor shook her voice, but it wasn't one of pain or sadness. The strain in her voice was pure fury. "I refuse to give her power over me. Not anymore. And I know you'll have a million questions, but I can't give you any answers, so please don't ask for more. I just can't."

Yeah, I had questions. A fuck ton of questions. But how could I be an ass and demand answers after she'd just been so brave to open up like that?

What she *had* shared, though, went a long way in helping me understand her. And while I respected her need to show strength, there was no chance in hell I was letting her step foot back in that club. This wasn't the time, however, to start that argument. And no matter how much I wanted to pull her into bed with me and hold her the rest of the night, that hardly seemed appropriate after she'd just told me she'd been raped.

That really only left me with one option. I got up and walked around to where she sat, holding my hand out for hers. She took it and let me help her to her feet. I led her into the kitchen.

"What are you doing?" she asked when I opened the fridge.

"Feeding you. You never ate any dinner."

"I'm not all that hungry."

I stilled, then looked back at her. "You're not going back to bed until you've eaten something."

Her brows knitted together. "I suppose I could have one of those bananas."

I followed her gaze to the fruit bowl that held two spotted bananas and an old orange. Not ideal, but it was something. I peeled back the top portion, then handed it over and leaned back against the counter.

She took a big bite, which didn't make my dick stir at all. Nope. That would have been tactless. But I didn't want her to be uncomfortable, so I averted my gaze off into the shadows of the living room.

"What about you? Don't you need to eat, too?"

"No need to worry about me," I murmured, amused that she'd asked.

"You get to worry, but I don't?"

"I look like I'm hurting for food?" I raised my arms out to the side.

She took another bite as her eyes raked over my chest, then wiped the corner of her mouth and shyly dropped her gaze to the floor. "Well, I may not look like an action hero, but I'm not hurting either."

"And I want it to stay that way."

Her jaw paused for a second as though she wanted to say something but didn't. I waited until she'd eaten the whole thing, tossed the peel in the trash, then walked her to the guest room. She could have her space for tonight, but that was about to change. A whole lot of shit was about to change.

"Good night, Lina." I placed a kiss on her temple once she was snug under the covers. "Get some sleep."

At least one of us should, and my night was just getting started.

# TWENTY-SIX

Sleep came remarkably quickly when I went to bed for the second time that night. After a deep and dreamless sleep, I felt oddly calmer when I woke the following morning. However, I wasn't used to sharing deeply personal information with anyone, and the vulnerability left me with a lingering unease about facing Oran in the light of day.

Would he act differently around me? I didn't want his pity or for him to treat me like I was broken. I also didn't want him to ask me questions, but I'd opened Pandora's box and had to accept that some sort of fallout would be inevitable. What exactly would that entail? God only knew. I just hoped I had a chance to get home and shower first. It was almost noon. I'd lost half a day, and while my schedule was flexible, I did have deadlines to meet.

I brushed my teeth in the en suite bathroom and looked around for the first time. The attention to detail and small touches that made the room homey were surprising. Tissue on the nightstand. A night-light in the bathroom. He even had a clock that doubled as a white noise machine. On top of all that, the decor was a blend of neutrals with enough variation that the room wasn't monochromatic. The feel was very Zen, if I was honest. The bedroom and bath were both spacious yet cozy. I was impressed.

I grabbed the sweatpants Oran had given me the night before. They still lay at the door where I'd left them. The waist bunched when I cinched the string tight enough to keep the pants up, making them bulky but functional.

Good enough for me.

I hadn't worn a bra with the red dress, so I didn't have one to put on. I was surprised at how much more exposed I felt braless in Oran's T-shirt than I had in the tight dress. The white cotton somehow felt more personal. More intimate. I suspected my emotional reveal last night was to blame rather than what I was wearing or not wearing.

I took one last deep breath, then left the bedroom in search of my fake fiancé.

I'd mentally run through a slew of possible scenarios that I might encounter when I saw Oran that morning. Unfortunately, I'd been so concentrated on what I'd say that I forgot to consider whether he'd be dressed. Oran Byrne stood in his kitchen wearing dress slacks with nothing else, sipping from a coffee mug and watching a news program. His damp hair was combed back. His feet were bare. His torso and arms could have served as da Vinci's model for the *Vitruvian Man*

—perfectly proportioned mature muscle rippling beneath smooth, unblemished skin.

The wiring in my brain popped and fizzled, rendering me temporarily dumb as a stump. I had to physically shake my head to rattle the thoughts back into motion.

"It's the dead of winter. Shouldn't you put a shirt on?" I blurted in greeting.

Oran peered over his shoulder at me, his eyes growing hooded. "I'm hot-natured. Does it bother you?" He smirked, clearly not caring if it did.

"Not at all. If you're comfortable flashing all that grotesque misshapenness, more power to you."

He tipped his head back and laughed at the absurdity of my comment. I'd known it wouldn't offend him. There wasn't a misshapen square inch on his glorious body. Not a tattoo or a single flaw that I could see, though I was trying hard not to stare and inflate his ego more than necessary.

"You could have woken me," I offered. "Sorry if I kept you from work."

"I got called away to handle something last night, so I slept in as well."

"In the middle of the night?"

Had he gone out after we talked? I hadn't heard him, but I'd been exhausted.

"It was more like early morning. I left a note in case you woke up while I was out, but you were still dead to the world when I got back."

He'd been busy, and I hadn't heard a thing. Wait, how had he known I was still asleep? Had he looked in my room? I hadn't locked the door. I'd been too emotionally drained to even think of it. An image of him watching me while I slept flitted through my mind, and instead of the unease I expected, my chest filled with a tingling warmth that slowly expanded into the rest of my body.

My stomach took that moment to chime in and remind me just how late it was with an embarrassingly aggressive rumble.

Oran chuckled. "There's protein bars, granola, or I can throw on some eggs."

"No Cocoa Pebbles?" I teased. It was my go-to defense mechanism. Feeling awkward or uneasy? Sarcasm and levity to the rescue.

Oran rolled with my comment, however, as though I'd been serious. "Just Frosted Flakes."

"Are you serious? You have Frosted Flakes?" I asked with genuine surprise.

Opening a cabinet, he took out a blue box with the familiar tiger on the front and set it by me.

"Milk?" I could hardly wait. I hadn't had a bowl of Frosted Flakes since I was a kid—before Eliza forbid Gloria from buying them because, according to her, cereal was making me fat.

Oran smirked with amusement as he brought over the carton, then watched me as I savored the first bite of sugary goodness.

"Anyone ever tell you staring is rude?"

"Anyone ever tell you not to chew with your mouth open?"

My eyes rounded. "I was *not*—" Instead of defending my meticulous manners, I inhaled a flake and devolved into a coughing fit.

Oran brought over a glass of water, shaking his head. "You're too easy to rile. Drink."

I did, clearing my throat.

"Jerk," I rasped, then went back to eating. I really was starving.

Oran turned back to the TV. "There's something we need to discuss," he said casually over his shoulder. "The work stuff that came up last night has changed a few things. We're going to have to adjust our agreement."

I stilled, spoon halfway to my mouth. "You mean ... you're changing the terms of your blackmail?"

His head slowly swiveled until his scathing stare met mine. His sudden intensity shocked me. It was the first time I felt a tendril of fear unfurl in his presence.

Why had my comment soured his mood so quickly?

"Adjust in what way?" I continued, hoping to smooth over my transgression.

His tightly coiled jaw muscle slowly softened. "I'm moving you into my place." He sipped from his mug as though he'd suggested I take a cab instead of the train rather than declare where I'd live for the foreseeable future.

"Move in? *Here*? For how long?"

He shrugged. "Can't say for sure."

"You can't expect me to agree to that," I balked.

"Two months." He said it like a counter, as though we were negotiating the price on a real estate deal.

*"Two months?"* Holy shit, that was a long time. Why the hell was he doing all this?

"You going to tell me what this is all about? It doesn't make any sense—you wanted to do business with Lawrence, but taking me from him put you at risk of losing that opportunity. And me moving in with you doesn't change anything where Lawrence is concerned. What aren't you telling me?"

"It wouldn't make sense to you," he replied dryly. "You're not a member of the boys' club."

I knew his reference was a turn of phrase, but it made me

think of Wellington and Gaetz and the Society. A very particular kind of boys club. One that I hated.

My appetite shriveled up and died.

I pushed my bowl away. "And if I don't agree, you'd really let them charge me with possession?" My tone was cool and even, but my emotions rioted.

I lifted my gaze to his. Any flexibility or reasonableness he'd possessed minutes before had fled, replaced with reinforced concrete, resolute and impenetrable.

"Some things require getting your hands a little dirty. I'm hardly asking too much of you."

"You can't possibly know what you're asking," I said quietly. Whether his motives were to protect me or control me, either way, he was getting in the way of me finding my sister.

Unable to look at him, my eyes cut to the side where his laptop sat on the counter. That's when I realized my emotions had clouded my judgment, preventing me from analyzing things clearly.

I'd worked for months to get access to Lawrence's personal life—his house or computer—anything that might give me a glimpse behind the curtain. With unsupervised access to Oran's world, the possibility of uncovering something about the Olympus Club's dark secrets improved drastically.

I jumped when his coffee cup clanked in the sink.

"It's not forever, Lina. You don't have to act like it's a death sentence." He was irritated, and if I didn't know better, it almost sounded like he was a little ... hurt?

"Okay, I'll do it," I offered softly.

He studied me. Intently. Warily.

I had a feeling we would feel infinitely better if we could get behind-the-scenes access to one another's thoughts, but that wasn't an option. Neither of us was ready to lay our cards on the table, so our uneasy truce would continue. The wolf and the fox walked in tandem, both wondering when the other might strike out unexpectedly.

"I've arranged for guys to meet us at your place in an hour."

Jesus, he didn't waste any time.

I had to snap my jaw shut when I realized my mouth gaped open. Not trusting myself to speak, I nodded, then tossed the rest of my cereal into the sink. Nerves had filled my stomach fuller than any food could have.

◊

"We'd already talked about me moving out when the lease was up in March. This just speeds things up a bit. I'll still pay my share, I promise." I rushed to explain the situation to my bewildered roommate as half a dozen men stood in the hall waiting to get started. I'd made Oran wait outside along with them. If he was going to push this on me with no warning, his ass could give me five minutes alone with my friend.

Jessa and I weren't super close, but we'd lived together for the past four years. We made good housemates. I didn't want to hurt her or give her the wrong impression. Not that it could be totally avoided. Bailing from the apartment without any warning was strange. Anyone with any sense would be suspicious.

"I get it, Lina. It's no problem, really. I'm just surprised."

"I know. I'm a little surprised myself."

Her eyes studied me, then cut to the door. "You sure you're okay?"

I held up my hand and gave the most genuine smile I

162

could manage. "I'm engaged to an incredible man. I know it all seems sudden, but it's a good thing. I promise."

I hoped that if I said it enough, I'd start to believe it.

An hour later, all my worldly possessions were piled into a small moving van. I was almost embarrassed at how little there'd been. What took the most time was packing up all the loose odds and ends. I'd been very particular about how my sewing supplies were packed, which is why I refused to allow anyone else to unpack those boxes once they were delivered to Oran's apartment.

I left Oran to deal with the rest while I set up a workstation for myself in the guest room I now occupied. I was so engrossed in my task that I didn't realize until I was done that none of my clothes or personal items were in the room. When I went in search of my things, I discovered that everything had been unpacked in the primary suite. Oran's bedroom.

I stood in the huge walk-in closet, staring at my clothes hanging across from his when I felt his looming presence approach behind me like a thundercloud electrifying the summer sky.

"They put my clothes in your closet." The array of luxurious fabrics surrounding us absorbed my softly spoken words, making me feel as though we'd stepped into a vacuum of time and space. Somewhere foreign yet familiar—frightening yet alive with possibilities.

Oran's knuckles trailed down my right arm. "I could hardly tell them to put your stuff in the guest room," he rasped, his voice like warm apple cider on a cold day. "You're my fiancée, remember?"

What was wrong with me?

Of course, my stuff would need to be with his. His family would ask questions if it wasn't. But I hadn't prepared myself for the logistics of exactly how this new arrangement would work. How it would feel to see my underwear in his drawers, and my toothbrush at his sink.

The most unexpected and confusing part was the tinge of disappointment that unfurled in my chest at the reminder that none of it was real.

"I didn't forget." My response sounded as hollow as my heart felt. I pulled away from him and grabbed a sweater off a hanger. "I need to shower, then get some work done."

Oran didn't move when I motioned to get past him. Slowly, I lifted my gaze to his and tried with all my might to keep him from seeing the tidal wave of emotions threatening to crash over me. He held me suspended in his stare. I couldn't breathe through the strain of maintaining my composure.

Reluctantly, mercifully, he stepped aside.

Ten more seconds, and I would have been at risk of passing out or devolving into a torrent of tears.

I took an extra-long shower in the guest bathroom. When I got out, a note lay on the bed. Oran had gone to work and wouldn't be back until late.

Again, he'd caught me off guard. I hadn't expected him to leave me alone in his home so quickly. Was it trust that enabled him to be so bold … or arrogance? Or maybe it was cameras. Would he have outfitted his apartment with surveillance equipment for my stay? Surely, he didn't live with cameras on him ordinarily. Or maybe it was all part of an elaborate scheme to drive me slowly insane with uncertainty because that was starting to happen, whether intentional or not.

I didn't know what to think. The self-doubt and second-guessing were killing me. I'd never had anyone else to rely upon in the past, but at least I'd been confident in my own abilities. Where Oran was concerned, I didn't even trust myself.

*Do his intentions matter? This is an opportunity you can't pass up.*

Right. I needed to focus on what was important.

Padding along the wood floors in my bare feet, I didn't make a sound as I went in search of a home office. A place this size had to have some sort of office. And it did, but it wasn't what I'd expected. The modern design suited Oran, but the use of framed family photos as the primary decor took me by surprise. One white wall was almost entirely dedicated to a collage of matching glass frames—all the same as though to minimize distraction from the photos themselves. Some images were candid while others were posed portraits. All of them held an element of joy and sincerity.

My gaze swept across the smiling faces, a stab of envy lancing through my chest. Aside from the awkward initial introduction at his cousin's wedding, everyone I'd met had been welcoming and kind. They seemed to be genuinely good people, which was ironic. But if Eliza Brooks could give to charity and be a celebrated member of society while secretly being Satan herself, then the Byrne family could be a loyal band of honorable criminals. If only I knew where I fit into the equation.

The opposite wall hosted a console with a credenza containing a few more framed photos. One caught my attention because of a pamphlet propped up next to it. A closer look unveiled that it was a funeral memorial. Brody Marcus Byrne. He'd passed away six months earlier, and he was the spitting image of Oran.

Reading the text, I confirmed that the man who had died at the early age of fifty-eight was Oran's father. The framed photo was of the two of them holding matching whiskey glasses as though toasting to the camera. They sat at a glossy mahogany pub table, their smiles radiating warmth.

I'd met Oran's mother at the wedding. She seemed somewhat solemn though kind, which now made more sense. She was still grieving. I imagined Oran was too, considering he hadn't mentioned his father's passing when introducing his mother.

I returned the memorial to its place of honor and peered inside the drawers of the console below. He was organized, I'd give him that. Two large file drawers full of alphabetized folders. Files for appliance operation manuals. Maintenance records for a personal jet. He even had a file to catalog news articles about local city politicians. All sorts of information, and none of it relevant to me.

The matching executive desk of glossy dark wood with a minimalist design spoke to understated elegance. Nothing about the room was flashy or braggadocio like Lawrence's had been. Oran's home base was functional and focused yet inviting. The surface of his desk was clear save for yet another framed photo, this one of Oran and his family when he was much younger, a rock painted hastily to look like a ladybug, and an electric bill for the apartment. All about as ordinary as I could possibly imagine. So ordinary it was frustrating.

He had to have a computer. Where did he keep it? I had yet to see him carry a laptop with him. And there was no sign of a docking station or desktop computer.

Undeterred, I continued my search. The top left drawer held office supplies, but the one below contained a small stash of papers. Finally, something with potential. One sticky note had the name of fellow Olympus member written on it. It also contained a phone number and the date December first —the first night Oran had attended a club dinner.

I had recognized the name but didn't know much about him. I took a picture of the note to look into it further.

There were two printed online articles, one about a hit-and-run accident two years ago, and the other was an editorial about the state of Russian organized crime in Moscow.

They were obviously of interest to Oran, but I had no clue why.

The remainder of the stack was a comprehensive background check on me. It was eerily thorough in some ways and woefully incomplete in others. The internet had a long memory, but not everything made it online.

I returned the papers to the drawer and finished my search, not finding anything else of consequence. Wanting a peek at the trash, I discovered that there was no bin under the desk. Odd. I made another scan of the room and almost missed the small metal container outside on the patio next to a set of lounge chairs.

I crossed to the glass door and fought the whipping wind to have a look. At the bottom of the black metal trash bin was a small mound of ashes and a few scraps of charred fabric. As a designer, my eye was always drawn to fabrics, which is how I knew with certainty these scraps had come from the shirt Oran was wearing the day before when we'd gone to the club for dinner.

He'd burned his shirt, and when I noticed a heavy crimson stain on one of the frayed scraps, I knew why. This shirt had been evidence. Of what, I wasn't certain, but something violent, without a doubt.

I'd known Oran was into organized crime, but seeing evidence of it gave meaning to the words. A tangible reality. Oran Byrne wasn't afraid of violence.

Did that change the way I felt about him?

I wasn't sure, but it reinforced in me a need to protect myself.

I took the small blood-stained scrap and went back inside. Taking a piece of paper from the printer, I carefully folded the fabric remnant within the paper and took it back to my room to hide away. I wasn't sure what could be done with the evidence, especially when I had no clue what crime had been committed, but it was leverage at the very least, and I needed to seize every opportunity available to gain the upper hand.

That night I went to bed in my new bedroom with a flickering sense of hope carrying me into my dreams. I could do this. I could not only survive what life threw at me, but I could use the circumstances to my advantage. I drifted off feeling bold and determined only to wake hours later with my heart in my throat and the shadow of a man standing over me.

# TWENTY-SEVEN

Even if I hadn't had business to take care of, I would have needed to leave the apartment to get away from Lina before I said or did something I would regret. I'd been aggravated by the way she'd fought me about staying away from the club and the way she'd recoiled at the notion of moving in with me temporarily. But neither of those things had bothered me as much as the utter despair that clung to her when she saw her clothes in my closet. That shit stung.

I didn't come home until I was certain she'd be asleep. I'd needed the time to cool off for two reasons. The first was illogical but present nonetheless. I was annoyed that she couldn't see all the things I'd done for her. That she still thought I was just an asshole manipulator. My secondary source of irritation came about when I faced the first because it made me realize that at some point my priorities had changed.

The last twenty-four hours had all been for Lina.

I wasn't sure of the exact moment my trajectory had shifted. My endgame was still the same, but I'd taken a detour along the way.

A shift in motivation was bad enough, the last thing I needed was to be upset about her perspective on the matter. Her feelings should have been irrelevant. Instead, I'd spent hours trying to talk myself down from the ledge. Commanding the wind would have been easier than reigning in my emotions. The past six months of grief and anger and betrayal had festered down deep where I'd banished them and were now threatening to consume me. And the one thing I shouldn't have cared about was going to be the tiny puff of air that tipped me over the cliff's edge.

Lina.

I wanted her to see me as more than her tormentor. I wanted her to acknowledge that buzzing intensity that elec-trified the air when we were together. Acknowledge the way her body listed toward mine of its own accord. I wanted her to want me, and that pissed me off more than anything. I didn't want to want anyone, let alone someone secretive by nature. What the fuck was wrong with me?

I poured myself two fingers of whiskey in my office and sat in my chair, eyes drifting to the skyline of twinkling city lights out the wall of windows. When I realized I'd left my trashcan outside, I went to retrieve it only to find the balcony door unlocked. I was rarely absentminded and had even been accused of being overly meticulous when it came to my habits, so I was confident that I'd locked the door the night before as always. I didn't care how high up we were, I locked every fucking door and window.

I peered back at my office over my shoulder and knew with a certainty that Lina had been snooping. It wasn't a shock. I'd expected it, but for some reason, I'd hoped that she wouldn't because what was the point? What had she hoped to achieve?

I sat back at my desk and opened the drawers, studying the contents with a critical eye. I wasn't worried she'd seen something she shouldn't have. I hadn't left anything incriminating accessible. I wanted to know if she'd just looked at the view from my balcony or if she'd truly been hunting through my things.

Using my phone flashlight, I looked for fingerprint smudges on the glossy console drawers. I hadn't opened them in weeks. The cleaners had been to my place multiple times since then and were exceptional about wiping off all prints from the modern lacquered finishes.

Smudges dotted every damn drawer.

A chilling savagery washed over me.

She wanted to think me a monster, then I'd show her how uncivilized I could be. I locked the balcony door and turned off the office lights then stalked quietly to the guest room.

I flung open her door, pissed that it was closed. She was sleeping so soundly that she didn't stir. I crossed to where I could see her face peeking out from beneath the covers. She was on her side with her hands up under her cheek as though she'd come straight from heaven. That only made me angrier. It wasn't right that someone so damn infuriating could appear so harmless and tempting.

*Time to wake up, little angel, and answer for your sins.*

As if she'd heard me, her eyes fly open an instant before I tossed the covers onto the floor.

"Oran? What's going on?" She sounded as innocent as she looked, and I want to shake her until the truth fell out of her.

"Why the fuck would you need to go through my office?"

"Huh?" She was groggy but coming around quickly, scooting to the end of the bed and rubbing the sleep from her eyes. "Your stuff? You practically kidnapped me, and you're surprised I went through your things?"

I couldn't help myself. I wanted her to see sense so fucking badly. My hand clasped around her throat, bringing her to her feet. She could breathe, I made sure of it, but her eyes were wide with worry. Good. I wanted to shred away her bravado and dig down to the truth. To the real Lina.

"What exactly is it about my actions that you find so offensive? The fact that I interrupted your geriatric dating strategy? Maybe the way I insisted you stay away from your toxic fucking parents? Or maybe it was moving you off a goddamn futon bed and into a luxury apartment that you find so appalling."

"You had me framed for drug possession with enough drugs to qualify for intent to distribute, and you think I shouldn't be wary of you?"

"Only because you wouldn't fucking walk away from him." I let go before my anger got the better of me and ran my aching hand through my hair.

"You ever think that maybe I had my reasons?"

"Trust me, I'd love to hear all about them," I roared back at her.

"I'm sure you would, just like I'd love to know why the hell we're in this fucked up arrangement to begin with."

I slowly turned and leveled her with a scathing glare. "Would it be so fucking hard to believe that I was doing it for you?"

"I'm supposed to assume everything you do is for me?

What about the blood-stained shirt you burned—was that for me?" She got in my face, thinking she'd pulled out the ace that would trump any argument I could possibly make. "Until I get some answers, I have no reason to believe you're looking out for anyone but yourself."

She wanted brutal honesty, she'd get it.

I took out my phone and did a quick search, handing her the device displaying the results—multiple articles dated from earlier in the day.

*California tech company reeling after tragic loss of CEO.*

Even in the dimly lit room, I could see the color drain from her face as she scrolled down and saw the smiling photo of Ron Gaetz.

"He's dead?" she breathed, a trembling hand lifting to her mouth as her wide gaze returned to mine. "They say it was a random mugging gone wrong."

"There was a report of a mugger using a knife in the area last night." Never thought I'd have been pleased about being mugged, but the guy made a perfect scapegoat after the fact.

Her eyes trailed down to my chest, drifting over the crisp lines of the dress shirt I was wearing, likely remembering the shirt I'd worn the night before. The one that was now a charred pile of ash.

"You wanted proof that I'm dangerous. Now you have it." Each guttural word clawed up from deep in my throat. "Not only did I kill a man I'd never even met before last night, I don't have a lick of guilt. Proof that I'm a monster."

Her head moved side to side in short, jerky movements.

"Now you can hate me more than ever." I inched closer. "Tell me you hate me," I demanded.

"I ... I don't hate you."

"Then tell me you fear me." I raised my hand to her throat again, this time gently collaring her, my thumb lazily caressing her smooth skin as she swallowed beneath my touch. "I want the truth."

"I should. I should fear you, but I … I don't." Her eyes shone bright blue with sincerity and fear. She was still scared, but not scared of me. What then?

"Prove it," I pushed. "If you don't hate me, and you don't fear me, then show me you trust me."

Her brows drew together. "How am I supposed to do that?"

"Stay with me." I leaned in close, my hand cupping the back of her head as my cheek came to rest against hers. "Sleep in my bed with me."

Her body began to tense, then suddenly softened on a shaky exhalation. "Just sleep?"

I breathed in the hint of jasmine that clung to her skin, my eyes closing. "Just sleep."

The moment I felt her nod against me, I bent and scooped her into my arms. The feel of her relaxing willingly into me had my heart thudding so hard against my ribs I wondered if she couldn't feel it from the outside.

I set her on the bed back in my bedroom. While I slipped off my clothes, she settled under the covers. She watched me with a curious stare. And for once, I didn't sense an undercurrent of suspicion.

*Thank Christ.*

I joined her in the bed and fought back the urge to pull her close. Fuck was it hard. *I* was hard, though, and I was trying to stay true to my word. It meant sleep would be a challenge. I wanted more than anything to feel her next to me and know that she was with me. Know that she was mine.

With Lina, I'd have to take what I could get.

I closed my eyes with that reminder and tried to be grateful the stubborn woman was here at all. But when the lightest touch of two words whispered past my ears, I lost my battle on restraint.

A sleepily murmured *thank you* erased the entire concept of self-discipline and had me hauling Lina into the curve of my body with a grunt. My arm over her waist, and my nose happily buried in her hair, I abandoned strategy and went with my gut. Minutes later, her body relaxed into sleep, followed quickly by mine.

Lina

# TWENTY-EIGHT

I woke in Oran's bed with him still soundly asleep next to me. I wasn't sure what to think about what unfolded in the night. A part of me was desperate to give into Oran's demands and trust him. To know for the first time in my life that someone was watching my back rather than trying to stab me in it. But the seventeen-year-old still hiding inside me was petrified that he was just as soulless as the rest, and the minute I gave him more than I should, he'd take everything. Every last bit of hope and strength I had left.

He'd admitted, after all, that his moral compass wasn't exactly standard issue. He'd stabbed Gaetz to death, and I hadn't even told him the whole story. Not that the piece I held back would have affected his decision. Hell, if anything, it would probably have reinforced his resolve.

*So why didn't you tell him?*

Because I knew how the Society changed people. How it warped their priorities. Until I knew for certain he hadn't actually come to Olympus to be part of the Society, or wasn't already somehow connected to them, I couldn't fully trust him. That was the harsh reality.

*But Gaetz had been a part of the Society. They'd never kill one of their own, would they?*

The depravity of that group knew no bounds. How could I possibly say what they would or wouldn't do?

For now, I could only rely upon what I knew as fact. I'd told Oran what Gaetz had done to me. I wasn't sure how, but Oran had gone out that same night, found him while he was still in New York, and killed the bastard. That pathetic excuse for a man didn't deserve to be alive, but Oran had taken a huge risk on my behalf, and I'd be forever grateful.

Looking at Oran's hand in the morning light, I could see busted skin on his knuckles. I hadn't noticed the scabbing before and could have sworn it hadn't been there. He'd made Gaetz suffer, and he'd done it all for me. Why? The whole thing was hard for me to comprehend. Was I so jaded that I couldn't imagine someone putting themselves at risk for me? Absolutely.

Yet he hadn't given up on me.

Before I consciously decided to do it, I took his hand, heavy with sleep, and brought it to my lips to place a delicate kiss on the scarred flesh. He didn't wake, but I still felt a wave of embarrassment when I reminded myself that Oran might have done a good thing, but that didn't make him a good man.

*He's dangling a prison sentence over your head, remember?*

Uninterested in having that argument with myself, I slid from the bed as quietly as possible so as not to disturb him. I made a quick trip to the toilet, and when I exited the restroom back into the main bathroom, I noticed a shopping bag on the vanity. It was a white sack with black paper, the shop name printed on the side just like the one he'd set on fire.

He had to have placed it there before bringing me to his room in the night. Was it for me? I hadn't even considered whether Oran might have anyone else in his life.

The thought pressed down on me like a cold wet blanket.

Too curious not to look, I went to the bag and peeked inside. When I saw red with black lace, I pulled out the contents to find the underwear set I'd loved so much along with two others. All were in my size.

Movement in the mirror drew my attention to Oran as he joined me in the bathroom wearing nothing but the boxer brief's he'd worn to bed. His body was even more spectacular in the soft morning light, though there was nothing soft about *him*—especially his impressive morning wood. The sight made my thoughts fuzzy and disjointed.

I cleared my throat and tore my gaze from his reflection. "Sorry if I woke you."

"Don't be. I would have stayed in bed if I'd wanted to." His sleep-heavy voice scraped across my skin like a warm wool blanket, bringing on an army of goose bumps.

"You have good taste in lingerie."

"They're yours. The sizes should be right. I went that same day to make sure the clerk remembered you."

I spun around. "You've had these this whole time?"

"Told you I didn't want anyone else to see you in it." He flipped on the light, then hooked a finger in the waistband of his briefs and slung them off in one swift motion.

I whipped back around like a spastic weathervane, only to be confronted with his smirking face reflected in the mirror.

"I have somewhere to be this morning." He walked to the glass shower door, his perfect ass on display. "You're welcome to join me in the shower." He peered over his shoulder, smirking when he caught me gnawing on my bottom lip, eyes glued to his backside.

"I'm ... my toiletries are in the other bathroom. If I used yours, I'd smell all wrong," I blathered with my two functioning brain cells.

"We couldn't have that, now could we?" he rasped, amusement coating his words like honey.

He closed the shower door and stepped into the spray. His hands lifted to smooth back his hair, and the movement drew my eyes to his flexing abdomen—water rivulets running down the carved dips and peaks of his chiseled muscles. The sight was mesmerizing, which was why he caught me staring when his eyes reopened. His darkening irises sparked with challenge as he held my gaze while spreading bodywash across his chest, arms, then down...

I couldn't resist. I was a weak, weak woman.

I tore my eyes from his and stared raptly as his hand encircled his engorged cock. The delicious Adonis V pointing down at the main attraction flexed more prominently as Oran began to leisurely stroke himself.

My fingers twitched with the desperate need to do the same—to touch between my legs and relieve some of the intense pressure he'd created. Instead, I spun around to flee so quickly that I bounced off the doorframe on my way out, a rumble of amused laughter chasing me back to my room.

I wasn't sure what sort of voodoo magic this man wielded, but it was strong. He had me so turned around, I didn't know which way was up or down. Even worse, I wasn't sure I cared. The temptation to follow him inside the steaming stone enclosure had been almost too overwhelming to resist. For a hazy second in that bathroom, I couldn't recall why showering with him would be so bad. We were both adults, right?

Oran was a raging river, and fighting the current was wearing me down. I was starting to wonder if the rippling torrent of water might take me exactly where I wanted to be. It was that, or I'd end up drowning. Either way, I had a feeling my course was set.

*Oran*

# TWENTY-NINE

I'D THOUGHT I WAS DREAMING WHEN I FIRST WOKE. THE BED WAS empty, yet I was engulfed in a hazy memory of lips pressing tenderly to the back of my hand. The touch was so light, so angelic, I'd assumed it had to be a figment of my imagination. But as I lay there, doubts set in. My dreams were rarely so chaste.

Lina would sooner chop off my hand than kiss it, wouldn't she?

I wasn't so sure anymore—about her or anything related to her—except that what I was about to do was necessary, no matter how seemingly repulsive. I had to find out more about Wellington and the Olympus Club. Something shady was going on behind the scenes, but I could only speculate what exactly that might be.

I couldn't get the tiniest hint of information anywhere I looked. Either everyone legitimately had no knowledge about secret club activities or they'd been highly motivated into silence. Normally, secrets didn't stay secret. People liked to talk. I might have been swayed by the stark absence of information if it weren't for the notably shady moral character of members whom I knew. That alone was enough to paint the entire club in a heavy coat of suspicion.

Lina was the only person who had made the slightest insinuation that Olympus was anything but an elitist social club. And every minute I spent with her left me more unwilling to discount her impression. Not to say I understood her complex feelings on the matter. She seemed to despise them yet couldn't stay away. It was a fucking mystery to me.

I knew of one person who might still have information. I hadn't gone to her yet because I knew anything she'd give would come at a cost. But if it meant freeing Lina of whatever shackled her, it would be a price worth paying.

♦

"Here to see Caitlin Byrne, detainee 563270." I handed over my identification at the jail registration desk. This was only the second time I'd come to see my wife and would hopefully be the last until her trial, assuming she had one. If she was smart, she'd take her plea deal. Then again, if she was smart, she never would have crossed me.

Once approved, I sat at the first visitation booth, each containing a phone receiver on either side of a thick plexiglass window. Ten minutes later, Caitlin walked into view and sat opposite me with all the borrowed haughtiness of a bastard royal—powerless and too dense to see it.

I imagined wrapping the coiled phone cord around her neck and cinching it tight until her body went limp. The visualization enabled me to produce a small smile as I brought the phone to my ear.

"I suppose you're here about the papers." Her voice carried through the line though she was sitting mere feet away.

"I'm curious how far you'll drag it out, but no. That's not why I'm here."

"I'll drag it out as long as necessary if that's what it takes to get what I'm owed."

Malice widened my smile. "You'll get what you're owed. I heard you got stuck in solitary for a while—two whole weeks, if I'm not mistaken."

Some of her smugness cracked and faded as reality dawned. "That was *you*," she hissed.

"Just making sure you get what you're owed, like you said."

She bared her teeth at me. It was almost comical considering only one person in this room held any power, and it wasn't' her. "I'll make your life a living hell, Oran."

"Save the threats for someone who gives a shit. What you should be more concerned about is whether you'll ever know life beyond cinderblock walls and razor wire. If I were you, I'd take every opportunity I had to improve my chances." She'd been framed for her own brother's murder, which was particularly fitting since she'd harbored an incestuous obsession with the man. A minor tidbit that would have been nice to know before I'd agreed to our arranged marriage.

The man was dead now, and I knew she was innocent in his death because I'd been the one to frame her. I also knew

I'd provided such an air-tight case against her that she had no chance of clearing her name. I'd considered simply killing her for betraying me, but death would have been too easy. She cost my father his life. That alone deserved a lifetime of punishment.

Her eyes narrowed warily. "You want something from me."

"There's a huge difference between minimum and maximum security facilities. With the right influence, a judge could be persuaded that you weren't a safety risk."

She mulled over the options, her face twisting with bitterness. Finally, she leaned back and lifted her chin. "What is it you want?"

"I want to know about Lawrence Wellington and the Olympus Club," I said evenly.

A glint of surprise flashed in her eyes. Her mind had to be racing with all the possibilities about why I cared enough about those two things to come here. To come to her.

"This about that server of yours? The one you say you hardly knew?"

"Doesn't matter what it's about."

"Sure it does. I don't know what to tell you if I don't have the proper perspective."

"You tell me everything you know and let me worry about filtering out what I need."

She shrugged a shoulder. "I don't know a whole lot."

I waited in silence until she sighed and continued.

"I don't know much about Wellington. I only came into contact with him because of the Russian."

"What about Olympus?"

"The hoity-toity club for the uber wealthy, right? The ones that have fancy dinners over at that building on the Upper West Side?"

"That's the one. And if you know that much, you know more than most."

"My brother heard about it and wanted to find out who the members were. He was always working hard to get in the right circles and make contacts. People with that sort of wealth always have money to throw at the sort of things my brother could make happen for them."

"What did he learn?"

"Not much about the organization itself. He was able to form a working relationship with one of the members. Met up with him after one of their Sunday meetings and said the old guy looked like he'd run a marathon. He told my brother he'd been learning to play pickle ball, but Flynn didn't buy it."

Sunday meetings? I'd been given a list of club events, and there weren't any activities on Sundays. And I also hadn't seen any sort of workout facilities.

"Could your brother have been mistaken about where the guy had been before they met up?"

She crossed her arms, agitated I'd insinuate anything negative about her brother. "The place is on Columbus Avenue, right? He said they met at a bar nearby. The only reason I know any of this is because Flynn thought it was all so strange that he told me the very next time I saw him. He didn't like to involve me in his business, but he wanted to know if I'd heard anything about them. That's all I know."

It definitely sounded odd, but everything she said was also a secondary account of events, neither source all that trustworthy. None of it was actionable.

"I told you what I could, Oran. Are you going to hold up your end of the bargain?" she pushed, leaning forward in her chair.

"Maybe. We'll see what the information turns up." I hung up the phone and stood.

Caitlin attempted to yell something through the thick plexiglass, but I'd already turned away and moved on.

♦

"You made this?" I trailed my fingers around Lina's waist as I circled her, admiring her incredible talent. The black dress she wore hugged her body perfectly. It was cut just above mid-thigh—short but still sophisticated—and the fabric was luxurious, but it was the neckline and sleeves that were most impressive. The front swept up and around her neck, leaving one arm bare, circling around and becoming a full sleeve on the other arm. I had no clue how she got into the damn thing.

Everything about the dress was mesmerizing—the fit, the design, the craftsmanship. Drawing out a concept on paper was one thing, but actually bringing the design to fruition was something entirely next level.

"Last year. It was one of the demos we used for a winter collection. That sort of thing makes up the bulk of my wardrobe."

"Why shop when you can create an original?" I murmured. "How did you learn to sew?"

Her shy smile and flushed cheeks sank hooks into my heart—the barbed kind that couldn't be removed without significant damage.

"I happened to see a sewing machine at a thrift shop one day. I'd always adored fabrics, the textures and colors. On a whim, I bought the machine and spent weeks cursing at it while I learned about bobbins and thread tension and a million other things. I suppose I fell down a rabbit hole and never really came back out. Six months later, I enrolled in design school, and the rest is history."

"You're very lucky. Not many people have a gift like yours, and to have discovered it at an early age is even more rare." I certainly had never found anything that captured me the way she described. The only thing that came close...

I watched the way Lina's right hand absently toyed with the ring on her left. An urgent need blazed through me to find a way to make the ring a permanent fixture on her finger. The urgency bordered on compulsion, which was a sensation I'd never experienced until I met Lina.

Okay, so the fixation she described wasn't totally foreign.

"I've never thought of myself as lucky. Quite the opposite, but I guess I've had my moments." Her eyes lifted to mine, and I'd be goddamned if they weren't shining with hope.

I hooked my hand around the back of her neck and brought my lips to her ear. "Lina, look at me like that again, and we'll both go hungry because the last thing on my mind will be dinner." I sounded like a fucking savage, my voice no more than a guttural rasp, but that's how I felt. One look from her, and ten thousand years of evolution went right out the window.

A shiver danced from her shoulders down her entire body before she nodded.

"Good girl," I breathed, giving her delicate neck a light squeeze. "Now, let's go before we're late."

She didn't move. "You sure this is a good idea?"

"Why wouldn't it be?"

"I don't think your family is a fan of me, and that's fine. They have no reason to be—"

"What gave you that impression?" I interrupted, tension coiling in my neck at the thought of someone making Lina feel unwelcome.

She shrugged and dropped her gaze. "When we first got to the wedding and talked to those two couples, I got the sense they weren't happy I was there—especially the one woman. The redhead."

"Her name is Rowan, and they were just surprised. My family is very tight and wary of outsiders at first. I promise it won't be an issue, though." A white lie. My family was close and didn't like outsiders, but the reaction Lina had sensed was actually grounded in who she'd been dating. I found out later that Rowan recognized Lina as the woman who'd been dating Lawrence Wellington. I didn't want to go into the connection and my family's past with Wellington, so I kept that information to myself. Lina would only ask more questions that I wasn't open to answering.

She nodded somewhat reluctantly, and I led her to the apartment door with my hand on the soft curve at the base of her spine. I'd made plans to meet my cousin Conner and his wife Noemi for dinner. I'd told Lina we needed to be seen together, but in reality, I'd simply wanted to take her out. I'd wanted her to spend time with my family and see there was more to me than what she might think.

Conner was five years younger than me, but I'd always felt like I could relate to him better than some of my other cousins. He ran the Bastion Club, which I often found myself at as part of my role of schmoozing the city's elite. I was the face of the Byrne family, and it was my job to foster connections with every possible individual of influence and power. Something about Conner gave me the sense that he knew what it was like to play a part. Keir and Torin and Shae—they were all perfectly comfortable being exactly who they were. Conner and I were different, and I appreciated our friendship.

I'd been a tad envious of him when he married Noemi. I could tell by the way he watched her that I'd never had with

Caitlin what he felt for his wife. I'd thought at the time that that particular experience was out of my reach, but as I helped Lina into the car on our way to the restaurant, I mulled over the unpredictability of life.

I'd thought after Caitlin, I'd never open myself up to another woman again. Now, I had the strangest feeling that things were unfolding exactly as they were meant to be. It felt fucking cliché to even think it, but it was true. The whole "things have a way of working out for the best" always felt like utter bullshit. It wasn't something you could understand until you'd lived it and experienced the feeling of all the pieces magically clicking into place.

I understood now, but it was all worthless if I couldn't convince Lina she felt the same.

# THIRTY

LUCK WASN'T JUST SUBJECTIVE, IT WAS A PERSPECTIVE. WITH A few murmured words, Oran had drawn back the curtains and helped me see my life in a whole new light.

There I sat in a beautiful restaurant with people who genuinely made me laugh. I was wearing a dress of my own creation, supporting myself in a career that was my passion, and falling more every day for a man who had literally *killed* on my behalf. But it had taken Oran's comment for me to see that my life wasn't just a series of misfortunes.

Of course, he was responsible for a good portion of my current circumstances. A month ago, I would have said he was to blame, but now I wondered if I'd look back and give him credit as the one to thank instead.

There was only one glaring problem. My heart was still in tatters.

I had a gaping chasm in my chest that needed to be closed, and that wouldn't happen until I had my sister back home with me or knew for certain that she wasn't ever coming home.

Did I trust Oran enough to risk telling him the truth? The fact that I was even considering it spoke volumes. I even genuinely liked his family, and I was generally highly suspicious of everyone. Sitting with Noemi on my right and Oran on my left, I'd been amazed at the ease of our conversation. Conner was a bit reserved, but Noemi seemed kind and surprisingly down-to-earth. I wasn't sure she could be hurtful to another human being if her life depended upon it. I didn't know people that pure existed.

"I think I may try the monkfish this time," Noemi mused half to herself.

"Have you been here before?" I asked, hoping she might have a recommendation.

She closed her menu and shot a challenging glare at her husband. "I came with a *friend* once. Conner threw a tantrum about it. Strangest thing—my friend ended up with a slashed tire that night."

Conner remained perfectly stoic. "She wasn't a *friend*, she was my very bisexual *cousin* who was practically salivating over you."

"Exactly. Your *cousin*, who had to deal with a flat tire out in the cold."

"That could have been any thug on the street out vandalizing cars." He sipped from his wineglass, his coy tone completely refuting his assertion.

Noemi snorted, making me like her even more. She leaned in conspiratorially, though she spoke loud enough for the guys to hear. "These Byrne men don't handle jealousy well. Just a heads-up."

My gaze collided with Oran's heated stare as I thought about the lengths he'd gone to to get me away from Lawrence.

*Would it be so fucking hard to believe that I was doing it for you?*

Oran's words whispered through my mind, causing a warm blush to kiss my cheeks.

"I've noticed a certain single-mindedness, that's for sure."

She winked and clinked her wineglass with mine. "I want to know all about your wedding plans! Have you decided on a date?"

"Sometime in the spring, but we haven't chosen a location," Oran cut in. He spoke so confidently, I wondered if he'd already thought about his answer to that line of questioning. I'd been too consumed with everything else to even play out the pretend scenario in my head. There wasn't going to be a wedding, but if there were...

"The Chinese Scholar Garden over at Snug Harbor—it's on Staten Island. I went years ago, but I remember feeling like I was in a whole other world there. It was the most serene and peaceful I think I've ever felt. If I could, that's where I'd get married."

"Oh! Do they have cherry blossoms? That would be so incredible to time the wedding for blooming season." Noemi's hand rested on her chest as though she could already see the ceremony play out and was overcome with its beauty. I had to admit, the image it conjured was breathtaking. So much so that my chest was left aching.

"I believe they did at the time. But like I said, it's been a while." I smiled and had a feeling Oran had seen through to the sadness beneath because he stared at me with such intensity, I had to look away. Fortunately, the server arrived at that time and began to list the specials of the evening.

The rest of dinner flowed with remarkable ease. I had a wonderful time—probably because I allowed myself to live in the moment for once. No reminders to stay on my guard or remember that the relationship was fake. I simply enjoyed dinner with good company, and it felt incredible.

When we stood from the table to leave, Conner cursed at his phone, causing us to pause. "Looks like I need to run by Bastion and open the safe."

"We could run over there." Oran looked at me. "If you're up for it."

I wasn't tired and the club had been intriguing. I hadn't been able to spend much time there at the masquerade. "Absolutely."

"Appreciate it, man. I spent three hours over there today and was hoping to be done."

"No problem at all."

We said our goodbyes to Conner and his wife, promising to have dinner together again soon. I wanted that to happen way more than I should have. I wanted all of it. The close-knit family. The lighthearted conversation. The security of a devoted partner. Those sort of luxuries weren't easy to come by, but once you had a taste, everything else paled in comparison.

I spent the short drive over to the club trying not to think about how I would manage once it was all gone. Oran must have been lost in his head as well because he was equally as distracted. The silence wasn't uncomfortable, however, and within minutes, we pulled up at the non-descript building I'd ventured to weeks earlier. I hoped that this time my visit to Bastion would be far less dramatic.

"Mr. Byrne, so glad you could join us tonight. It's been a

while." A beautiful woman smiled broadly from behind a counter in the lobby. Too broadly. I didn't like it.

"We're just popping in for a few. Ashleigh, this is Lina."

I extended my hand and spoke before he could continue. "Oran's fiancé."

The woman's eyes rounded as she shook my hand.

That's right, little miss. You can tone down the wattage on your fuck-me smile.

I took Oran's arm and prompted him to continue to the elevator, wordlessly dismissing the hostess. An amused chuckle rumbled from deep in Oran's chest. I chose to ignore it. Yes, I'd acted childish, especially considering the man wasn't really mine, but I didn't care. If I was trying to make this look real, like he'd wanted, then I couldn't tolerate such obvious flirtation. It was all part of the act. Obviously.

Oran's eyes heated to molten steel when the elevator doors closed behind us. Was that part of the act as well? It had to be, right? I wasn't sure how I was supposed to tell.

The way his eyes licked down my body felt as real as my thundering heart pounding in my chest.

"I was wondering if I'd get the chance to hear you say it."

"Say what?" I asked breathlessly.

"Introduce yourself as my fiancée."

I lifted my chin and asked with as much disinterest as I could muster, "And how did it feel?"

"Ill-fitting."

My spine stiffened reflexively. His unexpected response pierced straight past my armor to the soft insecurities beneath. "Sorry to disappoint," I said with forced calm, eyes dropping to the floor.

"I suppose I'll just have to be patient because I suspect it won't sound right until you're calling yourself my wife."

The elevator came to a stop, jarring my already shaky equilibrium.

*Did he say what I thought he just said?*

How incredibly presumptive and patriarchal. I should have been outraged. I should have balked and told him how absurd he sounded or laughed at the sarcasm in his tone. Only … the comment didn't sound absurd, and I couldn't detect an ounce of sarcasm. And when I met his steely gaze, I knew without a doubt that he was 100 percent serious.

Oran

# THIRTY-ONE

THIS TIME, LINA WAS THE ONE TO HIT THE EMERGENCY STOP button right before the doors could open.

"Why would you say that?" she demanded, eyes searching mine.

"Why? Because I meant it. I would marry you tomorrow if..."

"If?" she prompted, her voice a whisper of disbelief.

I was just as shocked at what I'd said. I hadn't put words to the thoughts, but they seemed to be pouring out of me like they'd been plotting their escape for days. They came so unbidden that I didn't have a chance to filter them. But now that they were out, I realized an explanation would be required, and I didn't want to get into the Caitlin issue right now. The night had unfolded perfectly, and Caitlin would only fuck things up. I should have already told Lina and would have if I didn't hate talking about it so damn much.

"If I thought you'd let me," I offered instead. It was a risk. If she agreed, I would have to come clean, but considering how resistant she'd been to any sort of relationship from the beginning, I wasn't too worried. I took Lina's hands in mine and held them above her head, her back pressed against the metal wall. "I have an entire list of things I'd do to you if I thought you'd let me—some of them unwise and most of them downright uncivilized."

Lips parted, she was on the cusp of begging me to show her when her gaze suddenly dropped to the floor.

"You wouldn't feel the same if you knew the things I've done," she whispered brokenly.

"Is this about that perverted bastard at the club? Because what he did to you doesn't change the way I feel. Not even a little." I wanted to kill the fucker all over again after hearing the pain in her voice.

She shook her head. "It's not that. I wish it was—I wish I was the only person who'd been hurt by my bad choices, but I'm not. I've done things…"

*Her* bad choices? Being raped wasn't a choice. Fuck, I hoped she knew that.

I needed her to know, not just that, but how much I wanted her regardless of whatever the fuck she thought she'd done. The intensity of my desire for her didn't make sense. I knew she was keeping secrets and that I didn't want that in my life, but it didn't matter. None of it did where Lina was concerned. I needed her to understand that. I had to find a way to show her. I'd done shit she didn't know about. Bad shit. And I still hoped she'd look past it just like I wanted her regardless of her past.

"You don't believe me, so I'll prove it to you the only way I know how." I hit the button to engage the elevator. When the doors opened, I gave the waiting club members a warning glare and pressed the button for the ground floor. Message received—no one tried to join us.

I held Lina's hand in mine on the way back to the car, my swift strides tugging her along with me.

"What about Conner?" she asked, growing winded. "Weren't you supposed to open the safe?"

"This is more important."

She didn't ask any more questions, though I could sense her anxiety. She sat with her hands tightly clasped in her lap the entire drive to the police station. When she saw where I'd taken her, I wondered if she might dart down the sidewalk she looked so panicked, though she seemed to remember my purpose for bringing her by the time I helped her out of the car. She'd calmed somewhat, eyes wide with a wary hopefulness.

"Is Casper on duty tonight?" I asked at the reception desk.

"Not tonight."

"What about Lieutenant Palmers?"

"Yeah, I believe he's at his desk." She motioned behind her to the open-area mass of desks.

"Thanks." I led Lina back to where Palmers was stationed, relieved to find him at his desk. He sat tall when he saw me approaching, eyes doing a quick sweep of the room. Plenty of these guys worked with us on the regular, but none of them liked to admit it.

"Mr. Byrne, this is unexpected."

"I just need a minute of your time," I told him. "I need you to pull up someone's record. Carolina Elizabeth Schultze."

Palmer took a quick look at Lina, then got to work on the

computer. After a minute, his brow furrowed. "There's nothing there." He angled the monitor so we could see it— Lina's perfectly clean record. "No charges or record of arrest. Was I supposed to find something?" he asked, confused.

I didn't answer, too focused on Lina as she processed what he'd revealed.

"You made me think…"

"I did what I had to do. No more."

I saw the second she realized and accepted that I never intended her any harm—not even the risk of harm. Her eyes filled with tears as she nodded, unable to speak.

"That's all we needed, Palmer. Thanks." I took her hand again, this time leading at a more casual pace. She stopped me once we were outside, pulling her hand free and facing me.

"What does this mean, Oran?" She looked so fucking lost and confused. I hated it but knew it was necessary. She needed to know the truth.

"I suppose that's up to you."

Her eyes dropped to the ring on her hand. I swore if she took it off, I was going to lose my goddamn mind, but she didn't. Instead, she covered it with her other hand. In protection or avoidance, I wasn't sure, and I didn't care so long as it stayed put.

"I don't know what to think," she admitted softly. "I don't know what to do. I don't even have a home anymore."

"*Fuck*, woman. Have you heard nothing I've said?" My frustration broke free. I yanked her to me and slammed my lips on hers, stealing the breath from her lungs in a brief but savage kiss. "I'm telling you that you belong with me. *I'm* your home, and all the other bullshit doesn't matter. Now, can we get out of the cold, or do I have to throw you over my goddamn shoulder?"

She sniffled and nodded. I thought she might have even smiled a little, but she was too overcome to know for sure. Once I had her in the car, I buckled her seat belt and turned on her seat heater before going around to the driver's side. She was more shaken than I'd ever seen her, and my protective instincts were screaming. I didn't like being the source of her tears.

The three of us rode back to the apartment—Lina and me and enough uncertainty to make the car feel suffocatingly small. I wanted to assure her everything would be fine, but how could I when I didn't know her half of the equation? I'd done everything I could. The ball was in her court now.

We stepped inside my apartment, both ambling slowly as though unsure what to say or do. When Lina reached the living room, she stopped, her gaze sweeping down the hallway to the spare bedrooms, then in the opposite direction toward the primary suite.

The room spun the tiniest bit, making me realize I'd been holding my fucking breath.

"Doesn't matter which room you choose," I told her. "The only place I'm sleeping tonight is next to you."

Her huff of a laugh and resigned shake of her head blanketed me with relief.

*Thank Christ, she isn't going to fight me.*

"Let me just grab a few things."

A primal part of me didn't even want to let her out of my sight. I used what little rational judgment I had left to force myself back to my bedroom. Minutes later, Lina joined me, setting her toiletries at the spare vanity. The one that used to be Caitlin's.

I really needed to say something about my ex, but the timing always sucked.

Lina was just starting to open up and trust me. Telling her

how I'd framed my ex for murder seemed like a conversation that needed to wait.

We brushed our teeth and changed for bed. I wanted to rip the T-shirt and shorts off her and demand she sleep naked, but that didn't seem to bolster my whole I'm-the-good-guy campaign. I was trying to prove that I wasn't a threat, so showing a little self-control might be a plus.

Unfortunately, no one got that message to my dick.

I tried to picture something that would be a turn-off—my nana, my ex, Lawrence Wellington. Even combined, they weren't enough to completely overcome my desire for the woman standing next to me.

Lina's blush indicated she hadn't missed the bulge in my briefs. "I hope you don't mind. I need to set an early alarm for a design meeting in the morning."

"That's no problem. I can give you a ride on my way into the office. I need to get some work done."

"Where's your office?"

"We own the building that Moxy is in and have offices on the second floor."

"Moxy?"

I turned when I heard the strange catch in her voice. "Yeah, it's a strip club."

"Your family owns it?" She made an effort to sound casual, but the color highlighting her cheeks moments before faded in a way that set me on edge. Did she have an issue with strip clubs?

"Yeah, we own Bastion, Moxy, and one other club in town. Moxy is the only one that has dancers. That a problem?" I asked warily.

She shook her head quickly. "No, no. It just caught me by surprise, that's all. I guess I don't really know much about your family."

I snagged the hem of her shirt and tugged her close. "You already knew I wasn't a Boy Scout," I murmured, my gaze trailing over her parted lips. "My family's no different."

Lina nodded with a smile. "I get it. The family I've met have been great. It's really not a big deal."

She was holding something back. I could feel it in every bone in my body, but I wasn't sure if it was best to push for an explanation or let it slide. We'd had an eventful evening. Something like that might be better to discuss once her emotions weren't so close to the surface.

I brought her forehead to my lips for a lingering kiss. "Let's get to bed. We can talk more tomorrow."

I assured myself that so long as she was here with me, everything else could be sorted out later and that the unease knotting in my gut was simply paranoia.

I should have known better than to ignore my intuition.

# THIRTY-TWO

"Honey, what is up with you? I might as well be brainstorming with that mannequin over there." Cosmo's botoxed brows attempted to express concern by listing toward one another without actually creasing any skin.

"I'm sorry. I didn't sleep well last night."

"You want to try again tomorrow? We have a little leeway in our schedule for this next collection."

"Yeah, that might be best. I've had a lot on my mind lately. Give me the afternoon to put pencil to paper, then I should be ready to collaborate tomorrow."

"Works for me. And no judgment here. You've never once let me down in the past. I know you'll bring your A game when you're able."

"You're the best, Cos. I knew I picked you for a reason."

"Girl, you did no such thing. You hardly said five words in that first class we had together. I scooped you up and made you mine—you never had a choice in the matter."

My lips quirked upward. "That's what you think. It was all part of my master plan." I slid my drawing pad back into my satchel and stood. "Identify most talented mind in the room? Check. Butter him up with flattery? Check. Scare everyone else away with vicious rumors behind his back? Check and check."

He attempted to raise a brow. "I am very susceptible to flattery."

"I know." I blew him a kiss. "See you tomorrow."

"Get some rest!" he called after me.

Rest. That was funny.

How was I supposed to rest when I might have been sleeping with my enemy?

I walked to the front of the building in a daze, the same hazy state of shock I'd been in since Oran mentioned Moxy. I was so out of it that I actually squeaked when my phone buzzed in my pocket. Heart in my throat, I checked the screen to see that Gloria was calling. That was unusual. No matter how many times I assured her that I was happy to hear from her, she worried about being a bother, insisting that a busy woman like me didn't need her old nanny checking in with her all the time.

A million and one reasons for her call flashed through my mind.

"Hey, Gloria. Everything okay?" I hoped she didn't hear the frenetic edge to my voice.

"Yes, everything is good, Lina. How are you?"

"I'm fine. Just wrapped up a short meeting with Cosmo."

"Yeah? Work is going well?" She sounded odd, like she was trying a little too hard.

"Yeah, work is great. You sure everything is okay?"

"*I'm* okay. I've just been a little worried about you is all."

"Me?" Why would she be worried about me?

"Yes, you know with Mr. Brooks's broken arm, I've been worried."

I was so confused. "Charles broke his arm? What happened?"

"You don't know?" she asked, a tinge of scandal showing through. "If you don't know, mija, I'm not sure I should say anything."

"Gloria Ruiz, tell me what on earth is going on," I ordered sternly. She might have been my nanny, but our dynamic had long since shifted to one of equal footing.

She tsked. "Your mother said it was the man you're seeing —he attacked Mr. Brooks. I'm worried for you, mija. She said this man is dangerous."

Oran broke Charles's arm? Would he have done that without telling me?

He'd gone after Gaetz, but as far as Oran knew, Charles hadn't done anything so deplorable. Why would he take it upon himself to hurt my stepfather?

I considered my mother's implication that Oran knew more than he let on. That he might have answers about the past. And then there was Moxy…

I needed her to explain. *Now.*

"I'm so sorry to worry you, Mama G, but I'm fine. Really."

"You sure, sweet girl? My sister used to show up with bruises but always insisted she was fine until her husband went too far and killed her."

"Jesus, Gloria." My heart broke for her and her sister.

"Oran hasn't touched me, I swear." If anything, he'd been even more compassionate than I would have expected.

*What about the strip club? How do you explain that?*

I couldn't. But maybe my mother could. I had to go get answers.

"If you're sure. You know you can always come stay with me if you need to."

"Thank you, Gloria. You're so good to me."

"You deserve it, mija. You're a good girl who deserves good things."

Tears clouded my vision. I swallowed down the rising emotions. "Thank you for checking on me. I'll be in touch soon, okay?"

"You take care and be safe. Te amo, mija." *I love you, my little girl.*

"Love you, too, Mama G," I whispered before hanging up.

I tossed my phone into my purse and charged across the sidewalk to flag down a cab. It was time to pay a visit to my least favorite place on earth. The house I grew up in.

◊

"Gloria said that you told her Oran broke Charles's arm. I know your propensity for making up stories that suit you, but this is ridiculous." I waited until I was inside with the door shut before I launched my attack. I wasn't worried about Gloria getting in trouble for telling me. I had a feeling that had been Eliza's intent from the beginning.

My mother dabbed at her perfectly coifed hair as though a strand might dare to be out of place. "If you were just going to hurl accusations, you could have simply picked up the phone."

206

"No, I couldn't because I want an explanation, and I want to see for myself that you're telling the truth." Eliza Brooks dabbled in lies so frequently that I needed to be in her presence if I had any hope of deciphering what was real and what was fantasy.

"I'm glad you did because I will get great joy in seeing you come crashing down from that high horse of yours."

"I'm sure you would."

A slow, vindictive smile slithered across her face. "What I told Gloria was the God's honest truth. Oran came by here the other day after we'd seen you at the club. He had the gall to threaten us to stay away from you." She scoffed. "As if he has any right to tell me who I can and can't see."

He'd warned them away to protect me?

Warmth expanded in my chest like a giant firecracker, fading just as fast as it split the sky with light. He'd warned them away, but what if his reason had been different? What if he had information about the Society and didn't want my mother and stepfather implicating him?

"Why would he do that?" I asked absently, my mind a flutter of confusion.

Eliza stilled, her narrowed eyes slicing back to me. "Why don't you ask him yourself?" she asked curiously. My mother knew better than anyone on this earth how to sniff out a person's weaknesses, and she was onto me. She could sense my uncertainty.

No matter how uneasy I felt, I couldn't give her that power over me.

"I plan on it, but if you hadn't noticed, he's not here right now," I shot back condescendingly.

She glared at me, then opened the door. "Then you best go find him. I have an invalid husband to attend to, thanks to your *fiancé*."

I was being dismissed. Fine by me. I didn't want to spend a single unnecessary second in her presence.

Chin raised, I turned my back on my mother and prayed I never had to see her face again.

◊

By the time I got back to the apartment, I'd lost my grasp on composure. Months of worry and frustration compounded until the pressure was unbearable. I had to know if I could trust him once and for all, or I was going to lose my mind.

I let myself into the apartment with the codes Oran had given me earlier that morning. I didn't waste a minute, immediately falling into the task of scouring the apartment. I didn't even attempt to hide my actions.

His dresser drawers.

His nightstand.

Under beds and inside closets.

I hunted with a single-minded determination to find anything that might tell me one way or another who to believe. Who to trust. I searched his freezer and inside the toilet tanks. If something was inside that apartment, I was going to find it.

I didn't stop to eat or clean up after myself.

I didn't check my emails or even look at my phone.

All I did for hours was comb through every single nook and cranny in his entire home.

I wasn't sure if it was pure exhaustion or an emotional release like a thunderhead finally relinquishing its hold on the rain, but when I circled back to where I'd started and realized I'd come up emptyhanded, every ounce of energy drained from my body. I folded onto my knees like a swath of heavy wool dropped to the ground.

I'd been so sure I'd find my proof if I just looked hard enough. Too much smoke surrounded Oran—that had to mean fire, right? I needed to rip off that Band-Aid and admit that I'd developed feelings for someone who'd lied to me. Someone who'd only been with me to use me. I was so sure that was the answer, yet when the storm cleared, and I looked back on the devastation I'd created, I had nothing to show for it. No evidence of anything but my own pathetic weaknesses. That and the cold, heavy pistol that lay in my hands.

I stared at it while desperation leaked from my eyes in fat, salty droplets, washing away what little dignity and self-respect I had left. When I heard the front door open and shut, I didn't budge from my spot on the office floor.

Let him see my disgrace.

The time for secrets was over.

"Lina?" Oran's frantic voice carried from the living room. "What the fuck? Lina, are you here?" He was moving quickly, probably worried his home had been robbed, considering the disarray.

"Lin—" He froze in the doorway, his cry cutting short at the sight of me on my knees.

I flicked the gun's safety mechanism on then off. On then off. On...

"Did you break my stepfather's arm?" The hollow words didn't sound like they came from me. They didn't even sound human. I didn't feel human. I felt dead inside, and it must have shown. When I raised my gaze to Oran's, he couldn't hold back a small gasp.

"I did," he answered tonelessly.

"Why?"

"To make sure he understood I was serious when I told him to stay away from you."

My mother had been telling the truth for once in her life, making my crushing disappointment ironic.

I should have known she'd be honest the one time I wished to God she'd been lying. Oran's need to control them insinuated they were a threat to him. And what could my mother do to hurt him except spoil whatever plan he'd had for me? That was the only thing that made any sense.

I slowly stood and cocked the gun. "You had no right to involve yourself." A thick vine of emotion slunk around my throat and squeezed off my airway, making the last words come out a breathless whisper.

Oran took a menacing step forward. "A day ago, you were ready to call yourself my *wife*, and you think it's not my place to protect you?" His words struck deep, triggering a gush of guilt and confusion that fueled a new surge of anger.

"Protect me from who, Oran?" I demanded, raising the gun.

*"From yourself, goddammit,"* he roared back at me.

He wanted to stop me from what I'd been doing—from finding answers. Stop me from finding my sister.

It was exactly what I'd feared. The very worst-case scenario.

My breath hitched as I took a small step forward. "You don't have to *protect* me anymore. Just tell me the fucking truth," I cried, my face twisted in agony. "Are you trying to get into the Society? Is that what this whole thing has been about?"

Oran's hands went up at his sides, his eyes widening. "I don't know what the fuck you're talking about. What society?"

*"Don't fucking lie!"* I screamed.

He charged forward, pressing his chest to the barrel of the gun. "I'm not lying, Lina. I don't know anything about a society, but if you don't believe me, then shoot me. *Just pull the goddamn trigger.*" He spoke with absolute certainty. No fear. No illusion. Oran was ready to die on this hill, so I did the only thing I could do.

I pulled the trigger.

# THIRTY-THREE

THE CLICK OF THE EMPTY PISTOL DISCHARGING SLICED THROUGH the air and severed the final threads holding me upright. My trembling body collapsed back to the floor, sobs bubbling up from deep in my chest like aftershocks from an earthquake.

"*Jesus*, Lina, baby. Come here." Oran lifted me into his arms and walked to the chair behind his desk where he sat and cradled me against his chest. He didn't say anything for long minutes, just letting my emotions take their course until I could breathe again and my body calmed.

My thoughts slowly returned as the emotional thundercloud dissipated, for better or worse. Now, I had to process what I'd learned and all I'd done. I'd almost been in a trance. That was the way the memories felt—as though I were seeing through someone else's eyes. But it hadn't been anyone else. I'd been the one with the gun, and Oran had told me the truth. He didn't know about the Society.

How could that be? It didn't make any sense. There were too many coincidences. I was missing some key piece of information, but if it didn't concern the Society, what then?

And where did that leave us?

I wiggled my hand down into my pocket, then handed him the five bullets I'd taken from the gun before he'd arrived.

"I knew I'd left that thing loaded." His rumbling voice vibrated from his body to mine, warming me from the inside out.

"You shouldn't have. Guns are dangerous," I said absently.

Oran choked on a laugh, hugging me closer and rocking us backward. "Woman, what am I going to do with you?"

"Be honest?" I suggested quietly. "Tell me the truth?"

He stilled contemplatively, then stood and eased me to my feet. "Okay. How about we start here." He walked to the bookcase and pulled it away from the wall, revealing a heavy metal door with a keypad. "If you're looking for something, this is where you'll want to start your search."

I stared in shock as he entered a code and opened the door to a smaller secondary office. It was more of a closet than an office, but the far wall had a built-in desk with a computer, and papers were haphazardly piled on either side of the keyboard. Above the desk were several shelves holding all sorts of foreign electronics with red and green lights. It looked like one of those safe rooms I'd seen in the movies.

This was his inner sanctum.

He was exposing his jugular in a show of trust, and I was so damn relieved I almost ended up back on the floor. Maybe my trust came too easily. His reveal wasn't an absolute guarantee, but somehow, I knew he wouldn't have shown me this if he wanted to keep me in the dark.

"You really are telling the truth. This isn't about the Society."

He cupped my face, his thumbs wiping away the remnants of my tears. "Having you here—everything I've done—it's all about you. I want you so fucking bad it hurts." He hadn't known I would tear his place apart. He hadn't prepped his little room first or planned to reveal his secret hideaway as a ploy to trick me into trusting him. Not only had he proved himself yet again, but he'd continued to be patient and forgiving despite all I'd put him through.

I let all my reservations about Oran fall to the floor. My doubts and worries. Everything.

And without their leaden burden, I practically floated up to kiss him. Or maybe he kissed me. I wasn't even sure. Suddenly, I was in his arms, my legs around his waist, and our tongues intertwined.

One minute, I was Lina, desperate and alone. The next, I was his.

Oran seared his name across the surface of my heart with the demanding press of his lips. He patched up my soul with pieces of his own—a unique custom weave that blended the two fabrics together in a way that could never be fully undone. No matter where we went from here, this man would always be a part of me.

He placed me on top of the executive desk in his main office, leaning against the side so his legs remained between mine. "You want honesty? What I want is *you*. I want you to give yourself to me in every way possible. Your body. Your trust. Your fucking *soul*. I want all of it, but I know some parts will take more convincing than others. So for now, what I want is for you to strip because you love having my eyes on your naked body. I want you to spread yourself wide because you can't wait to feel me inside you. I want you to scream my name as you come all over my cock because you know I'm the only man who has ever ... or *will* ever ... *own you*."

*Yes. Yesyesyesyes.*

The word echoed in my mind, resounding in every fiber of my being.

I wanted all of it. Everything he said. But I didn't know how to make it happen. How to make myself a normal girl without a mountain of baggage.

Hell, I couldn't even say the one simple word to tell him how I felt. Yes. YES!

Fear held the single syllable hostage deep in my throat, but I was more than my fear. I wouldn't let it control me. Instead, I slid from the desk.

Oran allowed me room to stand, stepping back a foot farther when I swept my shirt over my head. His ravenous stare devoured me piece by piece until I was fully exposed, bare before him. And he'd been right. I adored the way his greedy stare begged for more. I wanted to give it to him, so I did.

Once his eyes returned to mine, twin silver flames of desire, I lifted myself back onto the desk, scooting back before reclining to my elbows. Oran's body went inhumanly still. Every muscle was locked with restraint as he waited for me to give my final consent.

*...spread yourself wide because you can't wait to feel me inside you.*

I licked my lips, then slid my feet slowly out to the corners of the desk, opening myself to him completely.

Oran

# THIRTY-FOUR

My family owned a strip club. I learned at an early age not to unwittingly attach meaning to a woman offering up her body to a man. Sometimes sex was just sex, pure and simple.

This was different.

What Lina did by presenting herself to me was so much fucking more.

Knowing her and all that had passed between us, I recognized this gift for the treasure it was. I knew what it had cost her, and that alone made her actions priceless. The trust and vulnerability she displayed were so fucking brave. It was no wonder I'd been entranced by her from the moment we met. She wasn't an ice queen; she was a goddamn warrior.

I yanked off my tie and tore the buttons clean off my shirt, having no patience for unfastening them one by one. "I need to know that you understand how much I respect what you're offering," I told her in a voice sharpened by intense desire.

Lina nodded.

"I understand." Maybe she did to some extent, but her furrowed brows told me she wasn't certain.

I unbuckled my belt and let it clank to the floor, then placed my hand on the soft stretch of skin between her pelvic bones, just below her belly button. "It's important because this is mine now." I trailed my hand down until my thumb could roll gentle circles over her delicate clit. "And I'm going to fuck you without restraint. I don't want you confusing my actions for disrespect."

Her back arched off the desk as she moaned.

"*Jesus*, you're fucking magnificent." I brought my fingers to her entrance. "And so wet, baby. So fucking ready for me." I fingered her tight entrance with one digit, then eased in a second, her walls so snug around me that I worried I might hurt her.

I stilled. "How long has it been since a man was inside you?"

"A while," she breathed.

"You never fucked him." My disbelieving stare bore into hers.

Lina bit down on her bottom lip and slowly shook her head. I didn't understand it but also didn't care to. All that mattered was that geriatric bastard hadn't touched her. I was so goddamn relieved I could have screamed. Instead, I yanked her ass to the edge of the desk, then dropped to a squat. As she rested her feet on my shoulders, I flattened my tongue over her core, laying claim to what was mine.

Lina gasped and writhed above me. I didn't let up, licking and sucking and devouring her until her entire body quivered with the need for release. That was when I stopped and stood tall above her.

"No, no, no. Don't stop," she gasped, her breaths coming in shallow pants.

"Don't worry, I'm going to make you come so hard you'll forget your own name."

I kicked off my shoes and let my pants fall to the floor, finally freeing my angry cock. He'd been desperate for her for weeks and now demanded a taste. I gave myself a couple of strangled pumps to try to ease the ache, precum already dripping from me.

Lina stopped breathing. Her eyes rounded as she stared at my cock, her head starting to shake.

"Shh, I know." I soothed her. "It'll be a tight fit, but I'll take it slow. I promise."

The wary vulnerability in her azure irises fucking undid me.

*The things I would do for this woman.*

I fished a condom from my wallet and rolled it on, finally allowing the tip of my engorged dick to nudge her entrance as I guided her legs around my waist. Her radiant heat was an irresistible invitation. I wanted to sink inside her, but I knew I'd tear her wide open if I didn't go easy.

Leaning over, I rocked an inch or so inside her, bringing my mouth to her breast and sucking her hard peak into my mouth before releasing her and grazing my teeth over the sensitive flesh. I wove my fingers with hers and lavished her breasts with attention as I steadily rocked myself farther inside her.

"*God*, Oran. I'm so full. It feels so good," she said on a groan.

"Just a little bit more."

"More?" she gasped.

"You're doing so good, baby." My voice was no more than a rasp from the strain of my withering self-control. "Just a little…"

*Fuuuuuuck…* That was it. I was buried so deep inside her I could hardly breathe from the pleasure. My head dropped back as I wrestled for control over myself.

Once I had a tiny bit of blood back in my brain, I leaned forward over her and brought my eyes to hers, cupping the back of her neck with one hand. "This body is mine now. No one else comes near you. Promise me. I need to hear it," I demanded hoarsely.

"Yours and yours alone," she breathed, eyes wide.

"*Fuck, yes.*" I withdrew from her, then swiftly thrust back, but not too harshly at first. I did my best to give her time to adjust, but I only had so much restraint. Soon, I was fucking her with everything I had; my hand clamped tight around the back of her neck, and my other hand gripped her hip to keep her in place so my savage thrusts didn't send her off the other end of the desk.

Lina clung to my arms, her nails scraping at my skin as she moaned with pleasure. The room filled with the sounds of slapping flesh and panted breaths.

"Oh God. I'm almost there, Oran. Right there, just like—" Her words were cut short when her body seized tight, then erupted in an explosion of quaking convulsions. Lina threw back her head and screamed her release. The cry was raw and unbidden. It was the most beautiful fucking sound I'd ever heard in my life.

I came so hard my vision blurred, and my balls threatened to squeeze their way back up inside me. An electric surge of pleasure bolted from the base of my spine out to every extremity, leaving me gasping for air.

"Jesus Christ, I've never come so hard in my fucking life," I murmured after coaxing every last ounce of pleasure from our bodies.

Lina's response was no more than a garbled bit of nonsense.

"Oh yeah? You, too?"

She nodded, coaxing a smile from me.

"Oran?"

"Yeah?"

"I'm sorry I tore apart your place," she whispered.

"Our place," I grunted. "And it's fine because you'll help me put it back together. Later. For now, I need to get you cleaned up. You want a shower or a soak in the tub?" I knew she'd be sore regardless, but I hoped to minimize her discomfort.

"Actually, the tub sounds magnificent."

I lifted upright and disposed of the condom, then helped her up. We gathered our clothes and walked back to the primary bathroom. I cleaned myself off, then started the tub faucet. Sitting on the edge, I kept my hand in the water as I waited for the hot to kick in.

"I can do that, you know." She stood beside me, her hand resting on my back.

"I know you can, but I'm gonna do it for you anyway." I placed a kiss on her belly and watched goose bumps dance across her skin. "You going to tell me more about this secret society?" I asked just loud enough for her to hear me over the running water.

Lina stilled before escaping toward the toilet enclosure. "It's secret. I don't know much to tell you." She shut herself inside the tiny room. Technically, she needed to pee after sex.

I got that. But this felt off. It felt like she was avoiding me. Or was it the subject she was evading?

When she returned, she eased herself into the slowly filling tub, still not meeting my gaze.

"But you knew enough about it to think I was trying to join," I pushed. Surely, she could be open with me after everything we'd just shared.

She shrugged. "It made sense. Why else blackmail me into dating you?"

"And how exactly would that help me get into the society?"

"Maybe it was proof of your power over law enforcement. I really don't have any idea, but as a member of Olympus, you have the clout to find out." Finally, she peered up at me through her lashes. "You could ask around and see if someone is willing to tell you what it takes. See if anyone is willing to talk." An eager hopefulness made her voice breathy.

It didn't make sense. She'd sounded wounded before at the thought that I might have been associated with this society, but now she was suggesting I look into joining?

"If you don't know anything about this society, how do you even know it exists?"

A muscle in her jaw flexed. "I just do."

She definitely knew more than she was telling me. Why? Why the fuck keep secrets when I'd just put myself out there to prove I was on her team?

Despite everything that just passed between us, she still didn't trust me.

"I'm gonna start tidying up while you soak." I dropped a towel next to the tub and shut the door behind me, resisting the urge to slam the damn thing.

I couldn't believe this was happening. After our

confrontation with a fucking gun, and her tears, and then offering herself to me—how could she possibly still be holding herself back? *Why?*

This shit needed to end. All of it. My retribution. The secrets and lies.

I was done.

I needed it all to end so I could know one way or the other whether this thing was going to work between us. I'd already let myself feel more than I should have. I was done giving if she wasn't going to meet me halfway.

I went back to my office after getting dressed and into my hidden room, where I glanced over the collage of documents I'd been using to coordinate the systematic downfall of Lawrence Wellington. I was curious what she'd make of them. It would seem an odd mix of information to an outsider. Would she see his name and run to warn him? There was only one way to find out.

I'd told her she could look her fill. If I held good on that promise and gave her access to my secrets, I'd find out quick enough whether she was interested in betraying me. It pissed me off that I still had to question her at this point, but why else would she be keeping secrets?

*Maybe she has something going on that you know nothing about. Not everything is about you.*

No. I didn't buy it. Why not share with me if it wasn't somehow tied to me? Something continued to come between us, and I was sure as hell going to find out what.

# THIRTY-FIVE

I DIDN'T SPEND TOO MUCH TIME IN THE TUB BECAUSE I WANTED to help with the house. I hadn't exactly destroyed the place, but Oran kept a tidy home, and my search had definitely caused upheaval. I didn't want him having to clean up my mess alone.

We worked companionably together, then ate a quick dinner. He'd seemed quiet while we cleaned, but I assumed he was concentrating on his task. I knew he was upset when the awkward silence continued through dinner. I felt like I was in the middle of a gloriously hot shower, only to have the water suddenly run ice cold.

We'd connected in a way I hadn't experienced with another living soul. It was terrifying yet so incredibly fulfilling at the same time. To feel that newly formed bond slip through my fingers made me want to scrape and claw to get it back. Had the thief who'd stolen from me been anyone but myself, I would have defended my newly acquired emotional stronghold with feral tenacity. But there was no one to fight. No one else to blame.

Oran was upset that I wouldn't tell him more about the Society. The problem was that the one piece of information I possessed centered on the most shameful, heart-wrenching choice I'd ever made. I didn't want to keep secrets from him. I was sick of the lies and secrecy and desperately wanted to tell him everything, but I couldn't seem to do it. When he asked, I'd fought with myself over what to say. The battle had been vicious, but my shame had won in the end, insisting I stay silent.

*Better he think me a liar than know the truth.*

He gave me a chaste kiss good night before bed, then we kept to our separate sides of the bed, an ocean of biting cold between us. I'd done that. I'd driven a wedge between us, and I hated it.

Tears soaked my pillow. As I lay alone in the dark once again, I decided that what I should have done was at least explain my situation—tell Oran that I knew about the Society because of something I was a part of that was deeply embarrassing and ask that he not push me to go into detail. It seemed like such a simple solution, and I wasn't sure why I hadn't thought of it before except that I'd felt like a cornered animal desperate to protect itself. That was how I'd learned to survive through the years, but I was beginning to understand there were other ways.

I decided to take a chance and try that new route. First thing in the morning, I'd talk to Oran and explain what I could. With a plan in place and his soft snores filling the room, I finally gave in to sleep.

When I woke in the morning, however, Oran was gone.

No note. No indication of when he'd be back. I'd hurt him, and I hated myself for it.

Wanting to smooth things over, I called him on his cell but got no answer. The only other option I had was to wait for him to come home, and since I wasn't sure when that would be, I texted Cosmo and bailed from our rescheduled design meeting again. I felt bad for ignoring my work but had learned the hard way that work wasn't my top priority. Relationships came first.

I got myself some coffee and planned to sew for a bit when I made an unexpected detour to Oran's office. Curiosity drove me forward. Oran had cleaned up his office before I got out of the bath the night before, so I hadn't been back inside. I couldn't help but wonder if he'd closed up his secret room. He'd said I could look around, and he'd sounded sincere, but I was still shocked to see he'd left the hidden door open. Oran was intentional in everything he did. This wasn't an oversight. He was giving me free rein to look around unsupervised.

Rather than dive in, I chewed on the inside of my cheek and stared at the tiny room. If I'd been given permission, why did having a look feel so invasive?

*Because it's his private affairs, and if you trusted him, you wouldn't need to look.*

Except he might have pertinent information and not even know it. And what about Moxy? Maybe his club was connected without his knowledge. How would I know unless I took a peek?

I groaned inwardly and crossed the threshold into the closet office. To the right of the computer was an earnings report for The Blackthorn Group. I had no idea what the company did or any relevance it might have had. Inching it aside, the paper beneath was a nautical schematic of shipping routes. A stapled and highlighted stack of papers sat farther back and appeared to be some sort of printout of the federal tax code. Oran had OSHA listings for hazardous chemicals and printouts of various models of night-vision goggles. And that wasn't even half of the crap. I didn't know what I thought I'd find, but this wasn't it.

Resigned to let it go, I started to turn around when my gaze snagged on a photo peeking out from the bottom of a pile of papers. I used a finger to slide the image over for a better look, only to wish I hadn't.

My coffee turned rancid in my stomach.

The image had been clipped from the society pages of a local newspaper showing Oran attending the MET Gala ... with his beautiful *wife*.

*Oran Byrne and wife Caitlin arrive as part of the Friends of the Museum donor's club.*

The event had taken place a mere six months earlier.

I hadn't been so naive to think Oran wouldn't have a past, but a *wife*?

Holy shit.

Was he still fucking *married*?

With shaking hands, I pulled my phone from my back pocket and googled the New York State Department of Health—the entity that maintained searchable public record databases. When I input their names, I was only able to find one result. A marriage license. No decree of divorce. No death certificates.

Oran Byrne was married, and his wife was still out there somewhere.

There I was, beating myself up for a tiny white lie when

Oran had been lying through his teeth. I felt like such a fool to think he'd truly started to care for me.

*What an idiot!*

Was Oran simply two-timing his wife, or was this all part of a much larger con? I wasn't even sure what that could mean, and my emotions were entrenched in too much chaos to think clearly. All I knew was my heart hurt so fucking bad.

I looked down at the ring on my finger.

*He told you it was a fake engagement from the beginning. Why the hell did you pretend it was anything more? What is wrong with you?*

My eyes burned with tears. I wished they'd been out of anger, but the truth was, I felt absolutely gutted.

I took off the ring, set it on the photo, then shut the door behind me.

No more sacrificing myself only to get stepped on. If I needed information, I'd go straight to the source. I'd been playing it safe for months, trying to fly under the radar out of fear, but I was done with that. It was time to rock the boat and make some waves.

I threw as many clothes as I could fit in a duffel I found in the closet. I didn't know how I'd get the rest of my stuff, but that was a problem Future Lina could tackle. For now, I was on a mission.

Before I left, I placed a call to the number I'd seen on Oran's desk the first time I'd gone snooping. The one scribbled on paper along with the name of a fellow Olympus member.

"Hello, Mr. Paxton? This is Lina Schultze, Oran Byrne's fiancée."

"Oh, hello, Lina. How can I help you?"

"Oran has decided that he'd like to take his membership to the next level at Olympus," I said, giving my tone just a hint of innuendo. "He asked me to call and set up a time to come by and talk since you had already been so helpful." It was a risk assuming that this person had any role in the Society, but that was what it took to go on the attack. I was done playing it safe.

"I see. Of course, membership discussions are always held in person."

"Of course," I agreed readily.

"Tell Mr. Byrne he can come by this evening at seven. I'll make sure the proper parties are present."

"He'll be delighted. Thank you so much for your time."

"My pleasure."

The pleasure would be all mine.

I hung up, powered off my phone, and walked away from Oran Byrne for good.

# THIRTY-SIX

"I REGRET TO INFORM YOU THAT YOUR MEMBERSHIP WITH US AT Olympus has been revoked. All payments received will be refunded as the trial period was not successful." The aloof man on the other end of the phone was almost comical in his attempt to sound cavalier. Someone named Phillips had called out of the blue to tell me I'd been kicked out of Olympus.

"Trial period?" I'd never been told about a trial period. And why the hell was I being evicted? Not that I cared. I'd already achieved what I needed from my time at the club. In fact, the final stage of my plan had been set into motion that very morning. News channels were already starting to report on the container ship wedged in the Panama Canal, shutting down half the world's cargo ships, and the news that the New York district attorney had filed a dozen different criminal charges against Lawrence Wellington. Just wait until tonight when traffickers would be busted on one of his ships while yet another sprang a leak in the Gulf of Mexico. It was going to be a very, *very* bad day for Larry.

"Yes. That should have been explained to you upon signing the membership agreement. All memberships are subject to a ninety-day probationary period in which member fitness is assessed. It has been determined that Olympus is not the ideal organization for you. Naturally, that means the arranged meeting for this evening at seven with you and the future Mrs. Byrne has been canceled."

Meeting? I had no fucking clue what was going on, but I didn't want this dickhead to know that.

"Naturally," I repeated flatly. "Thanks for letting me know."

"Your cordial acceptance is appreciated. Goodbye."

I let out a wry huff of laughter when the line went dead. "Asshole." He probably expected me to put up a fight. Like I gave a fuck.

The only thing I wanted to know was what meeting. And he'd specifically mentioned Lina, which made me think it must have been something she'd set up. Why would she arrange a meeting at the club and not tell me? Was whatever she'd done the reason my membership was revoked?

Fuck. I needed to know what happened.

I got out my phone and discovered I'd missed a call from her. I called her back but was sent immediately to voicemail as if she were on another call ... or the phone had been turned off.

I opened my GPS app and verified that Lina's location wasn't available. Why would her phone be off?

I wasn't sure what was going on, but I knew I didn't like it. Something was wrong. I made it home in record time, calling out Lina's name as I walked around looking for signs of her. When I got back to my office, I saw that the hidden door had been shut. It had been open when I left that morning. I punched in the code and opened it just to be sure she hadn't somehow locked herself in. She hadn't, but she'd definitely been in there. The ring I'd given her sat on top of a photo clipping of me and Caitlin.

*Fuck me. What have I done?*

My pride had goaded me to test her, but I'd unveiled my own deception in the process. I had completely forgotten about the photo showing me with my wife. It had been mixed in with all the other papers, but Lina had clearly found it and figured out I was still married. And just when she'd started to open up.

I snatched the ring into my fist, then flung everything off the desk in a fit of rage.

What a goddamn hypocrite I'd been throwing a stupid fucking tantrum about her keeping secrets. I'd convinced her to trust me in the most intimate way possible, then shredded that trust in a matter of hours. Why the hell hadn't I told her the truth?

I had to fix this. *Now.*

I took out my phone to call Conner as I charged back out of my apartment.

"Yeah?"

"Everything in place to release the pictures taken of the girl from Wellington's attic?" I hated to use her, but she was already back in Russia getting top-notch services to help her recover physically and mentally. We made sure she was taken care of, and I needed the images to smear the last remnants of Wellington's reputation.

"Yeah, they're set to be delivered anonymously to the *Times* tomorrow. I've also managed to get the FBI to revoke his travel credentials."

"No shit? That came through?"

"Yeah, but you don't want to know what I had to give them in return."

"You're right, I don't." I had too much other shit to worry about. That could wait.

"Whispers of a fire sale are already circulating through our SEC channels for AIS Shipping, and Blackthorn stock is plummeting as we speak."

"Good, and the tax evasion charges will crumble his ability to take on more debt or secure investors. After that, anything remotely connected to the man will shrivel and die." I never could have taken down every individual piece of his empire, but with enough damage to the foundation, the rest would crumble. "Thanks for all your help with this."

"Anytime," Conner said readily. "And you keep your ear to the ground. Assholes like Wellington don't go down without a fight."

"Always."

I ended the call just as I reached my car. I needed to track down Lina. I wasn't sure where to look, but if all else failed, I knew where she'd be come seven o'clock.

Lina

# THIRTY-SEVEN

"I'm sorry, ma'am. Sundays are dedicated for certain members only." A young brunette with wide eyes crossed the lobby toward me as soon as I stepped off the elevator on the main floor where Olympus gatherings were held.

"Yes, I'm actually here for a scheduled meeting. I'm a bit early, so I'm happy to wait."

"I suppose you can have a seat over there." She motioned toward a set of club chairs.

I smiled and tilted my head conspiratorially. "If you're worried I might spoil the mood, I'd be happy to wait in an office."

An all-access pass to an office would have been incredible,

but it was too much to hope for. The girl shook her head. "No, this is fine. Please, have a seat."

I gave a tight smile and did as she instructed. The girl scurried back to her hostess station. Nervous energy buzzed in my veins, demanding I bounce my leg or chew my nails, but I steadfastly refused. The appearance of unshakable confidence would be necessary if I would get anywhere without Oran present. He was the member, after all. Whoever came to meet with us would be hesitant to continue when I informed them that Oran had been held up at work. I had to weasel out as much information as possible, and that would require a show of bullheaded entitlement.

A full fifteen minutes passed before a man exited the elevator and made a beeline toward me. Pious irritation wafted off him like bad cologne.

I stood at his approach and smiled.

"Ms. Schultze, Mitch Phillips," he offered in a curt introduction. "Did your *fiancé* not inform you that the meeting was no longer necessary?"

All my practiced confidence scattered to the sky like a cluster of startled pigeons. "I … No, I suppose my phone must have been on silent. What's happened?" How did Oran know about the meeting? They must have called him, and he'd known I was up to something, so he canceled the meeting. He'd told me before in no uncertain terms he didn't want me near the club. This was him holding true to his word.

Anger reared up inside me like a vicious cobra, neck spread wide and tongue hissing in warning.

Mitch glanced at his watch dismissively, oblivious to my growing wrath. "Perhaps you two should keep in better contact, then Mr. Byrne might have told you he is no longer a member at Olympus and saved you the trip over." He pinned me with an icy stare, dripping with arrogance and superiority.

Not a member? Oran had canceled his membership just to keep me away from the club. My only avenue for information, and he'd taken it from me. Without access to the club, I had nothing.

"Then I'd like to apply for my own membership," I shot back at him.

"That won't be possible."

"Who are you to tell me what's possible?" My eyes narrowed to angry slits. "You aren't the sole decision-maker for this club. My parents are members, you know."

"I am well aware of who you are, Ms. *Schultze*, and I think it's time you left the building."

His snide use of my biological father's name enraged me beyond comprehension.

I was no longer Lina.

I was a violent ball of vengeful energy ready to kick or bite or claw my way through the mounting army of enemies waging war against me.

I snatched Mitch's shirt into my fists, clutching so tightly my knuckles ached. "This isn't over. You think you're so fucking superior, but you're not. I'll burn this whole goddamn club to the ground if that's what it takes to get what I want."

Mitch yanked at my wrists to pull free of me, only I was a thing possessed and wouldn't release him.

"What in God's name is wrong with you?"

"Should I call the authorities, sir?" the young hostess called over to us just as the elevator doors opened, and Oran charged into the room.

Mitch's eyes widened. "Jesus, man. Get this woman off me."

"Lina, calm the fuck down and let go of him," Oran hissed, tugging at my shoulders. He might as well have painted a fat red target on himself. Every ounce of my fury refocused on him.

I whipped around to face him. "*You*. How could you?" My hands slammed against his chest, shoving him as violently as I could. "How could you do this to me?" Suddenly, it wasn't the club motivating me but the image of him in a tux next to his smiling wife. A barrage of tears blurred my vision. I rushed forward to push him again, only he bent at the waist and thrust his shoulder into my belly, sweeping me off the ground and folding me over his shoulder.

"We can discuss this in private," he hissed, a death grip around my legs to keep me captive as he marched us onto the elevator.

"I'm not doing *anything* in private with you." I slapped my hands against his ass because it was the only thing I had access to.

"You're going to give me a chance to explain, even if I have to force you."

"There is nothing you could say that I want to hear."

"That might be true, but you'll listen anyway." When the doors opened, he walked us out of the elevator and took us out onto the street, where his car was double parked, blocking the road.

"I knew you'd be just like Lawrence and the rest of them, using people for your own entertainment. Doing whatever the hell pleases you."

Oran opened the passenger door, then set my feet on the ground. "I didn't use you," he growled, his gray eyes almost black in the shadow of his furrowed brow. "I fucked up by not being up front about Caitlin. Yes, I'm technically married—"

"*Technically?*" I shot back with a humorless laugh.

He continued as though I hadn't interrupted. "But the divorce has been filed."

"There's no decree. I looked."

"That's because it's an ugly divorce. She betrayed my entire family—set my father up to be *killed*—so I had her put in prison for murder. That's why I didn't tell you. Seemed like a shitty selling point in my efforts to get you to trust me."

She set up his father's death?

I remembered back to the obituary and the picture of Oran with his father in a joyful toast. His own wife had done that? I thought back to his grieving mother at the wedding and how welcoming his family had been. Why would his wife have rejected all that?

I didn't know what I'd expected him to give as an explanation, but that hadn't been it. Some of the fight drained from my coiled muscles, though I wasn't totally ready to surrender.

"I told you how important it was to me not to run from my mother and stepfather and the club, and you took it from me anyway. How am I supposed to trust someone who ignores me?"

"I didn't take anything from you. I got a call out of the blue telling me I'd been kicked out and that *our* meeting was canceled. I didn't know what the fuck was going on."

"If that's the case, and you really don't care about the club, then why did you treat me like a lepper after I wouldn't tell you more about the Society?"

"Because you seem to care more about this fucking *society* than being with *me*," he bellowed, each word louder than the one before. His shout ripped through the night air, the city seeming to quiet in response.

My heart lurched to a stop in my chest.

I looked at the building in shock ... and fear. "We should go," I said softly.

"I'm not going anywhere. You started this, and we're seeing it through."

He was past the point of reason, whereas I'd finally begun to regain mine. I took a deep breath and brought my eyes to his. "I don't want to be a part of them. I wanted information from them. I've spent months trying to get access. Wellington, the club, everything I've done has been for a purpose, and now I've been cut off completely. Everything I've done was for *nothing*." A fist of emotions clamped tight around my throat, and tears burned the backs of my eyes.

"Why, Lina? What do you need information for?"

This was it. I had to decide whether I was willing to lay it all out on the line and tell him the truth. In reality, there was no choice to make. I needed help. And deep down, I wanted Oran to know the entire gut-wrenching story.

"Alright," I conceded quietly. "I'll tell you everything, but not here. Take me back to the apartment." I slid into the car. Oran thought for a moment, then closed the door and rounded to the driver's side.

The ride home was tense, yet I felt an odd sort of peace. Was that how people felt on their final walk down death row? No more option to debate. No more reason to fight. Just the simplicity of acceptance. It was freeing. I greatly appreciated the comfort it brought as I walked back into Oran's apartment without any guarantee about what would come next.

I crossed to the living room window and looked out over the city. It was easier that way—as though I was talking to everyone and no one at the same time.

"When I was seventeen, my mother sold my virginity to gain admission to the Society."

*Oran*

# THIRTY-EIGHT

*THE FUCK?* I KNEW HER PARENTS WERE SHITTY, BUT THAT WAS A whole new level of depraved.

And why? They had a fuck ton of money. My mind raced with the need to figure out what besides money could serve to justify such an atrocity, but then I realized that would be looking for sanity from the insane. The two simply didn't coexist.

I set aside my mountain of questions and braced myself as Lina continued.

"Eliza and Charles had joined Olympus a year earlier. I was told that there was a secret inner circle within the club called the Society and that my virginity was the only offering that would grant them access. I was stunned, of course. Eliza had been a terrible mother, but I never saw this coming. I panicked. My mother scoffed at me. She told me that my first time would be a disappointment anyway, and it might as well be for a good cause.

"I was already counting down the days until I was free of my mother and stepfather. I told her I'd run away, but she'd already planned for that and shrugged patronizingly. *I guess we could always offer Amelie instead.* Those words changed my life forever. I almost threw up on the spot because I knew she'd do it. Eliza didn't make idle threats.

"My little sister was six years old at the time. She's my half sister, and even though there are eleven years between us, she's the best thing to ever happen to me. I would have done anything for her. I still would." Lina's voice thinned with tension. She fought back tears, and I desperately wanted to pull her into my arms to comfort her, but I knew as well as she did that this story had to be told. She had to leach out the poison, or it was going to kill her one day.

"I thought about it for several days and eventually told my mother that I would do it under two conditions. I wanted five hundred thousand dollars and a promise that I'd never hear from her again. I also told her that if she ever tried to use Amelie in any way, I'd go to the cops about all of it. My sacrifice was also my leverage. That night, I was taken to a hotel room. I was blindfolded, and even though I technically offered myself voluntarily, every second of it scarred me beyond comprehension."

They were dead. All of them. I was going to kill them, but her mother would suffer the most.

"That's not voluntary, Lina," I said through clenched teeth. "That's *rape.*" I couldn't keep quiet any longer. The rage was too violent to fight back.

"I know, in a way. But I can't fully silence the voice that

reminds me that I let it happen. I didn't run away the moment she told me. I didn't even fight him off. I just … let it happen." She sounded so fucking hollow that it gutted me. She was always so feisty and strong, but all along, she'd been carrying this horrific trauma underneath it all.

*Such a goddamn warrior.*

"All this time, you never knew who the man was." And her parents had brought this man to her, knowing how it would affect her. It was beyond cruel. Sadistic.

"I was worried when I came to the club for the first time a few months ago. Every time I stepped foot in there, I was terrified I'd hear that voice. And when it finally happened, it was just as awful as I feared." She peered over her shoulder at me. "But now I'll never have to worry about that again because of you."

If it meant having her look at me like that again, I'd hunt down every goddamn Society member and flay them open neck to navel.

She turned back to the window and continued. "I didn't see my mother or stepfather again for ten years. I used the money they'd given me to go out on my own, as sparingly as possible, and the first thing I did when we started turning a profit at the design firm was pay back every cent. I didn't want any part of their blood money.

"Over the years, I kept in touch with Amelie—lunches with her at school or short visits at her dance studio where she took lessons. She knew that if she ever needed anything, she was supposed to call me. I also made sure our nanny Gloria stayed at the house to be there for Amelie. I knew Gloria wouldn't have stayed if she knew what my mother and stepfather had done, so I didn't tell her. All she knew was that we didn't get along and that I'd gone out on my own."

A horrible pit formed in my stomach as I thought about

why Lina had come back. She wouldn't have come near that place without a compelling reason. My thoughts turned to Amelie and her move to Paris. Something had to have happened.

"One day, I got a call from my sister. She was sobbing. My mother had done it again, only this time, she hadn't given any warning or choice. She'd taken Amelie to a fancy hotel suite and explained the situation. My sister had always been much more of a parent-pleaser than I was. Eliza counted on Amelie submitting. Thank God, she didn't. My sweet sister attacked the man who entered her room, ran as fast as she could, and called me using a stranger's phone. I picked her up and brought her to my place. While I'd desperately hoped she'd never have to know the truth about her parents, the time had come. I told her everything. She was devastated but agreed she couldn't go back.

"I'd already planned to move out of the apartment I shared with Jessa. I'm not wealthy like Eliza and Charles, but I've been making enough to live comfortably, so I rented a modest place where Amelie and I could live together."

"So she didn't move to Paris? When I looked up your family, I read that Amelie Brooks lived abroad with extended family."

Lina shook her head. "That's what my mother told the school and anyone who asked so people wouldn't ask questions."

"Did they try to take her back home?"

"I went to them first. It was the first time I had laid eyes on Eliza Brooks in ten years, and the only reason I did was to show her the results of the rape kit I'd had done a decade earlier. I told her if she so much as sent either of us a text, I'd file charges in a heartbeat. I was sure the threat would be enough." The last words were no more than a whisper. She had to clear her throat before she could continue.

"I planned to move my things to the new place so Amelie wouldn't be alone, but I was so busy working on a new collection that I kept putting it off. I'd worked so hard building a career for myself that it consumed me. Plus, I wasn't used to looking out for someone else. I'd been on my own for so long. And besides, everything seemed to be working out so well. Amelie was safe and thriving. She was using a pseudonym to make sure Eliza and Charles didn't track her down since she was still seventeen, though she didn't look it. She'd even been able to get a job waitressing." Lina quieted and finally turned to face me, her eyes glassy and red.

The pit in my stomach grew jagged thorns.

"Amalie had been so proud of herself. She'd gotten the job all on her own, and the bar wasn't far from our new apartment. A place called Moxy."

# THIRTY-NINE

Oran's entire body recoiled as though I'd physically struck him. It was an enormous relief. Since the moment I'd heard that he was connected to the strip club, I'd worried he was somehow tied to my sister. Even now after seeing his shock, I still struggled to believe that Amelie working at Moxy and Oran entering my life were purely coincidental.

I would ask him about it, but first, I had to force myself to finish the story.

"She only worked there a couple of months when…" My breathing hitched. I felt like I was reliving that horrible day all over again.

The day I figured out my sister was missing.

"We were in the habit of having Friday lunch together since she worked most of the weekend. I texted that morning asking where she wanted to meet, but lunch came and went, and she never responded." I wrapped my arms around my middle to help keep me in one piece because I felt like my heart was shattering. "The only thing worse than learning she was missing was figuring out it had happened two days earlier, and I'd been too damn preoccupied with my own life to notice." The words faded to a broken whisper as my tears got the better of me.

Oran crossed the room and wrapped me in his arms. It felt so damn good, but I hated that. I didn't deserve to be comforted. Amelie was alone out there somewhere, probably already dead, because I hadn't protected her well enough. I knew the chances of her being alive this long after her disappearance were slim. I was too much a realist to entertain ridiculous fantasies, and Amelie was too thoughtful to have gone off voluntarily without telling me. And besides, I preferred to think she was dead than trafficked. That reality was too horrific to even consider.

"Something terrible happened to her, and it was all my fault."

He pulled back and clasped my shoulders firmly. "This is *not* your fault, Lina."

I squirmed away from him, shaking my head. "Don't, Oran. Don't say crap to try to make me feel better. I knew she could be in danger from the Society and our mother. I should have kept a closer eye on her."

"No, Lina. Listen to what I'm telling you. It wasn't your fault, and it wasn't the Society."

I stilled at the remorseful timbre of his words. If he knew it wasn't the Society…

I looked back at him, my heart already rejecting the implication that he knew what happened to my sister. That this whole time, he'd known.

Oran ran an agitated hand through his hair, then sat on the coffee table with his elbows on his knees.

"You said she was using a pseudonym. She went by Darina, didn't she?"

My lungs seized, a vise clamping tight around my entire rib cage.

"Yes," I wheezed. "Darina Somova. It was the name of a dancer she'd idolized while growing up."

He knew her. Oran had known Amelie this whole time.

My shaking legs lowered me down to sit on the edge of the sofa as I waited to learn what had happened to my little sister.

"I don't have much to do with the operations at Moxy, but since I have an office in the building, I'm around often enough. One day, I was drinking at the bar when Darina asked if she could talk to me privately. We stepped out front, and she told me she'd talked to Torin and Jolly—her bosses at the club—and asked about dancing instead of waitressing, but they'd both refused. She wanted to know if I'd consider talking to them. They're both surly assholes, so I could understand why she thought I might be more receptive, but it wasn't my place. She told me she could use the experience and started tearing up. I didn't want the kid crying, so I tried to console her.

"What I didn't know at the time was that my wife was in the process of betraying me and my family. She happened to come by the club that night and saw Darina and me together, making the false assumption we were having an affair. Wanting to hurt me, Caitlin came back the next day and drugged Darina on her way in to work. Caitlin knew of a Russian man who was involved in trafficking, so she took the girl where she thought she could find him."

*God, no. Please don't tell me that was her fate. Not my sweet little sister.*

My hand clamped over my mouth to hold back the sob clawing its way from the depths of my soul.

Oran continued, his voice somber and foreboding. "Caitlin made an error, however. The house where she'd seen the Russian previously wasn't his. It was Lawrence Wellington's house. The two were doing business together." He paused, his eyes lifting to mine. "And before I say any more, I want you to know that I didn't figure out any of this until much later. It's taken months to sort through it all and involves so much more than you can imagine. I'll explain the rest later, but know that I interrogated Caitlin about what had happened after figuring out she was responsible, and I learned that Lawrence's son had been there the day she went looking for the Russian. He took possession of an unconscious Amelie."

Oran grimaced, slowly shaking his head. "It's complicated to explain, but it turned out that bastard was fucked up. He got off on torturing women, but he won't be hurting anyone ever again because he's dead now."

Dead? That couldn't be. "Lawrence told me his son had moved."

"Guess he and your parents had the same idea of pretending the kid moved and hoped no one asked any questions."

I was stunned. It had never occurred to me that Lawrence's son could have been responsible. "I tracked her phone GPS. The last known location was Lawrence Wellington's house," I said in a stunned, haunted voice. "I kept tabs on Olympus and my mother as best as I could. I knew he was a member. It seemed too convenient to be a coincidence, or so I'd thought. I thought the Society or Eliza and Charles had found a way to lure her over there and had taken her. My mother swore they weren't involved, but I didn't believe them."

"You had no reason to. The deductions you made were perfectly logical."

"But I was wrong."

He dipped his chin. "You never could have protected her from what happened because it was simply horrible, horrible luck."

"But ... what did happen to her?"

"I didn't find out Wellington's son had been responsible until after he'd already been killed, so I couldn't ask him what he'd done to her. But he was a twisted fuck, Lina. I'd say the fact that she's never been found gives you your answer." He spoke in a tone saturated with sorrow. It hurt him to say it almost as much as it hurt for me to hear.

My brain grappled with everything he'd unloaded, desperately trying to process it all. Lawrence's son, who was now dead, had most likely killed Amelie. It hadn't been Lawrence.

"But surely, he knew," I blurted. "It was his house. Lawrence had to have known what his son was doing."

"He did, but he didn't care."

"If you've investigated it all, then surely you have enough evidence to have him arrested." I stood, outrage giving me new strength. "I've seen how loyal your connections are in law enforcement. Surely, you didn't just turn a blind eye to Wellington's involvement."

Oran stood, his hands raised placatingly. "That's why I'm

here, Lina. That's where the connection lies—why it isn't all pure coincidence. I joined Olympus to make him pay in a way that he'd feel it. Some drawn-out lawsuit or even death was too easy for Lawrence Wellington."

Oran picked up the remote from the table and turned on the television to a news channel showing video of a giant chemical spill in the ocean trailing from a large ship. The program then showed an image taken from far up in the sky of enormous container ships dotting the sea just beyond where a green ship sat sideways in a narrow canal.

"What is this?"

"This is Lawrence Wellington's demise. His shipping company will be bankrupt soon. His assets have been frozen, and his passport revoked. And news of the Russian woman tortured in his home will be leaked later tonight. He will be a social pariah in a matter of hours. No money. No power. No options. It was the only thing that would truly hurt him the way he deserved."

I looked back at Oran, tears brimming in my eyes. "You did this?"

A single nod. "All of it. I only joined Olympus to get at him, as I told you. And stealing you from him was supposed to be just another piece of my plan."

Those tears tumbled down my cheeks. Oran had done it all to avenge my sister and the others Lawrence had hurt. I was so incredibly grateful, but that meant … he did have an ulterior motive for dating me. None of it was real, just as I suspected. My gaze darted to the floor, and I wiped hurriedly at my wet cheeks. "Of course, I understand," I said quickly.

He shot to his feet. "No, you *don't* understand. I nearly lost my mind seeing you with him. I couldn't figure out why you'd subject yourself to any of those people at that fucking club. I told myself that forcing you away from him was part of the plan, and that's why I couldn't quit pursuing you. But men like Wellington only care about power. If I'd been honest with myself, it was obvious that putting a ring on your finger had fuck all to do with him."

"*Oh*," I breathed, air suddenly in short supply.

"I know I'm technically still married, but I don't give a fuck. You're the one who's supposed to share my name. You're the one I should be calling my wife. You're *mine*, Lina Schultze. You have been from the minute I laid eyes on you. *That's* what you don't understand."

My tongue swept over my suddenly parched lips, my head spinning from such a chaotic swing of emotions. "I think I'm starting to get it."

Oran closed the distance between us. "Good." He held out his hand to help me to my feet. "Because there's only one place this belongs—" He fished the engagement ring from his pocket and put it back on my finger. "The next time you get the slightest inkling you might want to take that off, you come talk to me first, and we'll sort through it. You get me?"

I nodded. "Yeah, but I'm not used to relying on someone, Oran. It might take a little getting used to." I hated that I'd been conditioned not to trust and that it could push away someone as devoted as Oran. I didn't want to lose him.

"That's why I'm going to spend every goddamn day proving to you that I'm worth the risk."

We flew together in the same instant in a devastating kiss filled with a world of hopes and promises. I couldn't get enough of him. Of his taste and touch. His commanding perseverance and unquestionable loyalty to those he loved. I wanted to burrow deep in his soul where I could feel safe and cherished forever.

Oran swept my legs up bridal style and carried me to the

bedroom. We never stopped kissing. Couldn't. I was starving for him, and he was well on his way to owning me.

The second my feet touched the floor in the bedroom, we both began to strip like we couldn't get naked fast enough. Like every scrap of fabric was a loathsome barrier between us that had to be eliminated.

Once we were completely bare, I feasted on the sight of him. His mature, muscled physique called to a primal side of me that demanded a partner able to annihilate any challengers. Someone whose confidence showed in their every movement. Oran didn't need a title to be a king. The role was implied in every nuance of his being. I wasn't sure I could ever be worthy of such a man, but I wanted to try.

My gaze lowered to his cock when he took it in his hand and lazily stroked himself. "You aren't still sore, are you?"

I shook my head, transfixed, then went to him and dropped to my knees. I tried to take his engorged cock in my hands, wanting to taste him, but Oran took my hands in his instead and brought me back to my feet.

"Not tonight, little warrior. Tonight, we're equals." He pulled me into a kiss with his hand cupping the back of my head and his words cradling my heart.

After Oran guided me to the bed, we did something so magical together that it could only have been called one thing —we made love. It was a first for me. I'd never experienced anything like it—to be equals but still reverent of one another. And the emotions entangled with the physical? It was beyond intoxicating.

I was utterly addicted.

We came together three times that night, our bodies unable to resist one another. From just the slightest feel of him in the bed with me, I was instantly awake and craving more. He was just as consumed. The first time I woke, it was to the feel of his fingers sliding in and out of me, already drawing me close to orgasm.

The emotions swelling inside me were overwhelmingly intense. So much so that I was afraid to label them, but I knew one thing for certain—I never wanted it to end.

# FORTY

I'D HAD NO FUCKING CLUE WHAT I WAS MISSING. IF I'D HAD ANY inkling this sort of intensity of emotion in a relationship was possible, I never would have accepted a marriage with Caitlin. I hadn't even known something so profound existed. If I *had* experienced it before, I would have been married before I ever met Caitlin because I'd have locked that shit down faster than a warden in a prison riot.

Instead, I'd been trying to do what was right for my family. And without the perspective of knowing what I was giving up, I'd almost condemned myself to a lifetime without *ever* knowing.

I hated that my father had to die for me to walk this path, but at least his sacrifice wasn't in vain.

Lina lay sleeping, curled into my side. I felt like I could lie there all damn day and watch her sleep. It was later than she usually got up, but she needed to catch up on her sleep since I'd kept her awake half the night.

The ghost of a smile tugged at my lips as I thought of how my dad would have teased me relentlessly about being whipped had he been around to see me with Lina. And I wouldn't have minded because I knew he was devoted to my mother more than anyone. I learned about loyalty and commitment from him. I would always strive to make him proud, even if he wasn't here to witness my choices.

He'd definitely have approved of Lina. And when I told him everything she'd told me, he'd have been right there next to me when it came time for revenge, which it would ... soon.

Eliza and Charles Brooks were living on borrowed time.

Fucking secret society.

I'd had no goddamn idea, and no one I'd talked to had given any hints of its existence. Was it some sort of fetish club? How many members of Olympus were involved?

Whatever they'd done to silence people had been effective, but nothing kept people quiet when pain entered the equation. I'd learn what I wanted to know.

With a featherlight touch, I swept a strand of Lina's golden hair away from her face. She must have been close to waking, though, because her eyes fluttered open and met mine.

She smiled lazily and stretched, reminding me of a well-fed cat.

"Good morning," I greeted her in a husky tone. She was naked beneath the sheets, and just a glimpse of her full breasts as she moved hardened my morning wood to solid stone. I didn't think I'd ever get enough of her, but I was already concerned she'd have trouble walking today. Her body needed a break.

"Morning," she rasped. "You been up long?"

"No. I was just lying here contemplating breakfast." Not a total lie. I'd been thinking of eating something, just not food.

"Mmm ... you know what sounds good?"

*Sure do.* "What?"

"An omelet and a cinnamon roll with some fruit and maybe a side of bacon."

A huff of laughter rumbled in my chest. "Hungry?"

"I like breakfast on a good day. Today? I'm *starving.*"

I pulled her against me, a wolfish smile spreading across my face. "Sounds like I did my job."

"You, Mr. Byrne, were exceptionally thorough." She tucked her forehead up under my jaw and sighed contentedly.

I commanded myself to memorize every intricate detail of this moment—the midmorning sun lighting the room, the weight of her thigh draped over mine, and the miraculous warmth that filled my chest. I never wanted to forget the sheer perfection.

"Oran?"

"Mmm?"

"You think I'll ever be able to find out what happened to Amelie?" she asked quietly. "I know it's not good, but I think the closure would help. Not knowing is excruciating."

If anyone knew, it would be Lawrence Wellington. I had planned to let him flail in the agonizing uncertainty of watching his world crumble for some time before I did anything else. Getting him to talk, though, would take a good deal of incentive. I hadn't planned to move on to the physical torture part of my revenge until much later, but I hated to make Lina wait longer than necessary. She'd already gone through so much.

"Yeah, baby. I think I know a way."

# FORTY-ONE

ORAN DROPPED ME BY THE WORKSHOP ON HIS WAY TO MEET WITH some of his cousins. He said he'd have to work most of the day. I assured him a session with Cosmo could easily last until dark. After rescheduling twice, I was relieved to finally be in the right headspace to get some work done. Though, I had a feeling we would get off to a slow start.

I hadn't worn my engagement ring around Cosmo because explaining it all had felt like too much. An explanation was still going to be a little insane, but at least I didn't have to tell him I was being blackmailed into a fake engagement. This was real.

It boggled my mind, but Oran had made his feelings clear. He wanted me, and I was hopelessly lost for him. The uncertainty of such an intense, sudden connection was overwhelming, but we'd take it one day at a time. And today, that meant telling my longtime friend that I was engaged.

Of course, I didn't have to say a word. Cosmo's sharp eyes locked onto the sparkling diamond as if my entire hand had been gold-plated and bejeweled. His jaw hit the floor.

"It's costume, right? Tell me it's costume."

I laughed, running my thumb across the back of the band. "Funny story—it's been kind of a crazy couple of weeks."

"You met someone and got engaged in two weeks?" He slid into a chair. "Sit. Spill."

"I met him about six weeks ago." I set down my work tote and hung up my coat before joining him at the table. "So it wasn't just two weeks."

"Oh, thank *God*. A whole six weeks. I thought maybe you were rushing into something." Every word dripped with sarcasm. And just in case I didn't get the message, his eyes rolled so far into the back of his head that I worried he'd detach a retina.

"I know, I know. It seems really fast, but you know me, Coz. Have I ever done anything brash or committed to anything without thorough consideration?"

He studied me from the corner of his eyes. "You're the most ridiculously cautious person I know."

"Exactly."

"I'm not sure if that makes it better or worse."

I smiled. "It's all good, babe. I promise." The craziest part was I actually believed it. The world's worst cynic had somehow learned to have faith. Would wonders never cease?

"Well, then. I'm going to need every gritty detail." He leaned back and waved regally for me to proceed.

Grinning right down to my toes, I launched into a doctored version of my whirlwind romance with Oran. I tried to keep things simple—if only because we really did have a lot of work to do but also because it would make things easier to remember later.

After a half hour, Cosmo had heard enough to reluctantly allow me to redirect our conversation to fabrics and design. We spent the next two hours sketching, rummaging through fabrics, and laughing our asses off. Time with Cosmo rejuvenated my soul the way sleep rejuvenated my mind. I'd much rather have had a single Cosmo in my life than a hundred superficial friendships. No question.

We had decided to take a quick snack break when my phone rang. I'd half expected to see Oran's name on the screen, but it was Gloria, to my surprise.

"Hey, Mama G. What's up?"

"Lina! You'll never believe it. Amelie surprised us with a visit home. Maybe you already knew, but I wanted to call and make sure. I know you've missed her as much as I have." Her boisterous excitement was palpable even across the phone. I couldn't make sense of it.

"What do you mean she came home?" If there was any truth to what Oran had told me, the chances of my sister magically reappearing were almost nil. "That can't be right."

"It is, mija. I saw her myself. I know you don't like coming over here, but I'd love to have my two girls together again."

She saw Amelie? Gloria couldn't be deceptive if she tried. If she said she saw Amelie, then she saw her.

My heart forgot how to keep a rhythm, skipping and stuttering until my head spun.

I was scared to believe it was real, but my heart had held tight to a scrap of hope in the unlikely event that I received this very sort of call. Having Mellie back would be the ultimate miracle—practically impossible—yet my heart seized its chance to foster a new wellspring of hope, rejecting all logic to the contrary.

"Yes, I'll come by right now. As quickly as I can."

"Oh, good. I know she'll be delighted to see you, and I'll throw together some cookies. Good thing I got more eggs yesterday!"

I shook my head and smiled. "I'll see you soon, Mama G. Do me a favor, though. Don't mention I'm coming. I don't want to make a big deal of it."

"I won't say nothing to nobody. You know I always keep our talks private."

"Thanks, Gloria."

"Of course, mija. See you soon."

I leaned back in my chair, and my stunned gaze drifted to where Cosmo gaped at me.

"Tell me that was about Amelie. Tell me they found her." He knew she'd gone missing, and I'd done everything I could to find her. He didn't know all the circumstances but didn't need to. He knew what she meant to me. He'd been there through my tears and rage and had helped keep my spirits from falling into complete darkness.

"Gloria said she saw Mellie herself. She wasn't lying. I don't know how, but my sister's come home." I had to fight back a sob that hitched in my lungs.

"No shit." His tone was total disbelief.

"I need to go. I need to go see her." I shot to my feet, then froze. I wasn't used to reporting to anyone, but this was important enough that I needed to tell Oran. I wanted him to know.

He answered on the first ring. "Lina?"

"Hey, I'm sorry to interrupt—"

"You don't ever have to apologize for calling me."

Despite the torrent of emotions, he drew a smile from me. "Okay."

"Now, what's up?"

"Gloria, my old nanny called. She said Amelie came home. She saw her, Oran. Amelie's alive, and I'm going to go see her." Tears blurred my vision. I had to take a slow, deep breath to keep from becoming a blubbering mess.

"Whoa, okay. Let's slow down," he said in a calm yet wary tone.

"I know it seems crazy, but Gloria wouldn't lie to me. She saw Amelie with her own eyes."

"I hear you, and we can definitely go check it out, but we do it together."

"Okay."

"I'm going to come get you. You won't go without me, right?"

"I'll wait for you. I promise."

"Good girl. See you as soon as I can."

"Thanks, Oran," I said softly.

I heard a deep rumble over the line. "My girl's sweet when she's happy. I'll have to remember that."

My teeth grazed over my bottom lip. "Hurry, please."

"And impatient," he grunted. "Sit tight and try to keep a clear head. You know what they say when something seems too good to be true."

"Yeah, I know. I keep trying to tell myself that, but it's hard. I want it so bad."

"I know, baby. I want it for you, too."

"See you in a few."

Oran

# FORTY-TWO

I HAD A BAD FUCKING FEELING ABOUT THIS. I'D SEEN WHAT Wellington's kid was capable of. I knew how slim the chances were that Lina's sister was alive, let alone able to waltz back home like nothing had happened.

Where there was smoke, there was fire.

And the whole goddamn sky was black with soot from where I stood.

However, I understood why Lina needed to go see for herself. If I'd been in her position, I'd have been compelled to check it out, too. There were hardly two more motivating words than *what if*. When that simple phrase was given power by the mind, it could lead a person to incredible accomplishments or crippling devastation. Only time would tell which outcome would come to pass.

I ensured my cousins knew what was up before returning to the warehouse where I'd dropped off Lina. The second I texted to let her know I was outside, she burst through the front entrance and rushed to the car.

The twenty-minute ride over felt like an eternity. Lina practically vibrated with nervous energy, eyes glued out the window and her spine stiff as a board. I considered another cautionary warning, but she was too keyed up. Nothing would settle her except learning the truth, however good or bad that might be.

When we finally arrived, Eliza Brooks greeted us at the door.

"Carolina, this is a surprise. And I see you brought company." She looked me up and down in a way that made me want to take a bath in acid. "Please, come in." She held open the door and stepped aside. "Your father and I were just in the lounge catching up with an unexpected visitor. I imagine you must have heard, or you wouldn't be here."

"*Step*father," Lina corrected her as she led us inside. "Gloria called. Is it true? Is Amelie here?"

"It wasn't her, mija," the tear-filled voice of an older woman called from the other room. "I'm so sorry. I didn't know."

Before I could stop her, Lina shoved past her mother. I followed her into a large sitting room where Charles Brooks sat drinking a martini with an older Latina woman tied to a chair across from him.

"There's the little princess. So good of you to join us," he said dryly.

"What the fuck, Charles?" Lina cried. "Why is Gloria tied up?"

Gloria spoke before he could answer. "I don't understand, Lina. Why did they pretend that girl was Amelie? She looked so much like her, but when I went to her room to give her a hug and saw her up close, I knew." The woman's face was wrought with devastation and confusion.

Lina had to be heartbroken, but she was too busy comforting the older woman to let it show.

"It's okay, Gloria. I knew it probably wasn't her."

"Why, mija? Where's Mellie? What's going on?"

That was when Eliza pulled a gun from her pocket and pointed it at me. "You're a fool. That's what's going on," she said to Gloria, though she kept her eyes trained on me. "You were so damn gullible. You even believed Amelie up and moved to Paris out of the blue."

She stood about five feet away to my left with a small end table between us. Reaching her before she could pull the trigger would have been difficult, and the woman was deranged enough to make charging her too risky.

"What the hell is this about, Eliza?" Lina demanded. "What do you think you're going to accomplish with this? Oran isn't a member of the club anymore. You won already. I'm out of your life."

"If only that were true." Lawrence Wellington seized his moment and joined us with two gun-toting thugs behind him.

So that was the visitor Eliza had referenced. Clever.

I'd been ready to confront Lina's parents, but I hadn't counted on Wellington being present, let alone with reinforcements. This new arrangement left us woefully outnumbered. And when Wellington took the gun from Eliza, the glint of madness in his eyes set me even more on edge.

This was really fucking bad.

"Two for the price of one," he said through a tight smile. "You two did well."

Eliza preened. "Of course, Lawrence. You know we're at your service anytime."

I wondered how many times in a row a person could be choked to death and brought back. Maybe I'd use her to find out.

Wellington strolled over to where Lina still stood next to a sniveling Gloria and placed the barrel of the gun against Lina's head. He then speared me with his stare. "You don't fix what you've done, and I'll redecorate this room with the inside of her head."

Gloria whimpered and launched into what sounded like a prayer in Spanish. I didn't know how, but my little warrior stood perfectly still, nerves of fucking steel. I locked eyes with her, sending every reassurance I could. This situation was my fault, and I would fucking take care of it.

"I don't know what you're talking about, Lawrence."

"Don't play stupid with me," he hissed. "You can turn on any goddamn channel right now and see my face tied to one scandal or another."

I lifted my hands placatingly. "I get that, but I'm not sure why you think it's my fault."

He lashed out and slammed the butt of the gun against Lina's head. She crumpled to the floor unconscious. It took all my self-control not to roar with fury. But while I might not have made a sound, my entire body quaked with the need. Murderous rage was written all over me, from my clenched fists to the daggers in my glare.

"You want to blame someone for your failures, but I'm not the one who let my son rape and torture women. I'm not the one evading taxes and working with traffickers. I could understand if investors wanted nothing to do with you, and there's only one person responsible for that situation." I would have told the bastard anything he wanted to hear if it kept Lina safe, but the man had to know there was no getting the milk back in the jar once it was spilled.

I slowly eased myself farther into the room, drawing the two thugs with me as I moved closer to Wellington.

"Check him for weapons." Wellington snapped at the men behind me, turning his gun on me.

I exhaled harshly as they began to pat me down, removing the handgun holstered under my jacket. The same gun Lina had held on me two days earlier, only now it was fully loaded. I'd hoped he was enough of an amateur not to think to check me for weapons.

He might have been shady as fuck, but he wasn't the type to get his hands dirty. Pulling strings behind a desk was totally different from pulling a trigger. And if he hadn't been properly motivated, I would have doubted his ability to follow through. Insanity was a highly effective source of motivation. No threat from Wellington was idle at this point.

"Tell me how I can help you," I offered, trying to defuse the situation. As I spoke, I noted movement at Lawrence's feet, but I refrained from looking down. I prayed Lawrence didn't notice that Lina was waking up.

The muscles in his face quivered with rage as he snarled at me. "No, you're right. The only thing you can do for me now is to *die*."

"That's not true, Lawrence—" I never got to finish.

Two gunshots erupted in the air around us, quickly followed by lancing pain.

Lina

# FORTY-THREE

THE PAIN STREAKING THROUGH MY SKULL HAD ME WINCING before I'd even opened my eyes. Why the hell did my head hurt so bad? And was I on the floor?

Voices filtered in through my confusion. When I peeked above me and saw Lawrence Wellington holding a gun, everything came crashing back to me—Gloria's call, the fake Amelie, a gun being pressed to my temple.

Terror engulfed me.

But before I could panic about what to do, an explosion of sound lanced through my head. The pain was so intense, I had no choice but to scrunch my eyes shut and clamp my hands tight over my ears.

Gunshots. Glass breaking. Screams.

Wellington had been pointing his gun at Oran. Shots were fired.

Wellington shot Oran.

As my sluggish brain caught up, I pried open my eyes with a cry and searched the ground where I expected to find Oran bleeding on the floor, only he wasn't there. I scanned the area frantically to find Wellington's two bodyguards motionless on the wood floor. Above me, Oran now held Wellington's gun, waving it as he ordered the older man away from me.

I had no idea how it had all happened until Conner and another blue-eyed man walked in from the entry. Oran's family. They were here. They'd saved us.

"Stay put, baby. Just give me a sec." Oran was talking to me. I hadn't even realized I'd started to try to stand, still too dazed and overcome with emotions to think straight. "Conner, you take over here," Oran called, his voice sounding like he was talking from another room despite being right next to me.

Then Oran was helping me up, his arm supporting my back. "We have to hurry, Lina. The neighbors will have reported those shots, and the cops will be here soon."

I nodded and did my best to steady myself.

"What about these two?" the other blue-eyed man asked.

Oran and I looked at Charles and Eliza, who stood cowering next to one another.

"We need to move quickly, and two of them plus Wellington will slow us down." Oran lifted his gun and shot Charles in the head.

Eliza screamed, then turned her pleading stare to me, terrified she was next. As if I would ever have sympathy for her.

Oran's laugh was mercilessly cold. "No bullet for you,

Eliza. I have something much better in mind for you." He looked at the man I hadn't met. "Keir, one of you bring any tape?"

"Didn't have time, but they've got zip ties over here." He picked up a pile of white plastic ties and began to secure Wellington, then Eliza, who both looked at Charles's motionless body before reluctantly offering their hands in surrender.

"People will look for me, you know," Wellington snapped. "A man like myself can't just disappear without consequence."

"Well, fuck me," Oran said wryly. "He *does* understand the concept of consequences. He just doesn't think they apply to him. I've got news for you, Larry. I'm ready to accept the consequences of my actions. Are you?"

Wellington's nostrils flared before he made to charge at Oran.

The man named Keir caught him, swung him around, and decked him with a fist to the face in a matter of two seconds flat. Wellington crashed to the floor unconscious.

"Don't have time for this shit," Keir muttered as he bent over and lifted Wellington over his shoulder in a fireman's hold.

Oran nodded toward the front door, wincing from the movement. "Which one of you fuckers shot me?"

"It was just a graze. You were in the way," Conner grumbled.

I froze mid-step. "You've been shot?" I blurted.

"It's superficial—nothing to worry about. Just hurts like a bitch." He kept us moving, shooting a look at Conner. "I got them into the middle of the room for you. Least you could to was aim."

"Whatever, pussy."

Oran smirked, his teasing banter doing wonders to calm me. "Who's got a knife?" he asked when we neared Gloria.

Keir tossed him a switchblade, which he used to free Gloria from her chair. "Everything's going to be okay," Oran assured Gloria. "Lina will hook up with you later to answer your questions. When the police arrive, you can tell them you were in the kitchen and didn't see anything. All you know is that shots were fired, and when you came running, your boss and these other men were dead."

Gloria nodded, eyes seeking mine for confirmation. I wrapped my arms around her in a crushing hug. "I'll explain everything later, Mama G. Promise."

"Si, mija. Be careful."

"I will. Text me when you get home."

Gloria nodded.

Oran guided me toward the door with his arm around my back. "No more time, Lina. We have to go."

"Love you, Mama G," I called, blowing her a kiss.

Sirens began to wail in the distance, but we were gone before they were in sight.

# FORTY-FOUR

I HAD LINA GO WITH CONNER AND ELIZA TO HIS PLACE WHILE Keir and I took Wellington with us. Keir had history with the Wellingtons and practically demanded to be in on whatever came next. I appreciated his enthusiasm.

We debated the plan as we drove. Keir suggested we take Wellington to his house and chain him in the attic. I was a fan of the irony and liked it for the long term, but I needed information *now*. I wanted to give Lina closure regarding her sister.

In the end, we decided to take him to Bastion because it was closest. The old meat packing plant we sometimes used for this sort of thing was too damn far away. Wellington was quiet in the trunk for now, but who knew when he'd wake.

We parked out front and got him inside quickly. He roused on the way in but was still groggy, making it somewhat easier to get him down the basement steps to the multipurpose room that sometimes stored supplies, sometimes people.

"Don't know what you plan to accomplish with this," Wellington spat as we secured him to the small metal chair in the center of the room, fear clearing away the last of the cobwebs. "You've already taken everything from me."

I squatted in front of him like I was talking to a child. "We need a little information from you."

"Go to the press and tell them it was all a campaign of lies and fake news—I'll tell you anything you want to know." His fleeting grasp on reality was almost comical.

I shook my head with a humorless laugh. "That's not how this works, big guy." I patted his knee condescendingly. "But it was a nice try."

"I'm not telling you anything unless I get something in return. Hurt me all you want."

*Says the man who has clearly never suffered a minute in his life.*

"Happy to oblige." Keir swept in and bent Wellington's pinky finger with a crunch until it extended straight out to the side.

The animalistic wail that Wellington let loose hurt my damn ears. "Okay, okay. No more. I'll tell you anything, please." Pathetic blubbering—that was the only way to describe his pitiful begging. I had to stand and turn away before I put a bullet in his skull just to end my own suffering.

"Well, that was anticlimactic," Keir grumbled. "You sure you don't want to hold out a little longer?"

"No, no. I'll talk, just please. Put my pinky back. It hurts so bad." He devolved into a fit of tears.

*Jesus fucking Christ.*

I'd seen ten-year-old kids with more balls than this fuck-wad. I'd suspected he'd fold quickly, but this was pathetic.

"Back in early August, an unconscious girl was dropped off at your house."

Wellington's head snapped up. "Ha! I knew it." He laughed, a touch of madness setting in. "I knew from the minute I saw her that she'd be trouble."

"Why's that?"

"Drugged women don't just appear at random," he scoffed. "My son begged me to let him keep her, but I refused. She wasn't just some whore taken off the streets. There was no telling who she was connected to."

"You had no idea who she was?"

"No! I—" He stilled, gaze darting between me and Keir. "Why? Who was she?"

"Irrelevant at this juncture. What happened to her?"

He eyed me curiously. Keir paced around to the other side of Wellington and peered down at the man's one remaining functional pinky.

"I took her to the hospital," Wellington blurted in a rush. "I didn't know what else to do with her. She'd had some sort of reaction to whatever drugs she'd taken or been given, and there was a concussion—I don't know. She ended up in a coma for two fucking months."

I could hardly believe what I was hearing. Darina had been alive. I'd been so convinced Wellington's twisted offspring had gotten his hands on her and killed her that I never entertained the possibility of other options. Occam's Razor wasn't always right—the simplest explanation wasn't always the correct one.

"You say she was in a coma for two months. Did she wake up at that point?"

"She did. She woke up and had no fucking clue who she was, so I *still* wasn't able to escape her."

"Did you go to the cops?"

He sneered. "I'm sure the hospital covered that since she was a Jane Doe. No need for me to stir up a hornet's nest of rumors. You know how absurd the media can be."

"You didn't help to find her family at all?"

"I've been supporting the damn girl for months—paying her hospital bill and everything—isn't that enough? I knew if I didn't, it would come back to bite me. And *look*. That's exactly what happened." He spit on the concrete floor. "That's all I've ever done is damage control for that worthless piece of shit son of mine." He looked at Keir, snot running down his face. "You did me a favor by killing him, you know that? I know it was you. I don't care how much you deny it. Don't care that he's gone, either. He was a fucking *liability*."

Some people had issues. Some were a little damaged. Lawrence Wellington was fucking broken. He was missing an essential component of basic humanity. That was the only way to explain it.

How ironic that his inability to empathize was likely the very reason his son had turned out psychotic. And Wellington would never be able to see that he was the cause of his greatest disappointment.

None of that was surprising, considering his lack of self-awareness. However, I was shocked shitless that Amalie was theoretically alive and somewhere in the city. I wasn't going to fully believe it until I saw her with my own goddamn eyes.

"What's the address?"

"Let me go, and I'll take you there."

*Jesus, he was delusional.*

A merciless laugh rumbled deep in my chest. "Haven't

you caught on at this point? You're in no position to bargain —you're completely powerless. Period."

I cranked his other pinky to the side so that he had a matching set.

"*FUCKING CHRIST!*" His scream reverberated off the walls. "It-it-it's on 170th Street, Jamaica Hills, 89-12 170th, apartment 5B."

"That's Queens."

"Yeah, cheapest option I could find on short notice." He shook his head and started to sob. "Why don't you just kill me. That's what you want, isn't it?"

I squatted back beside him and patted my hand on his forearm. "No, Lawrence," I said softly. "I don't want you dead. I want you to suffer."

The man wept like a baby.

I stood. "We're heading out now, but someone will be back for you tomorrow."

"What? What do you mean you're leaving? What if I have to piss? And I'll need water at the very least."

Keir and I walked away, closing the door behind us. "He sure is a stupid fucker. No idea how he got so damn rich."

"Luck."

"Has to be."

We walked up the stairs to the ground floor, bolted the basement door, then returned to the car.

"Want me to drop you somewhere? I'm not telling Lina anything until I've seen her sister with my own eyes, so I'm headed to Queens."

"I'll ride with," said Keir. "I'm invested at this point." Aside from his personal vendetta with Wellington, he and our cousin Torin ran Moxy. Those two had known Darina better than I had. They'd both been shaken when we learned Caitlin had taken the girl and would love to know she'd survived.

"Works for me."

It took us over an hour to get from Manhattan to the far side of Queens. Fucking traffic. I could have walked faster. Eventually, we pulled up at the address Wellington had given us. The place was old—built in the seventies from the looks of it, but everything looked more shabby in the dark. The winter sun had set on our trip over, leaving only a soft turquoise glow in the sky.

"What's your plan here?" Keir asked.

"Fuck if I know." It might scare her to death if two strange men show up at her door, but I didn't want to end up sitting in the car for hours either. "Let's give it an hour. If we don't see her, we'll go knock."

"Got it." He tapped his phone. "Four forty-five now."

I sighed and dropped my head back on the headrest. Waiting was not my forte. Thank God we only had to sit for thirty minutes before we both bolted upright at the sight of a young brunette exiting the building.

"Tell me you see her, too," I breathed.

"Fuck yeah, I do. Jesus fucking Christ." His words sounded as shocked as I felt.

The girl we'd both known as Darina stuffed her hands in her coat pockets and started down the sidewalk, walking in our direction. We had a perfect view of her. There was no doubt.

I had said it would be a miracle if Lina's sister was alive.

It looked like miracles *did* happen.

Lina

# FORTY-FIVE

Noemi did her best to distract me—her efforts were truly heroic—but I couldn't stop worrying about Oran. I wasn't even sure what the hell I was so worried about. Wellington had been restrained and unconscious last I saw him. He didn't exactly pose a realistic threat, yet I couldn't shake the unease. It was like walking through a cobweb; no matter how well you swiped at the invisible strands, more took their place.

Eliza's looming presence likely didn't help. Conner had stashed her in a spare bedroom, but the woman was like a bad case of herpes—it was hard to forget she was there.

I was curious what the guys would do with her. Or maybe I wasn't. Maybe I didn't want to know.

"You think you can eat anything?" Noemi asked. "Conner is going to order something to be delivered. We can grab whatever sounds good to you."

"Now that you mention it, I haven't really eaten since breakfast."

A smile lit her face. "You tell me what you want, and I'll make it happen."

"Just something simple. Maybe ramen?"

"Oh, good choice! Conner loves the fried pork dish at Yanagi. Will that work?"

"Yeah, just have him get me the shoyu ramen." It was practically the same as chicken noodle soup—one of my favorite comfort foods.

Her thumbs went crazy typing out a text, and a knock sounded at the front door not thirty minutes later. Only it wasn't dinner, it was Oran. Seeing him alive and well made me feel like I could breathe for the first time in hours. I leaped from the sofa and gave him a full-body-slam hug.

"I'm so glad you're back." I relaxed my grip on him enough to look him over, only to see the dried blood on his shoulder and remember the poor man had been shot. "Oh my God. I'm *so* sorry! Did I hurt you?"

His arm tightened around my waist as he pulled me back against him. "I will be once you kiss me." His voice was as dark and decadent as pure melted chocolate.

I brought my hands to the back of his neck and pulled his lips to mine in a slow, sultry kiss.

"Mmm … that's more like it."

I felt his guttural rumble deep in my belly where a pool of desire warmed my insides. "Everything go okay?" I asked with a shy smile.

"It did, but I need to talk to you in private."

*Goodbye chill, hello nerves.*

"Yeah, okay." I nodded, my palms instantly starting to sweat.

He led me back to Conner's office and closed the door behind us. Meanwhile, my brain raced to predict every horrible scenario possible to help prepare myself.

"Is Wellington dead?"

*Jesus, Lina. Maybe at least try to be a tiny bit discreet?*

I cringed. "Sorry, I mean…"

Oran placed his hand over my lips. "No, he's not. And he might not be for a while, but there's no reason to worry about him. Okay?"

"What about my mother?" As much as I wished she didn't even enter my thoughts, she did.

"I suppose that's up to you. I could kill her, torture her, or drop her naked and alone in Afghanistan and let karma do its job."

So blunt wasn't an issue. Got it.

I shook off my shock and thought for a minute. While I didn't want Eliza in my life, I wasn't sure I could order her death or be responsible for inhumane suffering.

*You could always leave it up to him and turn a blind eye.*

I could, or I could follow Oran's lead and teach my mother a lesson she'd feel down to her bones. "The things you did to Lawrence—can you do that to her? Take her money and status?"

His smile was borderline unhinged. "With her in our possession for signatures and voice recordings, we could do just about anything."

I nodded resolutely. "Give it all to charity. I want Eliza stripped of every penny she's ever owned."

Hand fisted in my hair, he planted a kiss on my lips that I felt blossom deep in my heart. "God, it's sexy when you're vindictive."

"Not vindictive," I informed him haughtily. "It's karma, just like you said. Only, we're helping it along."

"Call it what you want. It still makes me want to fuck you raw."

Holy crap, did it suddenly get hot in here?

"I like your line of thinking, but I have concerns."

"Like what?" I asked, fighting back the lust-fueled haze in my brain.

"An enemy taken to their lowest can be the absolute deadliest. If a person thinks they have nothing to lose, they become infinitely more dangerous. If we strip Eliza of everything she has, including her pride, she'll suffer, but she'll also become a possible threat. I don't want to have to live every day worrying that woman will try to get revenge."

Hell, he was right.

If anyone was malicious enough to come after me for bankrupting them, it would be my mother. The loathing and fury would drive her insane—more than she was already. What options did that leave for me? She had to be punished, and I didn't want her to have the freedom to hurt anyone else.

I met Oran's sober stare and nodded. "Just get rid of her." Some souls were beyond redemption. I was ready for it to be over.

His lips touched mine again, but this time with exquisite tenderness. His kiss lifted away the thin veil of grief that tried to wrap around my shoulders. If only signing away her life was as effortless for me as it had been for her to sign away my innocence, but that wasn't the case. I supposed I was glad. I didn't want to be her breed of monster.

I smiled softly. "That everything?"

Oran leveled me with a sober stare. I was instantly back

on alert. My poor nervous system would need some serious time off when this was all said and done.

"I have something to tell you, but I need you to stay calm."

I gaped at him. "That's probably the absolute worst thing you could say to a person to keep them calm."

"Just shut up and listen, will you?"

I arched a brow in warning. He ignored me.

"Wellington told me what happened to Amelie."

My heart plummeted into my feet, along with all the blood in my body.

Seeing my reaction, Oran held up his hand. "Now, I told you to stay calm and hear me out, so let me finish before you freak out."

I had half a mind to tell him where he could stick it, but his next words left me speechless.

"Amelie's alive and well here in the city. I saw her myself. She was drugged when she was taken and ended up having a reaction. She was in a coma, and when she woke up, she had amnesia. Wellington was worried she could be a liability, so he put her up in an apartment."

Oh God. Not again.

I couldn't let myself have hope again, then see it dashed away.

My head shook in jerky motions. "No. It can't be. I can't do this again."

Oran cupped my face on either side and locked his gaze with mine, demanding my attention. "Shh, listen, Lina baby. I saw her myself. It's not a trick or a mistake. The girl I knew as Darina is alive and living in Queens."

I didn't shed a tear or cry.

I rocketed straight past both to spontaneous body-heaving breathless sobs, the ugly kind that leave you snot-covered and hoarse. Oran didn't say a word. He just held me as the wrecking ball of emotions ran its course.

Amelie was alive, really truly alive.

*This was what you prayed for—the girl who doesn't pray—stop sniveling and go get her!*

I wiped at my tears, a maniacal laugh bubbling past my lips. "Oh my God. Okay. Try to forget you saw that."

"No reason to be embarrassed about crying." He gave me a pointed look and waited until I nodded my acknowledgment. "As for your sister, you need to keep in mind that she may not recover her memories. I saw her, but I didn't talk to her. I have no idea about her mental condition."

"I don't care. I'm just so relieved she's alive."

He nodded. "Before we go back out there, you need to decide whether you want your mother to know."

I froze, eyes going wide. "I have no idea."

"Then let's not say anything for now. No reason for her to know."

I nodded, so relieved to have someone helping me for once.

"I know you probably want to see her right away, but she was leaving her apartment when I saw her, so she might still be out. Plus, it takes an hour to get over there, and two strangers showing up at her door at night might freak her out. I think it would be best to wait until morning."

"Okay." I frowned. What he said made sense, but I felt like I'd already waited so long. Another twelve hours sounded like an eternity.

We went back out to the living room, where Oran had a quiet word with Conner.

I rushed over to Noemi, tears flooding my eyes again. "My sister is alive. He's taking me to her in the morning. I can't even believe it, but Oran says it's true."

"Oh, honey. I'm so happy for you!" She wrapped me in a hug.

"Don't tell Eliza, though."

Noemi zipped her lips. "I wasn't planning on going in there at all."

"You ready, Lina?" Oran called.

I was *so* ready. I jumped up and followed him out, calling goodbye to Conner and Noemi.

He shot me a glance. "No questions or last-minute instructions?"

"Nah. I trust you." A smitten grin danced across my face.

Oran pulled me to his side and kissed my forehead. "Goddamn, it wasn't a fluke. My girl *is* sweet when she's happy."

I elbowed him in the gut.

"And feisty and impatient and sexy as hell," he added playfully.

"Don't you forget it."

"Wouldn't dream of it." He wove his fingers in mine, and I swore my heart went full-on Grinch and tripled in size.

I didn't get my ramen, but Oran picked up a pizza for us on the way home. I never did have to occupy myself that evening. As it turned out, when you were engaged to a sexy Irish gangster, killing time wasn't a problem. I was out like a light, naked and sated, not long after dinner. I didn't even stir until morning.

♦

*Please don't vomit. Please don't vomit. Please don't vomit.*

Saying I was nervous was like calling Mt. Everest a lovely little hill. I'd spilled my coffee at breakfast, stubbed my toe getting dressed, then forgot my purse when we left the house.

I didn't even remember the damn thing until we were half an hour into the ride.

Oran said he'd seen Amelie, but I couldn't help worry that it wasn't really her. And even if it was her, what if she didn't remember me? What on earth was I supposed to say?

Every minute that passed brought my meager breakfast closer to finding its way back up and out. By the time we stood at her door, there was a real chance I would pass out.

But then the door opened, and there she was. Amelie.

My mouth opened, but nothing came out. I had to rub at my stupid eyes when tears obstructed my view of her. Her head tilted to the side as she peered at Oran over my shoulder, then back to me, this time studying me closely.

"Do I ... know you?"

I nodded, a sob hitching in my lungs.

Oran put his arm around me. "Amelie, this is Lina, your sister. She's been looking for you since you disappeared. And my name is Oran. You used to work in a bar called Moxy—a bar my family owns."

She staggered backward a step, her trembling hands lifting to her mouth. "Lina?" she gasped, terrified eyes darting from me to Oran. The emotions flooding her eyes gutted me—so much fear and uncertainty—but the relief got me more than anything. She was desperately relieved to be found.

My sister's face crumpled as she leaned against the wall and let the storm of emotions overcome her. I lunged forward but stopped short of hugging her, choosing to lay my hand on her shoulder instead so as not to frighten her. The urge to scoop her up and whisk her back home was maddening, but I didn't want to overwhelm her. I wasn't even sure she remembered me.

"It's okay, Amelie. I'm here now. You're going to be okay."

She lifted her teary gaze to mine, bottom lip quivering. "Mellie. I'm Mellie," she breathed.

She remembered. Oh thank *God*. She remembered.

We fell into each other's arms, a knotted mess of sobs and elation.

Oran ushered us the rest of the way inside and closed the door behind us. We barely took notice, crying and holding one another for long moments.

Once we were able to breathe again, I pulled back just enough to see her beautiful face and wiped at her tears. "I missed you so much. I'm so incredibly sorry."

"What happened to me, Lina? These past six weeks since I woke up at the hospital have been so terrifying. How did I end up there?"

"I can't even imagine what that was like for you. I'm just so sorry."

"You don't have to keep apologizing. It wasn't your fault." That was my sweet Mellie. She didn't know what had happened, but she'd never voluntarily believe I was to blame.

"The story is complicated, more than I want to unload right this minute, but I'll tell you everything soon enough," I offered reassuringly, then paused, biting my lower lip. "What all do you remember?"

A shadow darkened her features, and her gaze dropped to her hands. "I think I remember most everything except for how I ended up in the hospital. I remember coming to you for help and us getting our apartment." She brought her eyes back to mine. "I remember working at Moxy and planning to see you for Friday dinner … and then … everything just goes … dark. Was it Mom?" she asked in a terrified whisper. "Did she find me?"

"No, Mellie." I shook my head and gave her a quick hug. "It wasn't them. It was a crazy coincidence, but everything's worked out just fine." I smiled warmly. "You're alive and well, and we're together again. That's all that matters."

She peered over my shoulder to the small apartment behind me. "I suppose I can let Lawrence know that I'm going home. I want to thank him for everything he did. I don't know where I would have gone if he hadn't helped me."

My eyes cut to Oran's. We would have to explain things to her, but not yet. Today was all about happy reunions. Reality could wait.

When Amelie turned back to us, her gaze snagged on Oran. "Lina, why is Mr. Byrne here? Did he help you track me down?" She looked so adorably confused that a fit of laughter overtook me. I could only imagine how strange it was to have one of her bosses show up at my side.

"Things have been a bit crazy since you disappeared. Oran and I sort of … got together. And now…" I held up my hand to show her the ring.

Her eyes bulged. "You're engaged … to my *boss*?"

"I wasn't technically your boss." Oran smirked.

"You're one of the owners, right?"

"Yeah."

"Kay, then. You're my boss. Or … you were. I suppose I lost my job when I never showed up." She grimaced.

"No need to worry, kiddo," Oran offered softly. "Having a job isn't an issue anymore."

Mellie looked back at me. I just smiled.

"How do you feel about staying the night at our place? I'm not ready to give you up yet." I hadn't thought to discuss it on the way over, so I hoped Oran didn't mind. There was no way Amelie was leaving my sight. Not yet. I would have checked us into a hotel if need be.

"By *our* place, you mean…?"

"Oran's apartment. I sort of … moved in with him while you were gone." God, it sounded crazy when I said it out loud.

"Oh…" Her brows arched high.

"I know, it's a lot to take in. We have plenty of time to sort through it all, okay?"

She nodded. "Let me grab a few things, and I'll be good to go."

We spent the rest of the day together. She called in and quit the job she'd been working at a greasy diner. I snuggled her close to me on the couch and kept a steady stream of chick flicks on the TV, though we spent most of the time talking. Oran gave us space, popping in to bring us food on occasion.

I would have preferred to wait for explanations and just enjoy each other, but Amelie insisted on knowing everything that had happened. I held her as she cried over Eliza and Charles. She'd grieved for them when she first ran away and learned the truth, but regaining her memories was like hearing it all again for the first time. My heart broke for her.

We covered topics large and small, including my relationship with Oran.

"Wait, isn't he married?" She bit her lip and glanced at my ring.

"Not long after you disappeared, he filed for divorce. It's … complicated."

"So did you meet while you were searching for me?"

My eyes trail away. "Sort of. That's also complicated."

She stared at me expectantly, so I launched into the tale. I had my Mellie back, and I wouldn't keep anything from her ever again.

"He *blackmailed* you into an *engagement*?" she cried.

I bit back a laugh. She had a right to be outraged, but I still found it funny.

"Romantic, right?" I teased.

"OMG. You're crazy."

I shrugged. "You're not wrong."

My lopsided smile drew out one of her own. "I missed you so much."

"I'm so glad to be back." She dropped her gaze. "Being alone was scary."

"I bet."

"It was like my entire life was just out of my reach. The only thing I knew was that I loved to dance. I danced every day, hoping it might help me remember. It was the only thing that brought me any comfort. In that regard, I was still me, whether I knew it or not."

"I'm super proud of you, Mellie. It's been one hell of a year, and you survived."

"Yeah, I suppose it has been."

"Well, things are going to be different going forward. I've learned how important it is to have my priorities in order, and *you* are my top priority. You aren't alone anymore. Never again."

Her eyes grew glassy, and her chin quivered. "Love you, Lina."

"Love you most, Mellie."

# FORTY-SIX

THE CHANGE IN LINA SINCE REUNITING WITH HER SISTER WAS astounding—like a stained glass window that couldn't show its colors until the sun shone through. She was playful and quirky in ways that made me want to get her naked. The cautious, determined woman I first met was still present but in a much softer, contented sense.

Seeing her with her sister was one of the most rewarding things I'd ever experienced. It was my new addiction. I wanted to find every way possible to bring that light into her eyes. More than anything, I wanted to know that every facet of that vibrant beauty was *mine*.

Not only was that legally impossible while I was still married, but every minute Lina wore my ring while Caitlin still shared my name felt like an unforgivable slight. I knew Lina didn't feel that way. She was incredibly understanding, but it bugged the hell outta me. I hated any implication that Lina was the other woman, even if only in my own head. I didn't care if everyone knew that Caitlin was in prison. I didn't want to chance disrespecting Lina in any way.

When I thought about it all, I realized that punishing Caitlin wasn't nearly as important as Lina.

I'd thought I wanted Caitlin to take the blame for her brother's death because it was a better punishment than death, but now, I just wanted her gone. She wasn't worth even the smallest nugget of my attention. And by keeping her around, I punished myself along with her.

I wasn't the masochistic type.

I grabbed my phone and placed a call to a number I'd labeled as Houdini. That wasn't his name. I'd never been given his actual name or even a nickname. Houdini had been the moniker I'd chosen for him because the man was fucking brilliant at making things disappear, whether problems or people. He was a fixer—an invaluable connection in my world.

I dialed the number. No one answered, but that was expected. Two minutes later, I received a call from an unknown number. That was how he did business. No direct contact. No names. No mistakes. Even his voice was electronically masked. I could have walked past the man on the street and had no clue who he was.

"Hello," I answered quietly. Lina and her sister were in the living room, well away from where I sat in my office, but I still wanted to be discreet.

"You called." Not a question. A demand. Get to the point.

"That black widow problem I had?"

"You want another capture and release?" Did I want Caitlin back in isolation? No.

"Extermination."

"Not an easy house to fumigate. Price is double."

"Invoice me."

The line went dead. I wasn't entirely sure why, but it seemed to take an especially strange sort of fucker to do that type of job. I'd never heard of one who wasn't maddeningly cryptic or eccentric. Usually both.

I slipped my phone back in my pocket and released a heavy sigh of relief. It was done. The call was made, and the deed would be soon to follow. I was almost free.

Fuck, it felt good.

I downed the last of the whiskey I'd poured myself earlier. It was time to call it a day. I was exhausted. The girls were still curled up on the sofa in the living room. I approached from behind them, placing a kiss on Lina's forehead.

"You two need anything before I head to bed? I'm beat."

"I'll come with you," Lina offered.

"You don't have to. I didn't mean to cut your night short."

"No, we were just talking about doing the same." She and her sister stood, Lina giving Amelie a hug. "You all good for the night?"

"Absolutely. You guys sleep well." She gave me a wave and trotted off toward the guest room she'd chosen for herself.

I rested my arm around Lina's shoulders and got out my phone with my other hand to set the living room lights on night mode. "I feel such an odd mix of exhausted and wired."

"It's been a crazy couple of weeks. That takes a toll even when the outcome is good." She didn't say anything more, and while we got ready for bed in the master bathroom, I couldn't shake the feeling that something was off.

"Things with Mellie okay?" I asked, watching her closely in the mirror as she removed her makeup.

"Yeah. It's incredible to have her back, but I guess I'm a little anxious about separating from her."

"Separating?"

"She's definitely not going back to live in the apartment Wellington provided, and we still have the place I originally leased for us, but it's awfully far away from here. She's only just turned eighteen, and after everything else … I just want her close," she concluded in a soft, sorrowful tone. Her eyes cut briefly to mine as though she were worried about my reaction.

"Already been working on it, babe."

She whipped around to face me, one eye smeared with half-removed mascara. "You have?"

"Yeah. I made a call earlier today. You have two options, and I'm equally good with both. Amelie can stay right where she is in our place until she's ready to go out on her own, or there's a one-bedroom down on the third floor that recently opened up. She'd be in the same building but have some independence. They're holding it for me, but if you'd rather have her here, it's no problem."

It didn't take a rocket scientist to figure out Lina would want easy access to her baby sister, and the girl was still awfully young. The situation was easy enough to fix.

Wide blue eyes stared at me before she jumped into my arms in a full-body hug, legs locked behind my back like a little monkey. "Thank you so much, Oran. I don't even know what to say."

I huffed with a laugh, my hands kneading at her ass cheeks. "First, you could tell me which option you prefer."

She pulled back, arms draped casually over my shoulders.

"I'll have to talk with her. I want her to have a say, and I think I'm comfortable with either."

"Works for me." I set her feet down on the cool marble floor and took the cleansing wipe from her hand. "We need to get this off you. Makes it look like you've been crying."

"You don't like it when I cry?" she asked softly, closing her eyes to let me wipe away the black smudges.

"Unless they're tears of ecstasy, you crying means I haven't done my job."

Her fingers trailed a path down my chest as a shy smile teased at her lips. "Sometimes things happen that you have no control over."

"Doesn't mean I won't take responsibility." I placed a kiss on one eyelid, then the other. "I take care of what's mine, little warrior."

Opening those blue eyes, bright as a summer sky, she peered up at me through her lashes. "And what if I want to take care of what's mine?" Slowly, she lowered to her knees.

My dick went hard so fast my head spun.

"I'm not one to argue."

She smirked and pulled down the waistband of my boxer briefs, freeing my cock. The damn thing looked like it was straining to reach for her, thick veins bulging with need. Lina bent to angle herself beneath him, looked up at me hungrily, then licked me firmly from base to tip.

My entire body trembled.

"You tryin' to kill me, woman?"

"Trying to make you feel good." She sucked the head into her mouth and circled her tongue around the tip.

I hissed. "Death by exploding dick. I suppose there are worse ways to go." I could barely get the words out as she eagerly sucked me down to the back of her throat.

There was real concern that at the very least I was going to come so hard my dick would break. Black spots dotted my vision. My blood pressure was probably low enough to convince most doctors I was technically already dead.

*If I die like this, it will have been worth it.*

I only allowed Lina to continue for another minute before I pulled her to her feet by her armpits and stripped her naked.

"That's better," I grumbled, then led her to the bed. "Lie on your back, head tipped back here over the edge of the bed."

I waited for her to get in position, then took her vibrator out of my nightstand.

"Hey, I was wondering what happened to that!"

"Now you know," I murmured distractedly, handing her the device. "Show me how you make yourself come."

I stood over her, watching hungrily as she inserted the toy inside herself, so wet already that she didn't even need lube. The device was a short J-shaped vibrator made of soft silicon with a butterfly on the short end. The wings, antennae, and other translucent silicon bits were meant to stimulate the outer clit while the other end worked her from the inside.

Once she had it situated how she wanted it, she pressed her thighs together, looked up at me, and parted her lips. I slid my cock against her cheek, the nearness of her velvet tongue an excruciating tease.

"Aren't you going to turn it on?" I asked, greedy to see her body writhe.

"The way I feel right now? I'll come too fast. I'm giving you a chance to keep up." She grinned mischievously.

"Even if I'm fucking your face at the same time?"

Her chest expanded, and eyes dilated a fraction. "Especially then."

"Show me." The words rumbled from deep in my chest where primal urges steadfastly refused to evolve.

She parted her lips, and I surged inside her mouth, the heavenly warmth making my spine tingle.

"Jesus, *fuck*, that's perfect."

Lina licked and sucked, taking me deep into her throat and following my lead with ease. When she finally turned on her toy and released a guttural moan, I had to fight savagely against the urge to come. I'd be damned if I let this end too quickly. I needed more time to watch her gyrate her hips forward and back, riding the toy. When her hands came up and began pinching her nipples, I thought I was a goner.

I sped up, gliding the head of my cock back and forth past her lips to lavish attention on the sensitive ridge. Lina reached back, gripping the base of my shaft with one hand and tugging on my balls with the other.

"I hope … you're good to swallow, baby," I strained to say. "'Cause you're about … to suck me dry."

My words seemed to coax her closer to release, her chest arching up with a moan. Her fist gripped me tighter, and her abs flexed. She was coming, and fuck was it beautiful. Her entire body quivered and quaked below me.

"*Fuuuuck.*" I surged one last time deep into her mouth, my body nearly seizing at the feel of her throat swallowing repeatedly, squeezing my sensitive tip.

Her hands released me and fumbled to turn off the device between her legs, though she continued to gently rock herself. We both languished in the lingering pleasure that pulsed through our bodies. I pulled free of her mouth as soon as I'd blown my load to give her a chance to breathe. I lowered to my knees and rested my forehead against hers as we recovered.

"That has to be the fucking sexiest thing I've ever seen," I told her.

"The view wasn't so bad from my perspective either."

I pulled back to look at her, hearing the smile in her words.

"I'm pretty sure my hairy taint doesn't even compare to those perfect tits of yours, not to mention the sight of that bright pink toy peeking out all naughty-like from between your thighs."

"I wasn't looking at your *taint*," she shot back playfully, smacking my arm.

"Smart. I can't imagine it's pretty."

Lina laughed. "Oran?"

"Yeah?"

"I don't think I can get up. I'm too tired."

"Then don't."

"I need to go clean this off." She held up the toy.

I stood and took it from her. "You stay there."

She shot me a thumbs-up, making me smirk. I cleaned off the vibrator, then wiped down my dick before wetting a washcloth with warm water.

"Spread," I instructed.

Her teeth grazed hungrily over her bottom lip as she complied.

"Don't look at me like that, or we'll never get any sleep." I gently cleaned between her thighs, ignoring the way my dick tried to perk up with interest. The damn thing didn't know when to quit. One more bout with her and he was liable to fall off. "You go ahead and get under the covers. I'm going to toss this."

"I'm not sure where my shirt and panties went."

"Good. You get cold, you stay close to me," I called over my shoulder.

"You're kind of a brute, you know that?" she teased.

I walked back to the bedroom and bent over her, slanting my lips over hers in an ardent, poignant kiss. "Only for you, baby. Only for you." I turned off the light and joined her in bed, pulling her snugly against me.

"Oran?" she asked again, this time more hesitantly, her voice barely a whisper.

"Yeah?" I murmured sleepily, breathing in the sweet scent of her hair.

"I love you."

The words hung in the air, stopping time and my heart along with it. I felt like a kid who'd caught a soapy swirling bubble on the tip of my finger, afraid the slightest breeze might cause it to burst. Elation brighter than pure sunshine filled my chest.

"I love you, too, Lina. More than you could ever comprehend." I rolled her onto her back and propped myself on my elbow so that I could kiss her with all the ardent devotion brimming inside me. I wanted her to feel my love for her with such unerring intensity that she never had to question it, no matter what the world threw at us. That would be the first thing on my to-do list every day, so long as I drew breath. And until that daily task was completed, my job wasn't done, because this woman was the center of my world. My greatest priority and my proudest accomplishment. I would never stop striving to be worthy of her love.

Lina

# FORTY-SEVEN

"I don't know what to say." Mellie looked worriedly from me to Oran and back. "Either option is awfully generous. I don't want to put a strain on you guys."

"That's sweet of you," said Oran, "but I'm not the type to inconvenience myself. I told Lina I'm good with either option, and I am. You just need to choose." He rinsed his empty breakfast plate in the sink, then placed it in the dishwasher.

I shot my sister a look. *See, I told you so.*

Excitement flashed in her eyes. "Well, if you really don't mind, the apartment here in the building sounds incredible. I've enjoyed having my own little space, and being so close to you guys would be perfect."

Oran took out his phone and dialed a number. "Frank, it's Oran Byrne. That apartment we talked about yesterday? I'll be by later today to sign the paperwork. How soon can I get access?"

Mellie and I exchanged beaming grins.

"That works. See you in an hour." He hung up and slid his phone back into his pant pocket. "They have to have a cleaning team go through tomorrow, but you can start moving in the day after. Just let me know of any other issues you notice after that, and I'll have them taken care of."

"Oh my God." My sister gaped at me. "Is he for real?"

I laughed. "Yup. He's a force of nature—there's no stopping him once he sets his mind on something."

Mellie smirked. "Funny, I know someone else like that."

I looked over my left shoulder, then my right, placing a scandalized hand over my chest. "*Me*? You can't possibly mean me."

Oran burst out laughing. "You can definitely stick around, kid."

When I gaped at him in outrage, he laughed a little more, then kissed my forehead. "I've got shit to do. You ladies be good." My mouth went dry at the sight of his expensive slacks filled perfectly by his muscular backside. *Good God.*

"Yeah," Mellie drew out slowly. "Having my own apartment is a must."

"What? Why?"

"The sexual energy between you two is so intense, I'm worried I'll end up pregnant just breathing the air in here."

It was my turn to burst out laughing. "Sorry about that." I shrugged. "We're still in that honeymoon phase, I guess."

"No apologies necessary. I'm so incredibly happy for you." She placed a hand over mine and squeezed.

"I'm pretty dang pleased for us both. Things are going to be freaking spectacular from here on out, I just know it."

She smiled, but her enthusiasm didn't match my own by a long shot.

"What is it?"

"Nothing. I was just thinking that I'll need to find a job again. I guess at least this time I can use my real name and documents." Amelie hadn't wanted the Brooks family money any more than I had when I'd asked her about it, though she definitely could have used it. I assured her that I wouldn't judge her at all if she used some—I'd done the same when I got started—but she stood firm with her rejection.

"I never got a chance to talk to you about it before, but Cosmo and I need to hire someone to handle administrative stuff for us. How perfect would that be?"

Again, she gave me a wan smile. "That would be awesome, Lina."

"Buuut?"

Her gaze dropped to her hands. "It's just that all I've ever wanted was to dance. I had to sneak around behind Mom's back to practice anything but ballet, and then I needed money too much to pursue anything in dance. I was just thinking that maybe with rent covered, this might finally be my chance. I could audition for shows and find a dance company to join. It would be a dream come true."

Amelie was an incredibly talented dancer. I would have encouraged her regardless, but knowing her ability made me that much more excited for her.

"Then I'd say that works perfectly. If you want to make some cash, you can do some work here and there for us on your own schedule. If you find something else in the dance industry, then I'll be the first to congratulate you. Life's too short, Mel. You should pursue your dreams every chance you get."

She slid off her chair and into my arms. "Thank you, Lina Bean. You're the best sister I ever could have asked for."

"Ditto, Mellie Bellie." The use of our childhood nicknames —the ones she'd given us when she was only a few years old —nearly brought me to tears.

The rest of our day was spent in shallower waters. No emotional heart-to-hearts or personal revelations, just good old-fashioned productivity. We had two apartments to empty in two days. She and I managed the Wellington place on our own since Amelie owned very little there. The next day, Oran helped us pack up the apartment Amelie had been living in when she disappeared, and the following day, we got everything moved to her new place.

The one-bedroom, one-bath apartment was incredible. Oran surprised us with the fact that he'd had the place furnished. It hadn't only been cleaners that came before we moved Mellie in. A living room setup, a small dining table with four chairs, and a full bedroom suite awaited us when we arrived. His generosity continued to humble me.

The apartment itself was better than I could have hoped. The high ceilings and large windows made the place feel even more spacious than its listed one thousand square feet. The corner kitchen had white granite counters, quality stainless appliances, and a small island with two barstools that separated it from the main living space.

And the very best part was that it was just one short elevator ride from our place.

Oran brought home takeout the first night she moved in, and the three of us ate together at her new table. I couldn't remember a time when my heart overflowed with such happiness. I didn't care what happened to Wellington or my mother—the only things that truly mattered were right there next to me, joining me in devouring a delicious bowl of queso.

The only piece of my heart missing was Gloria, and we went to see her the following day. She was beside herself with relief when I showed up with Amelie at my side. I was relieved to see that Gloria wasn't irreparably traumatized by what had happened at the Brookses' house. I'd reached out to check on her by phone, but there was no substitute for in-person confirmation. Gloria was tougher than I'd expected.

Oran and I had talked a few nights before, revisiting the matter of my mother and stepfather's money, and decided to put a substantial sum in an account for Gloria before donating the rest. She deserved the money more than anyone.

When I told her she'd been left money in Charles's will, she was shocked speechless. The realization that she wouldn't have to worry about working or money ever again brought her to tears. I'd never been so happy to see someone cry big fat heaving tears.

By the time Mellie and I left Gloria's, we'd all laughed, cried, and sworn an oath to keep in better contact. My family might have been small, but at least I had one. I wouldn't take that for granted ever again.

♦

"This is a regular Sunday dinner?" There had to be forty people crammed into Oran's grandparents' house. The place was a good size, but that was still a lot of bodies. I couldn't fathom being related to that many people or having a family who liked each other enough to gather in these numbers every single month.

"Yeah, just immediate family—the kids, grandkids, and great-grandkids."

If I hadn't known, I would have said we had walked into an extended family reunion or a big celebration. Instead, this was just another Sunday for the Byrnes.

Oran gently placed a finger under my chin and closed my gaping mouth as he whispered, "Don't want them thinking I'm marrying a mouth-breather."

That got my attention.

I swung around and smacked him in the gut. "Jerk," I shot back.

He wrapped his arm around my back and hugged me into his side, laughing heartily the entire time. I grumbled good-naturedly as he led us over to where Noemi and Conner were talking with Torin and Stormy, the couple whose wedding I'd inadvertently crashed on the first day of our fake engagement. Since finding Amelie, I'd learned that Stormy worked with her at Moxy, and the two had been friends.

I'd gone by the club when I'd first started looking for my sister, but the people I'd talked to didn't have any information on her. I hadn't gone back. I'd been so damn certain the Society was to blame—she'd been at Wellington's house, after all. Looking back, the web of connections astounded me. It was no wonder Oran and I crossed paths.

"Hey, you two," Stormy said with her trademark Southern lilt. "How's sweet Amelie doing?"

I gave her a hug followed by Noemi. "She's great. I would have brought her with us, but she was rehearsing for a big audition."

"That's exciting! I'm surprised she's already trying out. She's only been home a week."

"Dancing on a big stage is all she's ever wanted. The second she had the time and resources, she went straight to

303

work." I beamed like a proud mama because that's how I felt. I was so damn happy for my little sis.

"She gets a part in something, make sure to tell us. We'll all go for sure." Stormy nodded animatedly, and Noemi followed suit. The men at their sides didn't look quite so enthusiastic. I had to bite back a laugh.

"I'll shout it from the rooftops, trust me."

We spent a half hour talking and making introductions, some new and some repeated from the wedding I'd been to. He had so many damn relatives that it was hard to remember them all.

I had never experienced the sort of controlled chaos it took to get everyone fed at a Byrne family dinner. It was overwhelming yet thoroughly enjoyable. Everyone knew the drill. Dinner was served buffet style, which I loved. Why make things more complicated than necessary? No need to put on airs or impress anyone. The dinner was about having a reason to gather. It didn't matter that people sat on the sofa while they ate or that kids grouped in circles on the floor. The laughter and chatter all around us was the important part.

We managed to score seats at the main table in the dining room because that was where Nana and Paddy Byrne were sitting, and Nana had insisted we join them. Sitting in the spotlight would have been more stressful had Nana not been such a character. She was hours of entertainment all on her own.

"Oran," his mother spoke up after joining us at the main table. "Have you two thought about a wedding date yet?"

"April second," he replied naturally, not even pausing as he scooped up his next bite of food.

I was dumbfounded. He'd certainly never discussed a date with me. Hell, he hadn't even officially proposed—never mind the fact that he was still technically *married*.

"Assuming you get certain legal matters sorted," I pointed out, a tad miffed that he was making plans without me.

"Actually, I got a call this morning and hadn't had a chance to tell you. There was a riot at the jail yesterday. Caitlin was accidentally knocked over a railing in the scuffle and didn't survive the fall."

Our entire table fell into a shocked silence.

I had no idea how to respond, but the rest of the table felt no such uncertainty. They erupted into a chorus of cheers. I looked around in surprise, unsure if I should join in—a woman had *died*—celebrating that felt inappropriate, no matter how horrible she'd been.

Oran leaned over and kissed my cheek with a smile. "It's cause to celebrate, trust me."

Nana took the opportunity to chime in. "You bet your bleedin' arse it is. Leaving this earth is the only halfway decent thing the woman ever did. Good riddance." She raised her glass of whiskey and downed its contents in one gulp.

The rest of the table followed suit with ruckus cheers that rippled outward to the others seated throughout the house. They didn't even know what they were toasting, but the entire household joined in the celebration.

Their joy for one another filled me with warmth. Oran was blessed with an amazing family, and if I married him, his family would become my family. The possibility of being surrounded by so many supportive, loyal people immersed me in a wave of emotions.

My heart fluttered up into my throat as tears burned my eyes.

I raised my glass. "To new beginnings."

Oran lifted his glass to clink with mine, his silver stare sparking with admiration.

"To new beginnings!" The phrase echoed throughout the

house, filling my ears and nestling deep in my heart as his entire family cheered for us.

I'd never felt all that lucky before, but at that moment, I felt like the luckiest woman in the world.

Oran

# FORTY-EIGHT

Lawrence Wellington had thought himself untouchable. Wealth and power and privilege had lulled him into a false sense of security, leaving him at his most vulnerable. It was the worst mistake a man could make.

To help him reflect on all the ways he'd fucked up, we'd kept him chained in his own attic for the past two weeks. It seemed appropriate, considering he'd allowed his son to do the same to an innocent woman who'd been trafficked from Russia.

The operation had taken some finesse, considering the feds were still looking for him. I got a ridiculous amount of pleasure out of knowing he was hiding in plain sight right under their noses.

We'd provided entertainment, at least—news reports about himself played on repeat, detailing all the ways his empire had crumbled. All day and all night.

As I stood in the doorway of his makeshift cell and watched him sitting naked on the floor, rocking himself while staring at the wall, I could honestly say that Wellington looked like shit. He'd lost weight, though we provided ample stale bread and rotten fruit. He even had access to water in the toilet, so long as he remembered to drink before he took a piss. I thought the fact that we provided him with access to a toilet was rather generous.

Overall, Wellington was in rough shape, but there was still plenty of room for deterioration.

I considered what might come next to enhance his experience and came to the sudden realization that I didn't give a shit. So long as he wasn't out hurting anyone else, it felt pointless to spend any more mental energy on Wellington. *He* was pointless because he didn't matter. So why was I still over here spending time screwing with him?

We'd already extracted every ounce of information from him about the Society. The sick fucks were an island shy of being Jeffrey Epstein. Every one of them had some sort of perverted kink—things way beyond a little snowballing or toe-sucking. Wellington liked to degrade his women to the point of abuse. Like father, like son. Others were into children or other non-consensual situations. I wasn't even sure it could be called kink. These people found pleasure in the most cruel, inhumane treatment of others.

In that regard, they were all the same.

As was their solemn oath of secrecy, but only because they'd mutually agreed to provide blackmail material on themselves as a prerequisite of membership. That was the reason Eliza had offered up Lina's virginity. It wasn't about money. No money ever changed hands. It was about ensuring everyone stayed silent. If they were all equally at risk, they felt certain no one would talk. However, they failed to consider one important possibility. Torture.

The second one of them was forced to spill, secrets flowed like a burst water main. Not a single member was willing to go down without taking the entire group with them. Their *honor* system was no more reliable than a house built on a Hollywood hillside. Once the dirt started to slide, the entire foundation came crashing down.

We learned that they got together at Olympus headquarters on Sundays and planned their once-a-month fuck fests— secret nights filled with horrors and depravity. Though I got the sense their meetings were more about reveling in the anticipation than the actual planning. Not only did they keep one another's darkest secrets, they helped enable one another either personally or through contacts like my ex-wife's brother.

We had acquired a list of names and were working our way through it one at a time. We'd been discreet in our actions, however, so as to prevent them from catching on before we could dole out punishment. The Society's days were numbered.

Wellington was ruined.

The Society was crumbling.

Amelie was safely home.

And most important to me, Lina was mine.

It was time to end it.

"Lawrence, I've come to a decision," I said in a droll tone from behind him.

He rocked in place, not acknowledging me.

I took out my gun from its holster and checked the chamber. "I think we're done here. Do you have any last words you'd like to say?"

He stilled and slowly peered over his shoulder at me. If I wasn't mistaken, tears wet his eyes. He parted his chapped lips and—

With one swift motion, I cocked the gun, aimed, and put a bullet between his eyes.

"That's too bad because no one gives a shit what you have to say." I collected the discharged shell from the floor, holstered my gun, and walked away. As I exited the Wellington mansion, I put in a call for a cleaner, then went in search of flowers.

♦

"Oran, they're beautiful!" Lina leaned in and breathed deeply over the bouquet of long stem red roses. "And they smell incredible."

"Thirty-one roses, one for each day since you agreed to be mine," I explained. The florist had argued that it was too many stems for one vase, but I'd insisted she find a way to make it fit. The thing weighed a ton, but it looked spectacular.

Lina rocked on her heels and shot me a sheepish smile. "I didn't have much of a choice at the time." Her cheeks flushed. She felt awkward pointing it out and probably wished she hadn't, but I was glad she did.

"I realize that, which is why I decided that a do-over was in order."

"A do-over?" Her eyes rounded as I lowered to one knee.

"Lina Schultze…" I took her hand in mine. "Never in my life have I been more captivated by a woman. Your strength, loyalty, and exquisite beauty drew me to you, but I knew you had to be mine when I witnessed your compassion, talent, grace, and wit. I've already given you a ring, but I wanted to do something more—to make a statement about my commitment to you so you'd never have reason to doubt."

I unbuttoned the top half of my shirt and pulled back the left side to reveal a large gauze pad over my left pectoral. When I removed it, Lina gasped.

I'd had the artist start working on the design a week earlier, then had it tattooed that morning before going to see Wellington. The skin was still red and starting to swell a tiny bit, but not enough to detract from the incredible artistry now inked over my heart.

Two chess pieces—the king and queen—stood together, the king slightly taller and positioned behind the queen enough to highlight her prominence. A thorny vine of roses in full bloom dramatically circled the two, uniting and protecting. And the final touch, a perfect rendition of her engagement ring dangling from one of the vines.

The all-black design incorporated a gothic flare that offset the feminine nature of the flowers, giving the piece a decidedly elegant yet haunting vibe. It couldn't have been more perfect.

"Oh, *Oran*," Lina breathed, hand over her heart. "It's incredible."

"I wanted my queen with me always." I took her hand back in mine. "You're already a part of my soul, Lina Schultze. Tell me you'll be my wife as well."

She dropped to her knees and wrapped her arms around me. "Yes, I will absolutely be your wife." She pulled back, tears pooling precariously on her lashes. "Thank you, Oran. Thank you so much for everything."

"No need to thank me for treating you like you deserve to be treated."

"Oh yeah? What if I really, *really* wanted to show my

appreciation?" Her hand drifted down my chest toward my cock.

"Who the fuck am I to tell you what you can and can't do?"

She grinned, nipping at my bottom lip. "That's what I thought."

I nipped her right back, then carried her to the bedroom. She showed me just how grateful she was, and I returned the favor. Twice.

Afterward, we showered and cleaned up to get ready for a night out. I was done in a fraction of the time it took her, so I went to my office for a bit before checking back in on her. She was putting on the finishing touches of her makeup, her golden hair almost glowing in loose waves down her back.

I leaned against my vanity and watched her. "Wellington's gone. I thought you should know."

Lina's hand froze in the air mid-application of her mascara. "I suppose that's good," she said quietly. Her eyes caught mine in the mirror before she resumed what she was doing. "What about my mother?" The words were no more than a whisper.

We hadn't spoken about the woman since Lina consented to her death. I had started to assume that Lina wasn't ever going to ask.

"Gone, but we made sure that she transferred her estate to a living trust with Amelie as the beneficiary. The money will likely take a while to come through since we'll have to have her declared dead. There won't be any body." I'd considered making it look like an accident, but where would the fun have been in that? Lina had never told me to do it quickly. Eliza Brooks had needed to suffer. By the end, she begged me to kill her.

The past two weeks had been some of the most satisfying of my life.

"That's fine. Mellie's fine without it for now."

"She may be fine without the money, but she won't be fine without her sister, which is what will happen if you don't hurry. Ten more minutes and we'll be late."

"Crap! I'm ready, I swear." She ran the little wand through her lashes one more time, then slammed it back into its bottle. "Let me just put on my shoes and grab my clutch."

We made it to the car with three minutes to spare. I'd hired transportation, not wanting to mess with parking since we would be dealing with theater district traffic on a Saturday night. Walking would have taken less time, but at twenty-five degrees out, that wasn't an option. Instead, we sat in the back of a plush Escalade, watching others battle the cold.

After twenty minutes of Lina fidgeting absently with the zipper on her purse, I placed my hands over hers as the driver pulled up in front of the theater. She met my amused stare with wide eyes, then peered at our hands, unaware of what she'd been doing.

"She's going to do fabulous. This is what she's dreamed of doing." Amelie had unexpectedly scored a minor role as a dancer in the Broadway production of *Chicago*, temporarily filling in when the cast was hit with a wicked strain of the flu. It wasn't a permanent gig, but it would be huge for her résumé.

"I know, it's just that she's had so little time to learn the choreography. I'd be petrified."

"She's not you, Lina. Choreography is her life."

Lina nodded just as the driver opened her door. We exited the car and hurried inside the building. Winter was clearly not done with the city yet. Inside, an usher scanned my ticket barcode from my phone and showed us toward the hallway to our box seats.

"Just out of curiosity, are you going to be this nervous with our kids as well?" I asked, fighting back a smirk.

"Our kids?" she blurted, then slammed a hand over her lips and looked around to make sure no one had heard her.

"You adore Amelie, and with your age gap, she's almost like a daughter. Makes sense that you might want your own." I hadn't thought much about kids before Lina. Now that I'd witnessed her nurturing nature, kids sounded pretty incredible.

"I don't know. It didn't feel like much of an option before, so I hadn't put much thought into it. I suppose it worries me a little."

"What part?"

"Motherhood. What if I don't love my kids like I should?" Her whispered words were heartbreaking. I hated that her mother could make her doubt herself like that.

I smiled and shook my head. "Not possible. People either have a soul or they don't. Someone who loves as big as you can't just shut that off. You'd be the best mother in the world."

She stopped and looked up at me with glassy eyes. "I love you, Oran."

My lungs seized tight in my chest. "Say it again," I demanded, not sure I could ever hear it enough.

"I love you, baby."

"Fuck, I love you, too." I pulled her luscious body against mine and kissed her with every ounce of passion she inspired in me. I wanted her to feel as breathless as she made me. When I finally pulled back, her dilated eyes and pink cheeks told me I'd been successful.

"Oran, people are looking," she whispered, eyes cutting to the side.

My answering grin was positively diabolical. "Good. No reason the whole world shouldn't know that you're mine."

She grinned shyly. "You could always rent a billboard."

"What makes you think I haven't?" I said with absolute seriousness.

Her smile faltered before she shook her head in mock exasperation. "Good grief. What have I gotten myself into?"

I winked. "At least you'll never be bored."

"Heaven forbid."

"That's enough out of you." I swatted her backside playfully. "Let's get to our seats before we miss the show."

She yipped and hurried forward, shooting a glare over her shoulder. It was a nice try, but she couldn't completely hide the smirk that teased the corner of her lips.

The show was excellent that night. Amelie never missed a beat, and I'd never been so goddamn happy in my life. I wasn't exactly a fan of musicals, but that didn't matter. So long as I had Lina by my side, life was good.

# EPILOGUE

"LINA, THIS PLACE IS INCREDIBLE." AMELIE LEANED TOWARD THE car window as we drove up to the Chinese Scholar Garden within Snug Harbor.

"Isn't it? The first time I came, I never wanted to leave." Predicting the exact date of the cherry blossom bloom was impossible, and while we ended up on the tail end, it was still gorgeous.

We scheduled the ceremony for early afternoon to take full advantage of the daylight and the warmth. Early April in New York was just tiptoeing into spring. Planning an outdoor wedding during that time was risky, but the results seemed to be paying off. A layer of soft gray clouds blanketed the sky, laying a peaceful backdrop for an unforgettable day in the gardens.

"I mentioned this place to Oran when we first got together."

"When he blackmailed you?" She shot me a teasing look.

"Yeah." I sighed, smiling. "I never imagined he had paid attention or would remember months later. When he told me he'd reserved the place, I hadn't believed him. This is peak cherry blossom season, and at the time, the wedding was less than two months away. Yet he'd somehow made it happen." A part of me still hadn't believed it until now.

The driver parked, helping Amelie and me out of the car. We'd been waiting for our designated time to arrive at one of the on-site buildings. And this was it. The flowers I'd selected adorned the gated entrance to the garden, and just beyond the row of hedges, the most incredible man I'd ever met waited for me.

All of it seemed surreal.

After months of crippling fear that I'd never see Amelie again, not only was she alive, but she was here sharing the happiest day of my life with me. So much had changed in such a short span of time, and I had Oran to thank for all of it.

The thought made me miss him even more. I'd stayed with Amelie the night before, which was such a treat, but I'd quickly gotten used to having Oran around. Fortunately, we'd been busy enough that I hadn't had time to dwell on his absence. Amelie and I spent all morning at a salon getting ready. She was my maid of honor, and I couldn't believe how grown up she looked in the dress I'd designed for her. I designed my own gown as well. I'd never really thought much about my wedding, but Oran had a way of inspiring me. Once I started sketching, the dress had practically designed itself.

Now, I was in that dress and practically giddy to set my eyes on Oran in his suit.

"Gloria!" Mellie called.

I turned to see the wedding coordinator round the corner with Mama G on her arm. When it came time to choose someone to walk me down the aisle, Mama G was the obvious choice.

"Lina, you look like a princess." She looked me up and down, her eyes glistening.

"Don't you start crying," I chided her, my lip quivering. "The mascara's waterproof, but that won't stop my eyes from puffing up if the waterworks start."

"Don't be silly. I'm not crying; *you're* crying," she teased through her tears.

I laughed and hugged her, taking several deep breaths to stave away the emotions.

"Everything is ready to go whenever you are," said the coordinator with a broad smile.

I looked at my family, small but perfect, and my heart filled with joy. "Let's do this."

The coordinator, who looked like she had walked off the set of *Men in Black*, placed a finger on the earpiece of her headset and spoke into the microphone. "Bridal procession is ready in five," she said with military curtness, then handed her binder to Amelie and began straightening the short train on my dress. The woman was a machine. I didn't want to know what Oran had paid her to put all this together on such short notice. Whatever it was, it had been worth it.

The string quartet playing deeper in the garden transitioned from the filler music into an artful rendition of Pachelbel's Canon.

Amelie started down the path around a hedge row, and then it was just Gloria and me.

"I'm so proud of you, mija," she said softly, wrinkled fingers clasped over mine. "I wish you all the happiness in the world. No one deserves it more."

"Thank you, Mama G." My voice threatened to abandon me. "I never would have been the woman I am now without you. I owe you everything."

"I always knew God put me in that house for a reason. We were both grieving at the time, you and I, and when I saw the sorrow in your big blue eyes, I knew I had a new purpose in life."

I wasn't a believer like her, but I couldn't argue with her. If there was ever proof that guardian angels existed, Gloria was it.

"Love you always and forever, Mama G." The words were nothing but a whisp of air.

She wiped a tear from my cheek as her own fell. "Always and forever, mija."

"Okay, ladies. I hate to interrupt, but we have a schedule to keep."

Gloria and I both grinned, semi-delirious laughter taking hold of us.

"Deep breaths, please," the woman said sternly.

"Yes, yes. Lina, you don't want to be puffy." Gloria led me in a slow, deep breath.

"Okay, I think I'm okay now." I nodded, hoping if I said it, it would be true. Then I began my final walk as Lina Schultze.

When we rounded the corner that unveiled the site of the ceremony, my eyes only saw one thing. Oran, standing tall and confident without the slightest display of nerves. He'd been ready for this day for months. Conner stood next to him as the best man, opposite where Amelie waited for me in her role as maid of honor. We kept things simple. No ring bearers or flower girls. This was about our vows to one another and an epic party afterward.

My eyes held Oran's without wavering. His tailor-made three-piece gray suit was even better than I'd imagined, highlighting the shards of silver in his eyes. Eyes that swirled with so many emotions I could have spent all day trying to name them. I was utterly transfixed by the man, and he was all mine.

When we reached the end of the aisle, Oran gave Gloria a hug before she took her seat, and then the world melted away, and it was just Oran and me.

"Every time I see you," he murmured, "I fall in love all over again."

I blushed all the way to my toes, if toes could blush.

"Then we fall together because I can't help but go where you go."

His answering grin must have summoned the sun because I felt its warm rays fill my chest.

Oran turned us toward the Byrne family priest who led the ceremony. All my nerves melted away, leaving pure joy and excitement for what was about to unfold—our union but also the unveiling of a secret I'd been keeping. I could hardly wait to share it.

We recited vows that we'd written together in the weeks before our big day. When the time came for the rings, that was my cue. Amelie handed me Oran's wedding band, and after I spoke the recital and placed the ring on his finger, I turned over my hand to reveal a matching version of Oran's tattoo that I'd had inked on the inside of my left wrist the night before. I'd gone to the same tattoo artist to ensure it was drawn just right since the smaller size meant adjusting some of the elements.

I would never, ever forget the look in Oran's eyes when he

saw what I'd done. The enamored pride. The adoration. His love for me shone so bright it would have lit the night sky.

He cupped my face and pulled my lips to his in a passionate, unbridled kiss.

"Um, we haven't gotten to that part yet, sir," said the priest in a hushed, scandalized tone.

Oran ignored him, pulling away only when he'd had his fill. Taking my wedding band from Conner, he then looked at the priest to continue. Minutes later, we were pronounced husband and wife to a chorus of cheers.

After the ceremony, we mingled with our guests, enjoying cocktails among the cherry blossom trees. And when the time came, we moved into an enormous tent for the main reception dinner, which worked well because it began to drizzle not long after. We all stayed warm and dry and deliriously happy inside.

At one point, I sat with Nana and Paddy Byrne while Oran was off talking. I'd learned that Paddy didn't say much. He smiled a lot and enjoyed being around everyone, but Nana ran the show, and he seemed content with that.

"I'm glad you came over because we'll need to head home soon," Nana said. "Paddy doesn't like to be out late."

I peered over to the man tapping his foot to the music and grinning as he watched people dance. Someone may not like to be out late, but I wasn't sure it was Paddy. He looked like he'd go along with just about anything.

"I'm not one for late nights myself, anymore," I agreed. "And I'm sure things will wind down soon."

"Indeed. You did a marvelous job, lass. It was a beautiful wedding."

"Thanks, but Oran did a lot of the planning. He's pretty incredible."

"Aye, he is." She beamed at where he stood not far away.

"It's going to be interesting to see the family under his leadership—he and Keir and Conner, and even Torin. They seem to have settled into their roles nicely. This new generation looks at things differently—instead of outsiders, they see allies. I hope it continues to pay off for them."

"Outsiders?"

She discreetly angled her head toward the cake table. "The one there with the tattoos all up his neck. That's Renzo Donati. Italian." She said it as though it explained everything.

"Isn't he Noemi's uncle?" That was how he'd been introduced to me. I hadn't thought any more of it.

"Aye, but that's not all he is. He's the new head of the Moretti family—that's not something you want to forget."

"Oran said he helped bring down Lawrence Wellington."

"Very likely. Wellington was in shipping. The Morettis run the unions, including the dock workers. That makes them incredibly powerful. What happens if they notice the champagne on that table was imported illegally without their consent?"

I wasn't sure if her question was rhetorical, but I couldn't answer it either way. I had no clue what would happen.

"And you see that young man chatting up your sister?" Nana added.

I jerked upright and scanned the room for Amelie.

"That's Sante Mancini."

I relaxed a smidge when I spotted Mellie and the guy she was talking to. "He's Noemi's little brother."

"No, Lina." Nana took my hand in hers and leveled me with a hardened stare. "As Oran's wife, you can't afford to see things in such simple terms. You have to hear what isn't said and see what is hidden away. That young man has been Renzo's ward for the past year. He's been troubled ever since he learned that his father killed his mother. I don't believe time with Renzo is helping, and if I'm not wrong, he's been spiking your sister's punch for the last hour."

"What?" I gasped, my head spinning back toward the two young people.

Nana tugged at my hands to draw my attention back to her. "I won't be here forever, you know. Someone has to step up and keep this family running strong."

"*Me*? You ... think that person's me?" I gaped at her, still half focused on Amelie across the room.

"You're a tough one, lass. You have what it takes."

"You can't possibly know that."

"Oran told me what you did for your sister. That was confirmation enough for me. Everyone in this family is loyal, but not everyone can bring themselves to self-sacrifice when the time comes. It takes a special breed of person—a mental toughness and an aptitude for strategy—to help guide a family like ours. And who knows, with the quality of you young ladies entering our ranks lately, maybe you do the job together. Sometimes change is best. But know that the role will need to be filled, and I stand firm that the female mind is better equipped for such things." She gave a stern nod as though the matter was settled.

I couldn't necessarily argue with her on the final point, but I still wasn't sure looking to me to fill her shoes was the right plan. She had granddaughters who seemed plenty capable. Wasn't Mafia mentality all about keeping it in the family?

"I wouldn't even know where to begin."

"You pay attention," she offered simply.

"I don't know—"

"There's still time. I'm not quite on my last leg." She winked, leaning in conspiratorially. "You'll learn. Now, go rescue that sister of yours before he gets her alone in the dark."

I shot to my feet, then paused, looking back down at her. "Thanks, Nana. I'm not quite sure why you've chosen me, but I'll do my best."

"I know you will, lass." Her softly spoken words and kind smile filled me with a pride I hadn't expected. I wasn't sure why I cared what she thought of me, but apparently, I did. Nana was a badass, and if she thought I could follow in her footsteps and guide this family, I'd do my damnedest to live up to that standard.

I charged past two tables until I reached Amelie, taking her drink from her as I glared at Sante. "Excuse me, I think this one is done for the night."

"What? Lina Bean, what are you talking about?" Amelie was unquestionably tipsy.

Sante put his arm between my sister and me, trying to pull her closer to him. "It's all good. She's fine."

"*You* stay out of it." I glared at him. "You've done enough."

That was when Renzo Donati appeared. "Everything okay here?"

"This one's been spiking my sister's punch." I wouldn't have minded her drinking a bit, but sneaking it in her drink was unacceptable.

Sante raised his hands innocently. "It's just a tiny bit of vodka. No need to make a big deal." His eyes were red and glassy, denoting that he'd also been at the vodka, if not something more serious.

The murderous wrath that darkened Renzo's face almost made me feel bad for saying anything. Almost, but not quite.

"Can't fuckin' take you anywhere," he hissed through clenched teeth.

Sante sneered. "You mean you don't ever want me to have any fun."

Lightning fast, Renzo grabbed Sante by the throat in one hand and lifted the guy to his tiptoes. Sante had to be right about Amelie's age, which meant he wasn't fully mature, but he certainly wasn't small. The strength it had to take to lift him nearly off the ground with one hand was mind-boggling.

"What have I told you about disrespecting me?"

Sante clutched at Renzo's wrist. "*Just ... a little ... fun*," he wheezed.

"No, you're embarrassing our entire family, and now we're leaving." He dropped the kid with a little shove, then turned to me. "Lina, Oran, I'll make sure this is handled appropriately. You have my apologies."

Oran, who now stood hovering behind me, snaked one arm around me for Renzo to shake. "We're glad you could make it."

Renzo turned, motioning Sante toward the exit when Mellie reached out and snagged Sante's fingers. The two exchanged a look I couldn't quite read before he turned his back on her and walked away.

Mellie spun at me, her eyes glassy. "Why did you have to make a scene and get him in trouble? He wasn't hurting anyone," she snapped, then rushed into the crowd in a hormonal fit of tears.

My exasperation was mirrored in Oran's eyes. "Having kids can wait, I think."

His suddenly hooded stare grew sultry. "Doesn't mean we can't practice."

"Having kids?"

"Making babies." He grinned. My new husband had been enjoying his share of celebratory whiskey. I couldn't blame him. I'd enjoyed more than one glass of champagne.

I grinned back at him. "Practice makes perfect."

He swept me into a bridal hold. "Thanks for coming,

everyone," he hollered above the music. "I'm taking my wife to bed."

The entire tent roared with laughter and cheers.

I was a tiny bit mortified but too tickled to actually be bothered. Oran and I were married, and I adored that he wanted the world to know how much he loved me.

# BONUS EPILOGUE

"You seriously *still* won't tell me?" I stared at Oran with a bemused grin as our private jet lifted off the runway to take us on our honeymoon.

I knew we'd be gone for two weeks. I knew he'd told me to pack for snow and beaches and everything in between. That was actually helpful in eliminating options. I was fairly confident we were either heading to Hawaii or Europe— where else could you find those extremes in one place? Chile had mountains and beaches, but I didn't see Oran taking us to South America. Of course, I hadn't expected him to take me on a surprise honeymoon, either.

"You'll find out soon enough." His knowing smirk was both infuriating and sexy as hell.

I shot him an arched brow. "Well, I can at least figure out if we're heading east or west." I looked out the small window as we eased higher into the sky. The sun was just setting on our first full day as a married couple. We would be flying through the night, but in which direction?

Oran stood from his plush leather chair opposite me and leaned over me, his hands on my armrests. "Unless … I distract you." One hand slipped into his pants pocket and pulled out some black fabric—long and narrow like a necktie but soft satin. He kept pulling until a two-inch wide strip of fabric dangled two feet from his hand.

"You brought a *blindfold*?" I gaped at him. "You want to keep it a secret that badly?"

He wrapped the satin over my eyes and tied it behind my head, careful not to catch my hair in the knot. "Trust me, that wasn't the only reason."

Then I was being lifted into his arms. I squealed and clung to his shoulders, hoping turbulence didn't knock us into a wall. Fortunately, the plane wasn't very big, so it was a short walk to the luxurious bedroom in the back.

Oran squeezed us carefully through the doorway then lay me down on the bed. He stripped off my clothes, revealing that I'd worn the red lingerie with black lace that he'd bought me. It had been his favorite ever since the first time he'd seen me in it.

"You know I love seeing this on you, but this time, it has to go." He took off my panties, then flipped me over to take off the bra. He didn't flip me back over. I lay on my tummy and strained to hear what he was up to. I heard the slide of his shoes coming off, then clothes hitting the floor. My stomach fluttered when the next thing I heard sounded like him rummaging through a bag.

Did he bring toys? What did this man have up his sleeve besides a blindfold?

I had to force myself to lay still as he joined me on the bed. Something clicked open, then he straddled me, his cock resting heavily between my ass cheeks. I arched my backside up toward him. I loved when he took me from behind, especially when his body lay flat over mine. I wasn't sure why, except when we were like that, I felt so completely his.

I was reveling in that feeling when a stream of cool liquid dripped on my back and had me gasping.

"Wha—?"

Then Oran's strong hands were there, rubbing what must have been massage oil into my skin. I moaned, low and deep. He moved slowly with purposeful intent. This wasn't just a ploy to transition into sex. Oran was dedicated to his task, starting with my neck and shoulders, only moving lower down my back when every knot and kink was relaxed to perfection.

I'd just started to feel like I could drift into a deep, peaceful sleep when his hands began to massage my ass cheeks. I loved knowing Oran was getting glimpses between my thighs when my cheeks pulled apart. Little by little, his hands inched closer to my core as he worked, building an inferno of anticipation in my veins. I tried to hold still, but the lust pooling in my belly was overwhelming.

When his hands moved lower to my upper thigh, I started to worry he truly was simply giving me a massage. Then his hand grazed my folds as if by accident.

"*Oh*," I breathed.

"I'm sorry, I must have slipped." The rugged masculinity of his rasp raked across my skin.

"It's okay. I mean, I recently got married, and I'm not sure my husband would appreciate it, but it was an accident, right?"

Oran's hand swept strong and firmly up my inner thigh, this time slowing and his fingers splitting to sweep just outside my pussy lips along the crease of my thighs. "What he doesn't know won't hurt him. It can be our little secret."

*Oh, hell yes!* He was playing along, and it was so fucking hot.

My nipples puckered into leaden pebbles beneath me, and I arched to open myself further to him. He slid a single finger deep inside me.

"How's this? That feel good?"

*"Yesssss."*

He pumped his finger a couple of times. "This tight little body is begging for more. Think you can take two?" He didn't wait for an answer, inserting a second digit inside. "Oh, *yeah.* That's a good girl. Your pussy's practically begging for a cock to fill it."

"You won't tell him, right?" I whimpered.

"You just do as you're told, and everything will be fine." He pulled his fingers out, then lifted my hips to hoist my ass in the air, setting me on my knees while my chest still lay flat on the bed. "Hold still," he instructed sharply.

I felt so open and exposed, and without the ability to see, every nerve ending in my body came alive. At first, I couldn't tell what he was doing, then I felt his hair between my thighs and his breath on my core. His hands gripped my ass and pulled me against his face like a starving man at a feast.

I didn't want the flight attendant who'd been up with the pilot to hear me, but I couldn't help from crying out. It felt so damn *good.*

He licked and sucked my clit from beneath me, and I rode his face like I couldn't get enough because I couldn't. When he slid out from under me, I whimpered with frustration, hoping he was about fuck me. However, Oran was set on keeping me guessing. He pulled my legs straight, then flipped me onto my back with one commanding twist of my legs.

I squealed, biting my lip to keep from laughing.

"Shhh, we don't want anyone hearing you. If my boss knew, I'd get fired for this."

"I'll be quiet," I whispered.

"Yeah, you will." He crawled over me, straddling my body until he sat over my belly, making sure not to rest too much of his weight on me. Then more oil dripped on my breasts.

"Oh God. I need your hands on me." I arched, my breasts swollen and aching for his touch.

"You're going to get more than my hands, sweetheart. Just wait." He massaged and rubbed, pinching my nipples just often enough to make me feel like I might come without him even touching my clit. When I thought my mind might shatter, he inched forward until his scalding cock lay between my breasts.

"Hold those perfect tits together, beautiful, so I can fuck them."

I did as I was told, loving how, even when role-playing, Oran always made me feel like a goddess. He hissed with pleasure as he began to glide between my oil-slicked breasts. His finger hooked in the blindfold to lift it away.

"You need to see this. Your tits were made … for my cock." He struggled to speak as though fighting back the urge to unleash himself.

"Yes, baby. It feels so good." It wasn't the same as having his tongue between my thighs, but there was still pleasure in making him feel good.

I held tightly to my chest, hoping to drive him crazy. It must have worked. He groaned deep from his chest, then moved back down my body until we were aligned.

"Enough of that, I'm ready to fuck my wife." His lips crashed down on mine.

I wrapped my legs around his waist and ground my hips upward to press against his cock. One shift of his hips and he surged inside me.

We both gasped and stilled, our breaths coming in ragged puffs.

"Fuck me, Oran. Make me come so hard I can't see."

As if I even had to ask. That was his specialty.

My husband hammered into me with relentless intensity. All the buildup from our foreplay came surging forward like it had never receded, and in seconds, I was swept away in a flood of orgasmic bliss that left me gasping for air.

"That's it, baby. You squeeze my cock so good." His words were followed by a savage groan, and I could feel him swell impossibly larger inside me. His last thrusts came just as I thought I couldn't take any more stimulation.

I clung to him, my husband, my heart.

"I love you so much," I breathed.

"Love you more than life itself." He lifted himself enough for our eyes to lock before he placed a reverent kiss on my lips. "You go to the bathroom, and I'll grab us some food. We can eat in bed, then pass out."

"Works for me."

He'd fucked the fucks right out of me. I'd find out where we were going when we landed.

♦

Hours later—could have been a handful or a dozen, I had no idea—we touched down at our destination. We were surrounded by a large city, though we'd passed forested mountains nearby. Judging by the signs I could see, we were somewhere in Asia, though I wasn't informed enough to tell what country.

I'd been completely wrong. An Asian honeymoon had never even occurred to me.

"Where are we?" I asked, awe in my voice as we stepped down the plane's stairs onto the tarmac.

"For now, we're in Tokyo, but we're taking a helicopter to Hakone."

"A helicopter!" I'd never been on a helicopter. I'd never been to Japan either. "Oran, this is incredible!"

"Good." He brought my face around to his with a finger on my jaw. "Because my queen deserves incredible."

I smiled so broadly my cheeks hurt.

"We have a full tour of the country scheduled—more gardens than you can imagine—and we'll end at the beaches of Okinawa. Hopefully, the weather will be warm enough to enjoy them."

"I know I'll enjoy them regardless."

He tapped his knuckle to the end of my nose. "Let's keep going. We still have a bit more ground to cover."

I followed his lead to a porter who helped transport our luggage to a helicopter. The ride was unimaginable, especially as we left the city and entered the forested hills. Everything was so vibrant and green.

Oran had rented us a private house on a hillside for the first couple of days to give us time to relax and adjust to the time difference. I learned that one of the main draws to Hakone was the natural hot springs, called Onsens. They were public, separated into male and female pools, and clothing was not permitted. Lucky for us, the owners of our property piped in hot spring water to enjoy in a private setting. A large cast-iron tub sat on the balcony overlooking the tropical forest. If anyone could see onto our balcony, I'd never have known. The thick vegetation provided sufficient privacy for me.

Once we unloaded our bags and settled in, Oran suggested we soak. The skies had darkened with heavy rain clouds, making it look later than it was, though there was still plenty of light to enjoy the spectacular view. We could even hear the splash of a nearby waterfall. I couldn't imagine a more peaceful setting.

"Let's see how this works." He pressed a button that started a timed flow of hot spring water, which had a slightly sulfurous smell to it. "Shit, that's hot." He shook his hand. "I wasn't sure if we needed to add the cold, but we definitely do."

I turned the dial on the tap water until the two combined to make a comfortable mixture. As it filled, we undressed and settled into the water with me sitting between Oran's legs, reclined against his chest.

"I don't know how you came up with all this, but it's absolute perfection." My words were dreamy, in awe of the pristine beauty around me. Adding to the surreal magic of the area, a gentle rain began to fall on the leafy canopy of trees and vines. The whooshing sound of the shower filled the air.

Protected under an awning, we watched in reverent silence.

"You make me see the world in ways I never imagined possible," Oran said after a while.

"I think I know what you mean. Maybe we were both a little blind without one another."

"I had no idea of the beauty I was missing—what it felt like to truly love someone beyond all rational thought."

I rolled myself until my chest lay against his and gave him a gentle smile. "Hopefully not too irrational."

I'd meant to be lighthearted, but he looked more serious than ever.

"There isn't a thing in this world I wouldn't do for you. No act too violent or sacrifice too great."

His words left me breathless.

"I love you, too, Oran Byrne. My heart is yours and always will be."

Thank you so much for reading *Vicious Seduction*!
*The Byrne Brothers* is a series of interconnected standalone novels with *Craving Chaos* next in the lineup.

### *Craving Chaos* (The Byrne Brothers #5)

From bickering over a shipment of guns to fighting for their lives, rivals Shae Byrne and Renzo Donati find themselves stranded together in a frozen wilderness. Survival will test them; desire will threaten to change their lives forever.

*Silent Vows* **(The Byrne Brothers #1)**
Missed the first Byrne Brothers novel? In *Silent Vows*, Conner
chose his arranged marriage bride because she was mute,
thinking he wouldn't ever have to talk to her. But when he
learns Noemi was silent to protect herself from an abusive
father, he becomes obsessed with his new wife and vengeance
on her behalf.

♦

**Stay in touch!!!**
Make sure to join my newsletter and be the first to hear about
new releases, sales, and other exciting book news!
Head to www.jillramsower.com or scan the code below.

# ACKNOWLEDGMENTS

First and foremost, this book never would have happened if Oran hadn't evolved into such a compelling character that I *had* to tell his story. *The Byrne Brothers* series was supposed to end after *Ruthless Salvation*, but after writing *Corrupted Union*, I knew Oran had to find love again. Everything from there fell into place like it was meant to be, and I couldn't be happier.

My crew of alpha and beta readers were epic, as always. Sarah, my soul sister and partner in crime, gives the best alpha feedback a girl could ask for. And to Megan, Patricia, and Chris, your input is insightful and so incredibly appreciated. This book would not have been nearly as well-polished without you!

Jenny, you stepped up like a champ and did two reads over the Christmas holiday. That alone deserves a huge thanks, not to mention the masterful way you tweak my words to make them sound that much better. Thank you!!

More than ever, I want to thank my family for all their support and understanding during the writing process for this book. I'm the first to admit that I get a little crazy during a writing cycle. This one was extra challenging due to a barrage of life events that maxed out my stress levels. My husband and kids roll with the punches with such understanding and grace that I'm always in awe that I could be so lucky. Jasey, Tyler, Kam, and Landon, I love you with all my heart!

# ABOUT THE AUTHOR

Jill Ramsower is a life-long Texan—born in Houston, raised in Austin, and currently residing in West Texas. She attended Baylor University and subsequently Baylor Law School to obtain her BA and JD degrees. She spent the next fourteen years practicing law and raising her three children until one fateful day, she strayed from the well-trod path she had been walking and sat down to write a book. An addict with a pen, she set to writing like a woman possessed and discovered that telling stories is her passion in life.

## Social Media & Website

**Release Day Alerts, Sneak Peak, and Newsletter**
To be the first to know about upcoming releases, please join
Jill's Newsletter. (No spam or frequent pointless emails.)

Official Website: www.jillramsower.com
Jill's Facebook Page: www.facebook.com/jillramsowerauthor
Reader Group: Jill's Ravenous Readers
Follow Jill on Instagram: @jillramsowerauthor
Follow Jill on TikTok: @JillRamsowerauthor